THE MADDY SAGA

BOOK NINE

PONYGIRL PERIL

BY

I0630363

PAUL BLADES

Cover Art by Agnes Knox
agnes.knox@gmail.com

Dark Visions Publications
darkvisionspub@gmail.com

Previously published:

Watch for publication of the other books in the Maddy Saga:

Other books by Paul Blades:

Klitzman's Isle
Klitzman's Empire
Klitzman's Paradise
Klitzman's Pawn Parts One and Two
Slaver's Dozen- A Tale of Klitzman's Isle
The Taking of Cheryl Part One
The Taking of Cheryl Part Two: Slaver's Bait
Comfort Girl No. 4
Sacrifice to the Emerald God
The Blue Cantina: Anna's Surrender
The Warlord's Concubine, Books 1, 2, 3 and 4
Dreams and Desires, Books 1 and 2
Carmella Condemned
Carmella's Fate

CHAPTER ONE

Michael Burnham had good reasons to be self satisfied. All of his carefully laid plans of the last nine months were coming to fruition.

The most recent success story was standing in front of him right now. Nine lovely, young, Asian women were lined up, elbow to elbow, in the reception area of his new slave training center. Uniformly adorned with long, jet black hair and pleasant of face, they were dressed in a variety of short miniskirts, high heeled shoes and elegant, silk or cotton blouses. They were shifting nervously from foot to foot, hands placed behind their backs, eyeing their environs with growing apprehension.

About a half hour ago, they had pulled up in a black minivan. It was not the way incipient slave girls usually arrived. Normally, they were drugged and shipped in airtight containers from around the globe or stuffed into small cages and flown in on cargo planes from secret, temporary airfields. Uncrated by one of the dealers down in Dlitski, the capital of this Eurasian country that Burnham now called his home, they would spend several days being acclimated to their status as property and then sold off, individually or in lots, to the various slave dealers around the country. None, up until now, had arrived by bus.

Minivan, actually, a rental from the international airport down in the capital. They had made the three hour journey over the hardscrapple roads of the interior directly from there. There were no superhighways in Kalikastan and, if the powers that be had their way, there never would be. The country was a backwater from the word go, a breakaway republic from the old Soviet empire. Its nascent democracy had been crushed by a coterie of Russian gangsters who now ran the country like a Disneyland for ne'er-do-wells. They quickly established a national commission to regulate the criminal elements that flocked there, and divided themselves into clans, mixing with the already quite extensive native criminal groups.

Burnham had come to Kalikastan in search of his niece, Maddy, who had been kidnapped from her Tennessee home some ten months ago. Tall, big boned and pretty, the young girl had been 'recruited' to serve as a ponygirl, something that Burnham had never heard of until then. Burnham had hired Jake Barnes, a can do fixer, to track her down. When Jake reported that she had been shipped off to this remote, insular country, he had to go look for it on a map.

Rescuing Maddy was problematic. First of all, they didn't know who had her. There were over two dozen major estates in Kalikastan that ran and trained ponygirls and a number of minor ones. Just getting in to the country, for regular guys that is, was a near impossibility. Jake, however, came up with a plan. They would take over the US end of the slaving operation that had kidnapped Maddy and deal their way in. Posing as Amerikanski gangsters, they made contact with the slavers and, after assuring them that business would continue as usual, dropped a big juicy carrot in front of them in exchange for access to the country. A consortium of Western governments was funding a huge pipeline to deliver Russian and Ukrainian natural gas and oil to the developed west. Burnham, through his contacts, had won the contract to build it. It was going right through Kalikastan. When he promised to spread around the hundreds of millions in graft to be made, the Commission had invited him in.

The reality of female slavery had been quite a shock to the American billionaire. The institution was long a mainstay of Kalikastani life, that is before the fucking Communists screwed everything up, and the takeover of the small nation by criminal elements created a renaissance. The sport of ponygirl racing followed suit. His first blowjob from a naked, indentured, attractive, young female had been an eye opener, and shortly afterwards he decided to move his worldwide headquarters here.

He had since grown quite enamored of owning desirable female flesh. The Commission had awarded him his own estate about 75 miles from the capital. Now he had his own racing stable and had recently opened his own slave training center. In the spring, a huge resort he was planning was scheduled to open. He had arranged for the establishment of a syndicate so that underworld contacts from around the globe could do their banking here and trade freely in goods: heroin, pirated technology, slave girls, etc., without interference from international authorities.

The Administration in Washington had agreed to turn a blind eye to the goings on in exchange for the right to maintain secret prisons and so that major US corporations, whose ability to spread around the kind of juice that often made international markets flow was stymied by naïve, idealistic acts of Congress, could do business as it needed to be done. No congressional committee would ever set eyes on Kalikastani banking records and the FBI was barred from the country.

Right before him were some of the first fruits of his international endeavors. The nine nervous, trembling young women, diminutive and petit, their firm breasts apple like, their bare legs trim and shapely, would very shortly be introduced into their new status in life. Standing next to Burnham was Peter Wong, a lean, elegant Eurasian who represented a Malaysian syndicate. On the floor at his feet was a valise containing two pounds of uncut Thai heroin. He would take back with him, when he left, a valise full of cash and three young, recently trained, European women. The heroin and two of the pretty, slight, Malaysian girls would be dealt, after their training, to the Italian Americans for distribution to their friends. Two more of the new girls would be gifted to members of the ruling Commission and the other five would remain, for the time being, as Burnham's stock in trade.

The well built, American billionaire had rushed over to the training center as soon as he had heard that the new girls had arrived. The center was about a mile from his mansion and he had made the distance in a little over seven minutes driving hard the two, tall, broad shouldered, blond tailed, work ponies, Dora and Flora, that he kept around for his amusement. Too old for the racing circuit, having spent seven years at the bit, the pale skinned, big breasted pair was used by Burnham on his sojourns around his estate. One of Jake's men had developed an affection for the black hooded, ever silent creatures and took good care of them. Burnham loved to watch the rippling muscles of their powerful haunches as they trotted along in perfect unison. He gave no more thought for their long past, former human status than he would have for a dray horse, although he did fuck them every once in a while when the mood struck him.

Most of the other ponies were with their drivers returning, one by one, from the last race of the fall season to the ponygirl encampment adjacent to the stylish racing track and clubhouse he had had renovated at great expense. He would go there later to look them over. Chocolate, his 1500 sulky, had qualified for the Fall Tournament as had his four pony cabriolet team. The rest of his teams were nonstarters as far as the tournament was concerned. He was disappointed in their showing but he was determined, Steinbrenner-like, to pick up some new talent over the winter so as to make a better showing in the spring. He had been told by Irkut, his head trainer, that he had actually done better than expected for a new ponygirl estate, but that was scant comfort to a man who was used to winning every time he rolled the dice.

All that was far from his mind right now. Right now he was anxiously awaiting the denuding of his new property so that he could make a full assessment of their charms. The girls were obviously still oblivious to their ultimate fate although they were showing signs that they were aware that something was amiss.

Standing directly in front of the line of apprehensive, pretty, young girls was an Asian man, about 5'8" tall, broad shouldered and well muscled. He had short, grizzly hair and a square jaw. To Burnham he looked Korean, but he couldn't be sure. While Wong had come nattily attired in a sharply tailored, expensive suit, shiny black shoes and a paisley silk tie, the Korean was dressed in a tight fitting black t-shirt, blue jeans and heavy work boots. He had produced a three foot long quirt from somewhere and was tapping it on the side of his leg as he glared at his charges. The presence of the whip had not gone unnoticed by the frightened women.

"So, how do you like them," Wong asked Burnham in slightly accented, smooth English.

"They look fine, Peter," Burnham replied. "I was just curious, how did you get them here on a bus?"

"They were all recruited for overseas jobs as secretaries," Wong replied. "You can't appreciate how many pretty young, Asian women would jump at the chance to get jobs in Europe or America. All of these girls have gone to secretarial school in Kuala Lumpur and paid the equivalent of $10,000 for the chance at an overseas job. They all speak English and are very bright. So they should train well."

Burnham laughed. "So they paid the costs of their own transportation. That's funny. It'll give them something to think about while they're sucking cocks and spreading their legs. But what about their trail? Won't someone realize that they've been brought here? Won't they be missed?"

It was Wong's turn to chuckle. "No, there's nothing to worry about. Everything about their departure was totally above board. I have their passports and exit visas in my suitcase. It's just that the destination that they anticipated was slightly altered. Friends of mine in Hamburg will provide, if it ever becomes necessary, evidence that they arrived there on an international flight, were picked up by a van and then disappeared. But I doubt very much that that will be necessary. These girls' families just don't have the kind of clout or resources to do more than make a complaint at their local police station. All they will know is that the girls are gone and haven't been heard from since. The investigations will go nowhere."

"They all look delicious," Burnham observed. "Let's get a good look at them."

"As you desire, Mr. Burnham," Wong replied. He issued a curt command to the Korean, who looked back at Wong and smiled. He then returned his attention to the quailing young women all lined up obediently in front of him.

Some of the girls had apparently overheard Burnham and Wong's conversation and tears had started to flow down their pretty cheeks. Their skin was uniformly tawny and their eyes dark, almost black. They had cute, pert little noses and rounded chins. Their lips were mostly succulent and a few of the girls had wetted them nervously while awaiting the next act in the drama. None of the girls looked much older than nineteen or were taller than 5'4".

Several of Burnham's men, Barouf, the manager of the slave center, and his male, Kalikastani trainers, had joined the crowd. They were eyeing the girls with salacious intent. Burnham had begun to work a small revolution in the local female slave industry by importing non-European women in bulk. The chance to fuck the delightful, brown, yellow and black skinned girls was a novelty to the men and would be for the masters who eventually coughed up the substantial fees they would pay for them after they had been trained.

The Korean let out a loud, harsh, one word command to the girls in what Burnham assumed was Malaysian. The young women all jumped as one at the sound of the cruel, raspy voice. He followed his ejaculation with a few declarative sentences. The meaning of the foreign words were clear, even to Burnham, as a result of the girls' reactions. A few started to sob and tears filled all of their eyes. There was a look of fearful astonishment on their faces. They had just been told of the ultimate purpose of their journey to this strange place.

The Korean let his words sink in for a few moments. He then swished the whip he was holding in his strong right hand several times viciously through the air. The girls gave out moans of fear. All their eyes were pinned to the instrument as it made its violent journey back and forth. A couple of the girls looked like they were about to faint.

Seeing that his meaning had been fully understood by the pretty, trembling, young women, the Korean issued a command. The girls all looked astounded at his words. Their hands were still being dutifully held behind their backs as per an earlier order and several of the girls made slight, hesitant movements of them as if they were having trouble getting their hands to obey their instructions. The Korean man angrily repeated his command and swiped the whip three more times through the air while walking rapidly up and down the long line of pleasant, female flesh. This propelled the girls into frantic action.

Sniffling and crying, some of them sobbing, the women began to disrobe. Nervous, trembling hands pulled at the buttons of blouses or took hold of the hems of their brightly colored tops and began to pull them up over their bellies and breasts. As garments fell to the floor in front of the line of women, a wide array of dainty, lacy bras began to be revealed, firm, young breasts pushing out of them. The skirts were next and they were frantically, or here and there hesitatingly, unzipped or unhooked, as the case may be, and drawn down long, thin, tan thighs, over their graceful knees and then stepped out of. One of the girls, in her excitement, a short, slender delight, caught one of her fashionable high heels in the waist of her skirt as she was pulling it over her feet and fell to the floor. She gave out a loud, mournful wail. The Korean slapped at her bare back with the whip leaving a long, red trace behind it. The girl cried out in tearful pain and scrambled back to her feet.

The girls who had been hesitating, prolonging as long as they could the humiliation of showing their desirable bodies to these strange, fearsome men, increased the pace of their disrobement as the threat of physical violence had become a reality right before their eyes.

All except one. Third down in the row of young women from Burnham's right, she had managed to loosen the two top buttons of her peach colored, silky blouse and stopped. Her face, round and smooth, was a mask of agony. He jet black hair was cut short and stylish. She wore ruby red lipstick and had a slender gold chain around her neck. Her tight, short skirt was black and she wore matching pumps. Her small, delicate hands, topped with red painted, shiny fingernails, were joined together in front of her and were writhing like Lady Macbeth trying to wash off the evidence of her guilt.

The Korean took note of the girl's inaction and approached with a few inches of her face. She looked at him, misery in her eyes, tears flowing down her cheeks. She tried to murmur some plea to the powerful, angry man, but he cut her off with a harsh repetition of his earlier instructions.

The line of frightened women had come to a halt in their denudement. Some of the girls had already removed their delicate bras and tossed them on the floor in front of them to join their other discarded raiment. They covered their apple sized breasts with their slender arms, waiting to see what happened to the rebellious girl before going any further. The others either held their already loosened bras to their chests or stood there, arms wrapped around their slender bodies, dressed only in their intimacies.

"Excuse me," Wong said to Burnham. He stepped over to where the Korean man was confronting the reticent stripper.

He gently nudged the Korean aside and took a position in front of the girl. She looked up at him forlornly. Apparently, her need for modesty was immobilizing her. It was doubtful that she had ever thought that she would have to bare herself before a crowd of unknown men. The idea that her transformation into a sexual slave would soon follow was paralyzing.

Wong uttered some words in a low, gentle voice. The girl's misery seemed to increase as she took in his message. The Korean was hovering next to Wong and the girl glanced at the whip in his hand. She gave out a great moan of unhappiness and returned her supplicative gaze to Wong. She began to utter a plea for remission of her fate when Wong's right hand swiftly moved from his side and flashed across her face. A loud 'crack!' resounded through the room. The girl emitted a shout of distress and her head jerked to the side as she absorbed the cruel blow. Her crying became louder and she looked back at Wong, terror in her eyes. But she did not move to obey.

"Crack!" Wong's left hand repeated the exercise of his right. The blow made the girl sway and her knees weaken as her face jerked to her left. Just as she was about to collapse to the floor, Wang reached out, lightning like, and took hold of a fistful of her shiny, black hair, keeping her on her feet. Her cries of pain echoed through the room as her hands rose to try and assuage the pressure on her scalp. The other girls were sobbing and moaning as they took in the treatment of their mate. The girls to either side of her had moved away, as if fearful of catching the disease of disobedience from her.

While the rebellious girl flailed her soft, small hands at the powerful fist that held her head a prisoner, Wong said something to the Korean. Hooking the whip in his belt, he stepped behind the girl and reached around to her front. His large, strong hands took hold of the girl's silken, peach colored blouse and ripped it open. Buttons flew off as it was rent apart. The Korean grabbed the back collar of the garment and began to draw it down over the girl's flailing arms. She was crying and protesting in her native tongue and she tried to turn and twist her torso to resist the removal of her garment. With a brutal efficiency, the man soon had it down first one arm, and then the other.

Burnham was watching the display of brute force against the girl with untrammeled excitement. Watching the girl's futile struggles, appreciating her shame and humiliation at her abuse, had made him rock hard. He had had a blowjob about forty-five minutes ago while sitting at his vast desk in his office on the second floor of his mansion, but his lusts were enflamed anew by the tableau of the girl's suffering. He surreptitiously slid his right hand across his hip and gave his stiffened johnson a little squeeze.

The girl's firm, pleasant breasts swayed in the confinements of her lacy, white bra as she struggled to avoid the removal of her blouse. The tall, Eurasian man, Wong, just held her hair tightly in his fist, keeping the girl raised onto her tippy toes as the covering was pulled free of first one wrist than the other. As each hand was liberated from her elegant blouse, it flew back to her head in a desperate attempt to free her locks from her tormentor's grip while her body danced and she wailed plaintively.

Having removed the girl's blouse, the Korean used both of his powerful hands to tear apart her flimsy, lacy bra. He ripped each shoulder strap and then pulled the bra from the girl's body. Her breasts were handful sized, a little large for her slender, diminutive frame. Her areolas were wide and dark, darker than her tawny skin, and her nipples, fat and squat, had hardened from fear. She gave a desperate shriek as she felt her twin mounds bared. While her right hand maintained her effort to assuage the fierce grip on her hair, the other slid across her swaying mammaries in a vain attempt at covering them up.

The girl started to kick her feet at Wong, striking him solidly in the shin. Wong merely smiled and lifted the girl even higher by her hair. The Korean man proceeded to rip apart the waistband of her sleek, black miniskirt and then pulled it, together with the thin, white thong panties underneath, down over the girl's hips, along her thighs and down to her feet. He quickly flipped off one bright red high heeled pump after the other and drew the skirt and panties free of her feet.

She was now totally nude but for a pair of self supporting, sheer, beige stockings on her legs. The Korean had them off in an instant. The men all took a moment to appreciate her charms. Her torso narrowed enticingly to a pair of rounded hips and her belly was flat and tight. She pressed her legs together in an attempt to hide her sex, but the delicate entrance, two lines of soft flesh covered sparsely by finely trimmed black hair was revealed to all.

Burnham assumed that the parade of disrobing femininity would resume, but Wong had other ideas. He said something to the Korean who stooped down to the floor and scooped up the girl's delicate, white panties. He tore the waistband in two and then grabbed the girl's right arm and brought it behind her back. Her left arm still covered her breasts while he tied an end of the panties to her right wrist. Then, holding the right arm in place, he seized her left arm and pulled it behind her. When he had it in place, he used the panties to join her wrists together.

The girl's breasts were now free for closer examination. Realizing that her resistance had come to naught, the girl ceased her writhing and struggling. Tears were flowing down her face. Traces of mascara had flowed down from her pretty, brown eyes. Her face had a pitiful, mournful look. All male eyes were on her exquisite flesh.

Wong said something else to the Korean who moved from behind the now listless girl and retrieved a small gym bag that he had brought in with him. He carried it over to where Wong held the girl in place and opened it. He dug around inside and pulled out a thick leather belt that had in its middle a ring of soft, rubberized plastic. He turned back to the girl, an evil smile on his face.

The girl's eyes went wide with fright as she took in the instrument in the man's hands. When the Korean tried to introduce it to her mouth, she clamped her full, soft lips together and tried to twist her head away. The Korean looked at Wong and they both nodded. They were obviously men who had confronted this dilemma before, how to install a gag in a recalcitrant female. Wong took his free hand and pinched the girl's nostrils tightly together between a finger and his thumb. The Korean, seeing that the girl's access to air was limited to her mouth, gave the girl a sharp jab in her solar plexus.

Her eyes spread even wider and she gave out a deep moan of pain. Her lips spread apart as she gasped for air. While Wong held the girl's head steady, taking hold of her lower jaw, the Korean deftly placed the top of the ring behind her top teeth and then, bending the ring slightly, jammed it past the bottom ones. When the device was in place, spreading the girl's jaws widely as she continued to fight for oxygen, he buckled the belt behind her head.

"Would you like to make use of your new whore, Mr. Burnham?" Wong asked as he turned back to the American.

Burnham needed no encouragement. He stepped up to the unhappy, still recovering, young woman. She was panting heavily, desperately trying to recover her breath. Her eyes, tearful and plaintive, looked at the large Occidental demon in front of her. Being "made use of" was clearly not on the top of her list of priorities. She tried to form a word or words, but the sound emerged as, "Ahhhhhhhhhoooooooooooo!"

Wong had stepped aside and the Korean now had hold of her hair. Burnham took her firm, round breasts in his meaty hands and gave them a squeeze, gentle at first, as if weighing their mass and testing their softness, and then hard and harder still until the girl moaned in pain.

Satisfied at her response, Burnham moved his hands down over her hips and belly. The flesh above her barely shrouded loins was clear and soft. "Here's where my mark will go," he thought to himself as he allowed the tactile sensations of caressing the young girl's tender skin to excite him further. All the slave girls wore tattoos of their training houses on their bellies. It was the mark of pride of the slave houses. Burnham's was the snarling head of a black mastiff, its teeth and eyes bright red, its fangs exposed. Other houses used wolves, venomous snakes, lions, bears, any kind of beast that might strike terror in a helpless, young girl and be evidential of the house's brutal inclinations. It served as an ever present advertisement for the slave house's wares and an indication of where to return a slave girl for complementary, vicious retraining should she ever falter in her duties.

Burnham delighted at the thought that later, within the hour perhaps, the girl would be fixed to a specialized chair down in the lower level of the training center and her now, clean, smooth, bare flesh would be forever marred with the emblem of his ownership. When the mastiff was tattooed on her belly, her new slave name, whatever was chosen for her, would be emblazoned across her upper chest in two inch high, bright blue, scriptive letters. Finally, two disks would be affixed to her lower labial lips. They would be left blank for now. When she was purchased or converted to his staff after training, they would have etched on them the emblem of her current ownership. While the tattoos would stay, the disks could be removed and replaced as she was passed from hand to hand, from owner to owner. And if she managed to escape, a slim eventuality, when she was recaptured, a virtual certainty, her owner could readily be identified and she be returned for appropriately cruel punishments.

The girl's thighs were tightly clamped together as she suffered the hands of her new owner on her body. Her torso was twisting and turning and she struggled to free her cruelly bound hands behind her. Her mangled cries of distress and protest echoed throughout the room. Seeing that the girl was barring Burnham's desire to sample her black bearded slit, the Korean kicked her feet apart and then circled them with his own. Burnham, giving the Korean a little nod of appreciation, ran his hand between the girl's now outspread thighs and took possession of her delicate mound. He rubbed his fingers along her fleshy labia and the divide between them. He took his time in sampling the girl's sex, insinuating his fingers slowly along the gradually spreading gap. He teased the nub of pleasure at the crevasse's upper tip until the girl gave an involuntary moan. Her slit had moistened and Burnham felt a shiver of pleasure as his fingers slipped between her puffy love lips and inside.

"Auuuuuurh!" the girl moaned plaintively as she felt the intruders scour the interior walls of her cleft. "Ooooooooooo! Oooouuuu!" She struggled to bring her thighs together and tried to draw her hips back to take her pussy out of the man's reach. The Korean man held her firmly from behind and pressed against her hips with his, forcing her to remain in place. Some of the men behind Burnham laughed.

Having satisfied himself with his exploration of her flesh, Burnham was ready to sample the soft, warm, wet interior of her mouth with his cock. "Put her on her knees," he told the Korean as he lowered his zipper and freed his instrument from its dark environs. The Korean man pressed his knees into the back of the girl's, forcing her legs to bend and then pushed her down. Understanding what was about to happen, staring unbelievingly at the thick, long, stiff phallus that jutted out at her face, the girl tried to twist away. The Korean's grip on her hair held her still and she gave out a long, piteous moan.

Burnham waved his prick at the girl's face, enjoying her dismay. He rubbed it over her tear stained cheeks above the leather straps that crossed them. The girl's lips were distended into a wide circle. He caressed them with the tip of his cock's meaty head, circling his ultimate target, prolonging the girl's anticipation of her violation. Having so many well trained slave girls, it wasn't often that he could draw this kind of reaction from a pretty young woman and Burnham was reveling in the girl's distress. Then, having had enough, he slowly pressed his cock forwards. The girl became frantic with dismay. She strained to move the wide open target encircled by her distended lips by shaking her head violently, but her efforts at turning her head were fruitless. She pulled helplessly at her bound hands behind her. Her wails became louder and more desperate. When his cock breached her rounded lips, her body shuddered. Anxious to get his dick moist and hot, Burnham plunged himself in.

The callous American began his motions slowly and deliberately. He felt the girl's frantic tongue attempt to reject the intruder only, instead, serving to send a thrill of delight up his steel hard wand as it brushed over and along it. When Burnham pushed against the back of her mouth, at the edge of her narrow throat, the girl uttered a muffled, panicked, "Gaaaaaaaaaaa!"

Holding the girl's head by the sides, Burnham matched the rocking of his hips with a back and forth movement of the girl's mouth. He could feel the glans of his cock glide across the girl's tongue and the roof of her mouth as he went. His neck bent back and his eyes closed to slits as he enjoyed the use of his new slave girl. He jutted himself further and further within her, pressing deeper and deeper into her throat. Each time the bulbous head of his prick crossed the threshold of her esophagus, the girl coughed and sputtered as she struggled for air.

The room was silent except for the sound of the girl's sufferings, muffled by the huge male member in her mouth, and the soft sobbing of the female witnesses to their colleague's torment. Each one knew that her turn would come. They trembled and cowered, trying not to look at the display of male cruelty before them. Tears were being shed all around. What had started as a hopeful journey into a prosperous and secure future had turned into a nightmare.

Burnham felt his juices beginning to build. "Ohhhhhh-hhhhhh," he moaned as his testes tightened and his cock began to vibrate with anticipation of his climax. "I could never give this up," he thought as his pleasure washed over him. "And if everything works out, I will never have to."

While his cock began its dance within the girl's mouth, Burnham issued loud grunts of satisfaction. His pace had quickened as his need had built. The girl's voice, now muted, continued a soft, "Gaaaaaa!" every time his cock jammed home. His hands clamped down hard on the sides of the girl's helpless head and he buried his cock deep into her throat. She wailed and struggled, her face pressed against his belly, as he let the product of his passions jet directly into the narrow passageway en route to her stomach.

When his cock's convulsions ebbed, Burnham let it sit encapsulated by the girl's throat while he reveled in post orgasmic bliss. He was dragged from his reverie by the girl's frantic squeaking and desperate movements to free her head. He didn't want to suffocate her on her first day, that would be a foolish business loss, and so he reluctantly drew his softening piece from her mouth.

Burnham stepped back and zipped up his fly. The Korean released his hold on the girl's hair and let her body sag towards the floor. She was sobbing forlornly and she bent over, her breasts touching her slender thighs, her face turned downward. Her shoulder length, black hair made a curtain around her face. Her prettily decorated hands lay limp amidst the sparkling white remnants of her panties fastened around them. Her graceful back was arched, revealing the little bumps of her slender spine and the soft, round, enticing orbs of her rear. Her body shuddered as it recorded each heartfelt sob.

Suddenly the Korean sprang back to life. He shouted out a command to the other half naked women. He took the whip from his belt and lashed out at two of the girls, making them scream with pain. It was if a spell had been broken. The shapely, brown skinned girls moved frantically to obey the harsh Korean. Bras, panties and brightly colored high heeled shoes quickly joined the piles of clothes in front of them. One or two of the girls were wearing pantyhose and they struggled to draw them down over their hips as quickly as they could. No one wanted to experience the travail of the now defeated rebel girl.

When the eight other slender, diminutive, young beauties were fully naked, the Korean ordered them to put their hands on their heads. The girls all complied with alacrity and the raising of their arms caused their enticing breasts to lift up in presentation position. Wong guided the sated Burnham down the line of beauteous female flesh. The American measured the girls' breasts, squeezing them and pinching at their fear stiffened nipples. He paused here and there to wander his hand across a taut, brown belly or to delve between a pair of graceful, thighs.

The girls shifted their legs readily to give him access to their loins, afraid of the rebel girl's fate. Their lips were all trembling with fear and their eyes, if not tearful, were watery and sorrowful. Although at first glance they had all looked alike to the American tycoon turned slavemaster, at closer look, he took note of their differences. Each girl had a distinct personality revealed by the evidence of their fear: the biting of their lips, the nervous flicking of the eyes. One had a longer face than the others; another's lips were more puffy and pronounced. One had high cheekbones and another, thick, dark eyebrows. The breasts, although on the small size by European standards, were plump and firm, some larger than the others. Almost all of the girls had trimmed their pussy hair and a few had denuded it completely. Their dainty, hairless mons accentuated their little girlish aspect.

One girl, who had long, black, thin hair that reached behind her to her waist, had breasts no bigger than inverted teacups. They were so cute that Burnham could not resist, much to the girl's dismay, placing his lips upon them and suckling at her sharp, fear stiffened nipples.

When he was finished with his inspection, he turned to the Eurasian gangster who had dutifully followed down the line behind him. "So how many can we expect a month?"

"We'll be sending nine a week at first. They won't all be Malaysian. We have operations in Indonesia, Thailand and Burma. We're working on a Cambodian and a Vietnamese connection as well."

"That's fine," Burnham responded. "The market for them is huge. And as we discussed, we'll be able to match one for three in Caucasian whores. The ratio reflects the relative market supply and difficulty in transport you understand, not a comment of relative value."

Wong laughed. "You don't have to be politically correct with me. Mr. Burnham. I understand supply and demand."

In the meantime, Barouf's men had gone to work in preparing the sniffling, frightened young women for their journey down into the bowels of the slave training center. They would all start out on level three and work their way up as their training progressed. If they had any true conception of how harsh and painful their training would be, they probably would have all made a mad dash for the door regardless of the chance of escape. Little in their life would have prepared them for the experience of being reduced to chattel and converted into exquisite creatures of subservient sexual service.

Four of Barouf's men were going down the line of women. The first one held a black velveteen bag and the girls were ordered to throw all of their jewelry into it. He was followed by the other three. Each held a box of that they would put down next to a girl, retrieve the implements of servitude contained within and attach them to the girl's body. One went behind the girls and, taking their hands from their heads one by one, attached thick leather cuffs and then joined them behind the girls' backs. Another was in charge of the ankle bracelets and, when they were affixed, he bound their ankles together with an 18" long chain. The third was responsible for slave collars and gags.

After encircling each trembling girl's neck with a three inch wide leather band with gleaming, brass rings embedded in front and behind, he took out a leather belt with a long, fat, leather prong attached and inserted the business end into the frowning, but obediently opened, mouth. Once the alluring, bound and gagged young women were all suitably prepared for their journey into hell, even the still quietly sobbing rebel of a little while ago, they were ordered to turn to their right. A chain was fastened between each one's neck. Barouf clapped his hands and uttered a command and the line of nine sobbing, naked, former aspiring secretaries meekly and despondently shuffled off to the elevator and to their unknown, dismal fates.

CHAPTER TWO

About 150 miles southwest of the Burnham estate, a slender ponygirl, new to her bit, was undergoing a workout. She was one of the newer ponygirls belonging to Axmail Grobgy, a notorious Russian gangster. Grobgy, among other things, controlled much of the drug trade within Moscow and St. Petersburg, owned a chain of whorehouses and strip clubs and dealt in just about every variety of contraband that could be transported and sold. He was a former sergeant in the KGB.

When the Evil Empire collapsed, he and a few of his cronies shifted their allegiances from Karl Marx to themselves. Being ruthless, and knowing where all the bodies were buried, they had no trouble carving out criminal empires. A few, of course, had fallen along the way. Disputes between gangsters, especially in the early days, were resolved by a pistol, a stiletto or a garrote, or maybe a few ounces of plastic explosive. Now things were more settled with the Commission and all that. So the heavyset, late fiftyish, black haired and bearded man spent most of his time on his estate in Kalikastan watching over his ponygirls and enjoying the sweet life. He was standing there now at the rail that surrounded the little training paddock, watching what had been until little more than a week ago a pretty young girl, being put thorough her paces.

The girl and her boyfriend had been caught abusing one of Grobgy's prime ponygirls, Lightning. They had bribed their way into the ponygirl encampment at night and had hauled her into the woods to make use of her. Doubtless the boy would have bragged for years about the time he actually fucked the famous 3000 meter sulky. The girl had objected at first but, seduced by the available flesh and the thrill of doing something outré, she had joined in. When they had been caught in the act, the boy paid with his life for his violation of the ponygirl. The girl's body had been too enticing to be disposed of so casually and Grobgy had decided that if she wanted so badly to see what ponygirls were like, she could become one.

It was a violation of the rules of the Commission to enslave Russian or Ukrainian women for use in Kalikastan. They didn't want to do anything to endanger their tenuous and always precarious relationships with the large former Soviet republics to their east and south. Although the ruling powers in those countries worked hand in glove with the gangsters most of the time, the idea of Russian or Ukrainian women serving as sexual chattel was thought to be a little too provocative. The same pertained to local girls. There was no sense stirring up rebellion within the local population who mostly benefited from the expenditure's of the criminal gangs' largess within the country. Besides, who wanted slave girls or ponygirls who spoke Russian or even Kalikastani? Keeping them largely ignorant of what was going on around them made their situations seem all that more hopeless. Russian speaking girls might escape more easily back to their native lands and raise a ruckus. Slave girls were spoken to mostly in English, the lingua franca of their enslavement. Ponygirls were taught just enough Russian command words so that they could perform their duties: running, fucking and sucking.

Grobgy had made an exception for the pretty, brown haired Russian girl who had crossed the line of propriety that night. She had seen her boyfriend's throat slashed by Lightning's driver, a four foot tall dwarf named Jerzi. She couldn't just be let go. So, although she was more slender than and not quite as tall as the typical human female recruited for such purposes, she had been stripped and hooded, tattooed and ringed. Her hair, but for a thick strand in the back of her head, had been shaved as had her delicate, little pudenda. She wore a blue, neoprene hood at all times except for cleaning and grooming purposes. The tight fitting hood conformed to the contours of her face and tied off at the thick, chin uplifting ponygirl collar that she wore. It had an opening for her mouth and nostrils, but ponygirls never were permitted to speak. They wore continuously either a thick leather plug ensconced in their mouths which was attached to a broad leather shield that covered their lips and chin, or their steel, leather encased bits for when they were training or racing.

All humanity had been stripped from the former, pretty young woman. No one, especially her, would ever see her face again. A large golden ring had been fit into her septum and her hands were kept fastened behind her to a strap that ran down from her collar. Ponies didn't have hands and females who had become ponies had no use for them.

Grobgy had been present when the artisan he employed on his estate had etched the emblem of his estate into the girl's flesh. It was a snarling, rampant, yellow wolf, its front paws raised ominously. The girl had struggled and cried as the electric pen sent the ink into her pores. Grobgy didn't know the female's human name, such things were not important. He had her christened 'Suki', and the two inch high, blue, Cyrillic letters had been added to her upper chest.

Standing in the middle of the ring, wielding a long dressage whip, was a tall, lean but well built man dressed in black. This was Anton Drabik, Grobgy's second in command, chief killer and his best ponygirl trainer. It took a heartless soul to be a good ponygirl trainer. The former women needed to be well acquainted with the whip and totally devoted to their new life. Competition on the racing course was intense and ponygirls had to be ready to give their all. It took a strict regimen of discipline and abuse, unrelenting, to tear away from the dehumanized creatures all thoughts of return to their former lives. Acceptance of their new status as mere beasts was crucial to their development. Drabik's cold, steel heart was perfect for the task.

The killer/ponygirl trainer was conscious of the watchful, eyes of his employer. Drabik was a former colonel in the red Army. When the Soviet Union collapsed, he had been left unemployed. Since killing was what he knew best, he turned to a life of crime. It rankled him though to serve under the command of a mere sergeant. Some months ago, he had decided that he had had enough of service to the former apparatchik and had put plans into motion to overthrow him. The time was coming soon and he was having a hard time waiting. Even now, he resented the presence of his master while he worked. But the old fuck would get his soon. That was for certain.

Since Suki was of insufficient size and strength to make a good racer, the racing carriages were heavy and needed ponies with great endurance and stamina, Drabik was training the new pony for show purposes. It was a recent fad and Suki, with her graceful, delicate lines, was perfect for it. She was circling the paddock, her bit chained to a revolving arm overhead, lifting her knees high at each step in a prancing mode. Her back and rear were spotted with bright red, painful looking wounds denoting where she had suffered Drabik's lash for faltering in her rounds. Her naked body was covered with sweat. Her ample, bare breasts flopped and danced on her chest attractively as she kept up her pace.

"So what do you think, Anton?" Grobgy finally called out. Drabik gave him a harsh look. Usually speaking one's mind around a ponygirl didn't make much difference. None of them could understand the guttural Slavic tongue. This one was different and communicating in her presence worked against Drabik's efforts to complete her dehumanization.

The black clad killer turned to the machine which drove the overhead armature and snapped it off. He turned back to the ponygirl and yelled, in Russian, "Halt!" one of the seventy five or so words in Russian that ponygirls were taught.

The grateful ponygirl came skidding to a stop. Her chest was heaving from her exertions and she swayed on her thick, tall, black ponygirl boots. The chain to the armature kept her head tilted firmly upwards. Her sobs and moans of unhappiness had been drowned out by the humming of the small electric motor that controlled the overhead pole. Now that it was stopped, her caterwauling could be distinctly heard. Drabik shook his head. After two weeks of training, the pony should be further along than this. Unlike the others, this one knew precisely where she was, that her home and her family were probably, at the most, a hundred miles away, that people would be looking for her, wondering what had happened to her. And hearing her native language spoken all around her was preventing her from making the separation that she needed from her former self to become a well adjusted pony.

Drabik let the pony stand at rest and walked over to his master. "I wish you wouldn't talk in front of her," he said churlishly. He kept his voice low so that the pony, who was standing on the other side of the paddock, could not hear them. "It makes my job all the harder."

Grobgy was slightly taken aback by his employee's hostile tone. Something was going on with him; Grobgy sensed it. His attitude had changed over the last few months. He would take careful watching.

"Relax, Anton," Grobgy replied. "I just want to know how the pony is doing."

Drabik reigned in his animosity to the bear sized gangster. "It's like I've been saying. It's going to be awfully hard to break her completely in this atmosphere. Every time she hears someone speak in Russian, she's reminded of who she used to be. I think that we need to sell her off."

"To who?" Grobgy asked. "I don't want anyone to find out who she was. I've got enough trouble with the Commission as it is." Someone had been knocking off Grobgy's drug dealers and making off with millions of dollars. Grobgy had struck back at the most likely suspects and his escalation of the rivalry between gangs was causing some dismay down in the capitol. "It's nothing I can't handle, but I don't want the annoyance of an investigation,"

Drabik smiled. He knew the troubles Grobgy had been having. It was he who was ripping off and killing Grobgy's drug dealers. He needed money to buy the loyalty of enough of Grobgy's men to make his move. And he needed the permission of the Commission, whose consent was more easily obtained after the submission of a substantial gratuity. No one took out a gang leader without their tacit acquiescence. Grobgy didn't know it, but Drabik had gotten the green light a few days ago.

"I've made contact with some of the Arabs who've been given export licenses by the Commission," Drabik replied. "One of them is interested." Since 9/11, the means of acquisition of ponygirls for the Arabian market had all but dried up. Security in all of the Western countries was too tight. Through Burnham's deal with the American government, flights between Kalikastan and the Middle East were left untouched. The Commission had issued a small number of licenses to Arab buyers so they could replenish their stock.

"It's the perfect solution," Drabik continued. "Since she can't understand Arabic, she'll be able to settle down and become a good ponygirl. Once she's somewhere that doesn't remind her of home, she'll lose any ideas of rescue or escape."

"Okay," Grobgy said. "Do it."

"He's coming around this afternoon," Drabik informed his erstwhile leader. "I'm going to ask for fifty thousand, but I'll settle for thirty."

Grobgy gave a nod of approval. He was miffed that his minion had made arrangements for the pony to be viewed without getting permission. It was another thing to keep in mind. Tall heads needed to be chopped off every once in a while. Drabik was getting too powerful. And he was fucking his daughter.

Anya Grobgy, 23 years old, was the apple of her father's eye. She was tall and thin and beautiful. She had been practically raised on the estate and was as callous and brutal in her use of slave girls and ponies as any of the men. He didn't mind that. Everybody needed a hobby. But Grobgy drew the line where men were concerned. A few who had had the temerity to sample the shapely young woman's charms were lying under several feet of sod out on the steppes. It wasn't just his antique morality. The daughter of a prince was a valuable commodity. Whoever took Anya's hand would be heir apparent to the throne.

For a while, Grobgy had done nothing after he learned of the regular trysts that his daughter was having with his chief enforcer. He was getting on in years and maybe it was time to think of the future. Drabik was smart and ruthless enough to be a gang leader. In the last few weeks, though, he had been having second thoughts. He was too young to retire. He had at least ten good years left. And who's to say whether Drabik would let him go. He might put a bullet in him just to make sure that his retirement was permanent. No, once the pony racing season was over, Drabik would find his own six by three foot hole out in the steppes.

Grobgy left to go back to the mansion leaving Drabik alone with his troublesome charge. The killer stepped over to where the new pony was standing disconcertedly, having recovered a semblance of her breath. She gave a little shiver as she sensed her trainer approaching. Contact with the trainer could only mean two things. One was that it was prefatory to some new, painful abuse, or, two, a continuation of the seemingly almost constant assault on her sexual senses. Rarely was the contact innocuous.

Drabik had retrieved the large plastic jug of water used to keep the workout pony hydrated. It had a long, narrow snout so that it could be poked between her lips and over the leather covered steel bit in her mouth. Suki had only started using the bit a day or so go. Until now, her exercises had been conducted with the mouth filling, leather gag. Covering the lower half of her face, or where her face would have been had she still had one, ensured that the pony would start breathing through her nose during the workout. This helped attain the anaerobic state needed for good training, the point where the pony would have to give more than she thought possible, passing the point where the oxygen in her bloodstream was replenished.

It also taught her, when the bit was installed, to breathe through both her mouth and nose when she ran, since the bit itself hindered the free flow of air. This in turn generated the horse like snorts from the ponies when they raced that aficionados of the sport are all too familiar with and, in fact, serves as the basis for much of the public's conceptions of these marvelous animals. No human makes a sound like that when they run and so, ergo, ponygirls weren't human.

Suki had learned, to her disconcertment, just how unhumanlike she had become. Aside from the permanent loss of the use of her hands, the worse was the inability to communicate with her handlers and abusers. It was something that she just couldn't get used to. The cruel man who was her trainer had driven her hard this afternoon. It was the hardest workout she had had yet, and that was saying a lot. Her thighs were burning from exhaustion and her lungs ached. The 'ggggghpf, ggggghpf, ggggghpf,' sound that she made when she ran tormented her. Even to her protesting mind, the fact that she was snorting like a horse made her realize that her humanity was slipping away.

She had heard the voice of the man talking to her trainer and had heard his inquiry as to how she was doing. She recognized the voice. It was the large, black haired man with the full, bristling, fierce beard who had enslaved her on that terrible night when her boyfriend, Sergei, had been killed. She feared that the men were planning some terrible fate for her. She had tried her best to comply with her trainer's cruel demands, really she had! If he would just let her rest, she could do better!

Another thing that was eroding her sense of her former self was the new name the men had given her. She had seen it in the full length mirror in the ponygirl barn that was used to demonstrate to new ponies just what they had become and to renew the memory of older ones, from time to time. They had tattooed it on her chest. The vision of herself hooded, tattooed and ringed, naked and hairless down below, was shocking and she almost fainted when she saw it. Could that faceless, blue hooded creature really be her? She had to cock and sway her head to get the full view of herself through the tiny, dime sized holes in her hood over her eyes. The golden ring they had placed through her nose glimmered in the dim light. Little golden disks dangled from the smooth, soft lips of her sex. Although the letters etched into her upper chest above her bare breasts were backwards, she could read them easily enough, even if the man had not reinforced her awareness by pointing to them and pronouncing her new appellation.

It was "Suki this," and "Suki that" now. When the men were fucking her in the ponybarn, they cooed her name as they plowed her fevered canal, "Good Suki. Pretty Suki." Fixed motionless, her legs spread wide by chains on her ankles and one leading from the demeaning ring they had placed in her nose to the blank wall in front of her stall, leaning against a thick beam that ran across it at the height of her waist, she received their hard, conscienceless shafts helplessly. Her disobedient cleft reveled in the caresses that the men gave it and, try as she might, she could not fight off the paroxysms of pleasure that they induced in her. She cried out in her mind as the unknown, anonymous men fucked her from behind, "I'm Zhanna! I'm Zhanna! My name is Zhanna!" When the men left, sometimes abandoning her to incomplete pleasure, she cried and cried until her tears would come no more.

Standing now in the training paddock, Suki dreaded the thought that her trainer would resume her terrible journey around it. Her neck ached from its awkward and demeaning position. The smooth, featureless blue hood that she now always wore confined her vision so that, with her head perched upwards by the chain connecting her bit to the infernal machine, all she could see was the chain above her head, a small portion of the wooden pole to which it was connected and a tiny, round background of lightly clouded, blue sky.

She gave a jump when the man approached her and started to moan her unhappiness. The man introduced the nozzle of the watering jug to her mouth and poured the lukewarm liquid in. Due to her posture, the water flooded her mouth and she had no choice but to swallow. She, in fact, welcomed the tepid sustenance. Her throat was dry and her body felt weak. She swallowed as fast she could, but even so, a good quantity spilled over her lips and ran down her neck and her bare chest.

When the man thought that she had enough, her withdrew the nozzle and placed the jug back in the center of the ring. The former young woman panicked at the thought of another training run. Forgetting the lessons that the men had taught her through their ever present and always ready whips, she started to call out a plaintive entreaty to the man in her native tongue. Her voice was garbled by the fiendish bit between her teeth. "...eeeeease! eeeeease! oh ore! eeeeease!" As soon as the sounds of the mangled words escaped her lips, she regretted it.

Drabik heard the pony's attempt at speech. He turned on his heels and stepped over to her. She was sobbing, realizing her terrible sin. He seized one of her breasts with his left hand, cupping it underneath and easing the soft, spongy mass from her body. He gave it a fierce, resounding slap with his right. The pony jerked and moaned at the pain. He then lifted her other breast and gave it the same treatment. The contact between his powerful hand and the surface of the pony's delicate breasts made a loud 'crack!'. The former human female jumped and howled at the pain. Drabik repeated the punishment, once again to each breast, and then took hold of the pony's nipples and squeezed them cruelly. Suki danced and screamed behind her bit as the awful sensations of having her nipples crushed and twisted coursed through her.

The newly dehumanized pony gave out a gasp of relief when the man released her nipples. Her breasts were on fire from where they had been slapped and she still suffered from the residue of the abuse to their tender points. "Bad, Suki! Bad!" the man said, like she was some kind of little girl or, worse yet, a dog or other disobedient pet.

The man took repossession of the pony's ample breasts, but this time he was satisfied with caressing and massaging them. His touch was gentle and strangely soothing. He leaned over and took her nipples in his mouth, one at a time and gave them each a long, strong, pacifying suckle. Despite her pain and humiliation, Suki felt a tug at her loins as the man's lips pulled at her teats. His hand wandered down her tattooed belly and pressed itself between her long, graceful thighs, capturing her smooth, hairless mons. He stroked it as his lips and tongue teased her nipples and the pony realized that her sex was responding to the man's caresses. A thick finger slid along the divide between her labial lips, gathered some of her incipient moisture of arousal and then spread it over her tingling, disobedient clit. Suki had learned quickly not to try and close her legs when a master wanted to caress her there, yet she yearned now to shut them to protest against her callous treatment and, more importantly, ashamed at her powerlessness, to stop the rebellious arousal that her body was experiencing.

Drabik felt the pony's body tremble as he massaged her crevasse. He took his time, exploring and caressing the cleft until the portal was wet and soft. The pony's breathing had become deep and heavy, even as she whined her unhappiness. Her knees bent and her body started to sag. She began to emit a low pitched, distraught moan. When he had her good and aroused, he pulled his hand from her loins and took his lips from her teats. Pleasure and pain were the tools of ponygirl subjugation. One complemented the other. She could be a good ponygirl and experience, from time to time, exquisite, conscienceless pleasure as anonymous, uncaring men used her, or she could suffer unbearable pain.

The killer lifted his hand to the nostrils on the pony's forcibly uplifted head so that she could get a good whiff of her own arousal. She needed to learn that others controlled her body now. She was its mere occupier.

Suki gave out a morose whine as the odor of her juices floated to her nose. The point had been made.

Drabik returned to the center of the ring. He picked up the dressage whip and started the motor of the armature. The pony felt its tug on her bit and gave an unhappy groan. "Go!" Drabik yelled as he cracked the whip across her buttocks.

The sharp pain jolted the bound, naked and hooded ponygirl into motion.

CHAPTER THREE

Jake Barnes was lying on his back in the large, four poster bed of his bedroom in the upper floor of the guest cottage on the Burnham Estate. His mind was struggling to consciousness. Slowly, he recorded the warmth of a soft, female body next to him. A small, delicate hand had hold of his cock and was gently stroking it into hardness. The girl was lying against his right side, her breasts pushed against his upper arm, her upper thigh sliding back and forth languorously across his. He could hear her lust charged breath from her mouth near his ear and could feel her chest rising and falling against him. Groggily, keeping his eyes closed, he tried to recall which of the pretty, subservient slave girls he had brought with him when he decided to take a little nap this afternoon. She was blond, he remembered that. No, not really blond, her hair was kind of a silvery color. He remembered that now. Burnham had brought in a hair stylist from New York and some of the girls were wearing some unusual colors these days. Streaks of garish red, green or blue, stuff like that. It did make the slave girls look more exceptional and exotic.

Jake concentrated his mind. He had had so many of the delectable creatures over the last many months. It was hard to distinguish them as individuals. He was determined to bring the girl into recall before he opened his eyes. It was kind of a test, to see if he was really so far gone that he could not think of them as people any more. He and the girl had fucked for about an hour before he drifted off into his nap. He was pissed at himself that he could not remember who she was or what she looked like.

Her face and body began to come into his mind. She was about 5'4" tall and she had an impertinent demeanor. Her breasts were midsized, very firm, almost like two torpedoes jutting from her chest. They were the same breasts that were rubbing against his arm, the nipples hard. She wore the same, standard, circles of leather around her wrists, ankles and neck as the other slave girls. Marlee, that was her name. Marlee. He recalled the florid, blue letters tattooed across her chest.

She was not one of Burnham's trained girls; their names were all etched into their skin in scriptive English letters. Burnham was determined that his buyers know that their purchases were the result of good old American know how and efficient, proper corporate management. This girl's name was spelt out on her upper chest in bright blue, two inch high, Cyrillic letters. She had obviously been picked up by Burnham here or there, a casual purchase at a slave auction, perhaps a gift from a fellow estate owner. Although, at first, the strange, seemingly hieroglyphic letters were impenetrable to Jake, he had, over the last seven months or so, learned to decipher them. Marlee, her name was definitely Marlee. Now, if he could only recall the tattoo of her training house etched on her belly, he would be satisfied.

The expert manipulation of his hardening tool was making concentration progressively more difficult. The soft hand eased itself up and down his shaft, the small, nimble fingers fluttering over the soft, sensitive skin. When it reached the narrow band of flat, red flesh that demarked the edge of his cock's fat helmet, the fingers lingered there, drumming softly on the supersensitive surface. Each time the girl did it, he gave out a soft sigh and his breathing became just a little more deep, his blood just a little hotter.

The girl was taking a bit of a chance in her immodest advances. Slave girls were not permitted to touch a master without permission, nor to act out their own sexual desires. But Jake and his Amerikanski crew had gotten a reputation among the estate's servile sluts as easy marks and they often competed for the chance to serve in the small guesthouse that served as their headquarters. It was better than the rude treatment they normally received in the mansion proper from the Russian guards, the Kalikastani staff or even from Burnham's mostly American complement of corporate employees. Maybe it was the fact that Jake and his crew perceived their stay in Kalikastan as temporary and they wanted to be able to assuage their consciences when they returned to the real world where such things as female slavery was looked askance at. Feeling free to urge Jake to a resumption of their passionate coupling, the girl was making her wants clearly known.

A snake. Suddenly Jake remembered the girl's tattoo. It was a green and yellow, coiled cobra, its head proudly raised, its tongue lashing out provocatively, two long, sharp, exaggerated, yellow fangs protruding from its mouth. Jake felt better. His was a dangerous business and attention to detail was a large factor in his survival to date. His body, which had been drawn into tightness when he first awoke and felt the girl's supplicative advances, loosened now and he relaxed, committed to enjoying the upcoming intermingling of their flesh.

The slave girl took the softening of Jake's muscles as permission to accelerate her attentions to his pleasure. Her soft, plump lips pressed against his shoulder and then, dragging her breasts across his arm, she moved her mouth to his chest, nibbling at his rigid nipples. Her tongue flicked at them and her grip on his cock became a little more firm. It was tall and hard now, ready for action.

Jake moaned as the girl drifted her lips down his belly, kissing and licking his tensile skin along the way. She was kneeling now at his side, her head pointed towards his feet. Her firm breasts with their stiffened nipples coursed along his flesh, giving no doubt as to her prominent and aroused femininity. Her hair was just long enough so that Jake could feel it drifting along his torso, curtaining the girl's face, producing faint quivers of his skin.

When the silver haired slave girl's mouth reached its goal, she took a few moments to massage the bulbous head of Jake's rampant meat with her thick lips and tongue and then, slowly, her lips tightly gripped against his shaft, she lowered her mouth until the thick, reverberating pole was firmly ensconced within. His groan of pleasure was met with a syncopated moan of delight from the female. Jake lifted his hand, which had been pinned to his side when the girl had lain next to him, and caressed her soft, firm rear cheeks. Her skin was smooth and hot and the girl's body welcomed the contact. While she worked expertly on his pole, her hand cupping his trilling soft stones, her tongue dancing and swirling on his meat, Jake let his hand drift between her widened thighs and captured, from behind, her soft, engorged, hairless mons. The girl's body shuddered with grateful echoes of her pleasure when he slipped two thick fingers into her moistened and hot crevasse. The unmistakable, fecund, musky odor of her arousal wafted up to his receptive nostrils.

Jake had been surprised at how readily the slave girls took to their new roles in life when he had first arrived in this lawless paradise. As he came to learn more about their intense training, he began to understand how they seemed to uniformly be able to shift their bodies into an aroused state at will, for god help the slut who could not. And since the opportunity for frequent, intense sexual pleasure was perhaps the only redeeming feature of their embondment, the slave girls responded uniformly with alacrity to any male advance.

But for some, there was something more. A number of the girls, more than you might have expected, descended into a kind of psychotic reaction to their cruel captivity. Whether formerly, loose liberated and licentious or prim, modest maidens, with maybe one or two prior occasional sexual partners, or, perhaps, none at all, they became ravenous sirens. You could see the glint of constant desire in their eyes as you passed them in the hallways, kneeling and chained in place awaiting someone to take an interest in them, or passing them in the hallways of the mansion on their way to one work assignment or the other. Marlee was one of these. Jake had taken note of her a couple of times as he perambled through the mansion on his way back and forth from Burnham's office on the second floor. He had always been on his way somewhere and so had not had the opportunity to sample her. But late this morning, he had seen her chained to a column in the great hall, kneeling, her hands locked behind her, her knees spread wide apart. Their eyes had met and the invitation to make use of her had been crystal clear. Jake had not been disappointed.

Marlee's hips began to rock in time to Jake's sawing of his fingers back and forth along her enraptured canal and she was giving out moans and squeals of appreciation as she continued to suck at his cock. Suddenly, she withdrew her lips from his tool and turned her torso, throwing her leg over his thighs. Jake had kept his eyes closed up till now, but he opened them in reaction to the girl's quick, deliberate movement. Her pleasing face was alight with her passion, her mouth distended in a mischievous, delighted smile. Her chest was flushed red and her breasts were hard and pointed. Her eyes were wide and watery. The golden colored ring that emerged from the thick leather collar around her throat glinted in the afternoon light.

The girl had hold of Jake's rigid shaft with both her hands and she slid its head along the gates of her crevasse. Jake could feel the warm moisture of her arousal as the soft, slippery surface of her love lips glided along the head of his cock. He groaned with appreciation and his hips rose to encourage the girl to suffuse his manhood deep within her. The girl seemed to be enjoying the tantalizing effect of her little trick. She slid his cock two more times along her distended love lips and then, her mouth forming into a little 'o', her features drawn tightly together in impassioned enjoyment, she lowered his hips slowly and deliberately until Jake's prick was incased fully within her.

The soft, moist heat of the girl's cunt sent a thrill to Jake's prick that passed from his belly, up his chest and into his almost delirious brain. The girl began to ride him slowly, her pussy muscles clenching his manhood firmly on each upwards stroke and then releasing his shaft and letting the soft, cushioned interior of her sex flow over him. Her satisfaction at Jake's thick, long manhood was evident on her face and she gave a low moan each time that she lowered her hips as it scraped across her engorged clit. As her passions rose, so did Jake's and soon her motions became faster, more needy. Jake thrust his hips up to meet hers when she pressed her pussy down, slamming her love lips against the base of his cock. He reached up and took hold of her full, conical breasts and squeezed them hard, making the girl throw her head back with pleasure.

"Ohhhhhhhhhhh! Ohhhhhhhhhhhh! Master! Yes! Yes! Yes!" she called out loudly as her lusts overwhelmed her. Her body shuddered as her orgasm shot through her, apparently triggered by the manhandling of her hot, blood filled peaks. Jake felt his crisis rising. His balls tightened and a tantalizing tingling spread along his shaft. He felt his head swim as his blood concentrated in his loins.

When his ejaculations began, Jake gave a great shout. His hands tightened even more firmly around the girl's ample breasts and he pinched her nipples, grown as hard as buttons, between his thumbs and forefingers. His loud expression of delight was matched by the girl's scream of pleasure as her cunt's contractions began anew and intensified. Jake felt his spume flow along the length of his jumping, jerking member. At each spurt from its end, he gave a heavy moan and his hips slammed upwards. The intense pleasure seemed to last minutes, rather than seconds, sending fierce jolts of pleasure to his brain. Ultimately though, his pulsing manhood waned and his forces faded.

The girl's body was gleaming with sweat as she slowed her cunt's ministrations to his cock. Her hands were planted firmly on his shoulders. Her tongue licked across her plump lips which were spread widely in an appreciative smile. She lowered her torso so that her breasts mashed against Jake's chest and she nuzzled her lips against his neck. "Ooouuuuu, master," she moaned.

Jake had no idea where the slave girl was from, how long she had been a prisoner, what she was really like. He had spoken no more than four or five words to her. He did know that he wanted to fuck her again. For now, though, he had other things to do. His boys were probably all waiting downstairs for their meeting.

Reluctantly, Jake pushed the slave girl aside and rose from the bed. A pair of dismayed eyes peered up at him from a small cage in the corner of the room. His slave girl, Dana, crouched inside, a gag across her mouth and her arms bound behind her. She had been a gift to him from one of Burnham's contractors. It was the second slave girl that he had owned. The first, Klara, a blond Dutch beauty had been stolen some months ago. He had become enamored of the girl and was manic with rage when he found out that she was gone. He had, initially taken it out on the dark haired American girl who had become his property around the time of Klara's disappearance. He had been determined that he would form no more emotional attachments to slave girls. The buxom, succulent young woman had suffered greatly. For the last several weeks, though, he had softened his treatment of her. She had undoubtedly expected some sexual relief from him when she heard him coming through the door earlier and had become frustrated and needy as she heard the frantic coupling on the bed, the silver haired girl receiving repeatedly what she considered her due.

Jake ignored her for the moment and retreated into his bathroom. He used a wet cloth to wash away the slimy remnants of the girl's passions mixed into his thick, curly pubic hairs. He pissed into the bowl, rinsed his hands and then reemerged. Marlee was kneeling on the bed, a lascivious smile across her face. Dana was peering at him from behind the slim, silvery bars of her confinement, her unhappiness clear in her eyes. Jake had learned that owning a slave girl brought with it responsibilities. Even the most dedicated and energetic slut would lose her sheen if not treated properly. Once he had drawn on his clothes and slipped on his heavy work boots, he decided to grant Dana some respite.

He opened the cage and signaled her to emerge and get up on the bed. He loosened her braceleted hands from behind her back and, after she had stretched out her cramped muscles, had her lie down on her back, refastening them to the headboard. He removed her gag and tossed it on the side table. Moving to Marlee, he took a chain from the foot of the bed, attached to one of the tall, thick posts, and connected it to the hook in her right ankle cuff, locking it in place. Marlee's eyes spread wide in quick understanding. She lay herself down next to Dana and ran her dainty hand across her belly and breasts.

The insatiable Marlee would be free to pleasure Dana as much as she wanted, but her own lusts would go unsatisfied by Dana's mouth or hands. Dana, Jake knew, was in for one hell of a ride. He watched as the girl placed gentle kisses on each of Dana' thick, flat teats and then, circling her arm around the young American woman's leather collared neck, planted her mouth on the girl's lips. She spread them and slipped her tongue into the girl's mouth. Dana, giving out a happy moan, spread her lips to accept the silver haired girl's proffer of pleasure. Jake watched as Marlee slid her body atop the other woman's, marrying their breasts together. Dana spread her pale, graceful thighs apart, allowing Marlee's legs to rest between them. In spite of his recent orgasm, his cock stirred at the sight of the deliciously formed women's embrace. Shaking himself from his reverie, he left them to their devices.

Downstairs, his boys were waiting. It was unlike Jake to be late. It was just one more example of the changes that had come over him since he had come to Kalikastan. It had been supposed to be a short run thing, in and out. But Burnham had put the nix on a snatch and grab of Maddy, once Jake had located her. He sensed that the billionaire had been corrupted and he now suspected that the saving of his niece had become secondary to his desires to spend the rest of his days as a slavemaster. Jake had proposed an alternative to the forcible liberation of Maddy. Her owner, Grobgy had turned down an offer to buy her, which would have made things simple. So when simple won't do, complicated has to take its place.

The scheme was to challenge Grobgy, Maddy's owner, to a stakes race after the end of the racing season. He was known as a great gambler and a proud aficionado of the sport of ponygirl racing. His teams had won the spring overall championship this year. If Burnham could develop a pony to challenge Maddy, now known as Lightning, to a match race with Lightning as the prize and millions of dollars of graft Burnham's stake, and they could win the race, they would have possession of Maddy. Her death from some staged accident could be faked and she could be smuggled out of the country.

They needed a ringer. Jake had known a young hooker back in Chicago, his home stomping grounds, who had been a track star in high school. He had helped her out of a jam and she was intensely loyal to him as a consequence. He proposed to her, in consideration of a million dollars, that she should allow herself to be brought to Kalikastan, converted to a ponygirl and then trained to challenge Lightning. Jackie was tall, amply endowed and broad shouldered, a perfect physique for a ponygirl. She had agreed without hesitation even though Jake had warned her about how difficult the life of a ponygirl would be.

Jackie's kidnapping was faked, just so her bone fides would not be questioned, and she was shipped off to Kalikastan to be made into a ponygirl. She was listed as a special order for the Burnham estate and there she was hooded, ringed and marked. She underwent an extensive and excruciating round of training to run the 1500 meter sulky, a one pony race in which Lightning had championed in the spring. The idea was that Jackie, renamed Chocolate because of her deep brown skin, would fight her way to the finals in the Fall Tournament and then the bet would be made with Grobgy, since Lightning was sure to be the other finalist.

Things went haywire when it was discovered that Lightning would be running the 3000 meter instead. It was too late, according to Racing Commission rules, to change Chocolate's designation and so the pony had to train for both races, one in the open and one surreptitiously. The plan was now that if Chocolate championed in the 1500 meter, Grobgy would be enticed to match Lightning in a 3000 meter stake race. But if Chocolate did not win the 1500 meter championship, all bets would be off. She was doing fine and had qualified for the Fall Tournament. She had finished strong and was positioned well to champion. Her training in the 3000 meter was going well too and she was sure to give Lightning a run for her money. But that was not what was worrying Jake right now.

The deal with Burnham had been that Jackie would be released win or lose once the Fall Tournament was over. Jake had his suspicions that Burnham would be unwilling to set the ponygirl free. He was too caught up in the whole thing and he had acted funny when Jake had tried to get him to make plans for the smuggling of the two liberated ponygirls from the country. The billionaire had cozied up to some of

the Russian security people he had hired and Jake was wary
that he and his men would meet a violent end if they resisted
any effort on Burnham's part to keep the ponygirls in his
barn.

To Jake, a job was like a solemn oath. He was committed
to freeing Maddy, whatever it took. And there was the fact of
all that he had done: facilitating the kidnapping of innocent
young women and participating in the exploitation of dozens
of the beautiful, well trained subservients. He did not want to
have to face himself if it all went for naught. It was a slim
moral justification. Why did so many other women have to
suffer so that Maddy could go free? Well, some of the
women, most of them probably, would have been kidnapped
and enslaved anyway, that was one rationalization he
sometimes used in his mind even though he knew that with
one phone call to the FBI he could have put the slaving
operation out of business at any time. And the slave girls he
used, well, they were already slave girls weren't they? And they
were typically subject to much worse use than he ever put
them to.

Jake had set up the takeover of the Elizabeth, NJ slaving
operation and hired an associate, the tall, beautiful, blond
lesbian, Mary Ellen, to operate it while he and Burnham were
in Kalikastan. Mary Ellen was as ruthless as any woman he
had ever known. She and her small gang of fellow lefties had
done a number of jobs for him before and they took no
prisoners. But, like him, Mary Ellen held ironclad the
principle that her word was her bond and Jake knew that she
could be trusted to end the slaving operation when the time
came. Once they had made contact with the suppliers for the
operation, Mary Ellen's girls drove the specially designed
uniform van around the eastern half of the country collecting
unfortunate young women for shipment off to Kalikastan.
There had been some other customers of the operation, but,
at Jake's instructions, Mary Ellen had squeezed them out.

Now all the girls who ended up in the basement of the work uniform warehouse that served as the front for the operation were destined for export to Kalikastan.

Mary Ellen had confided to Jake one day that Burnham had approached her about expanding the operation to the American Midwest and the West Coast. She had declined. She wasn't especially enamored of being a slaver, she, after all, had some sisterly compassion for the poor young women torn from their homes and destined for lives of sexual slavery. But a buck was a buck, however you made it, and Jake had offered her and her girls a ton. On the other hand, she would be happy to wind the operation up once Jake's purpose of rescuing Maddy had been served. She had some scruples after all.

Yesterday, Jake had sent word to Mary Ellen that she could soon terminate the operation. The Fall Tournament was less than a week away and would last three days. On the fourth day, they anticipated holding the match race between Chocolate and Lightning. One day after that, according to Jake's plan, if all went well, the young women would be on their way home. He told Mary Ellen not to do anything to give their hand away and to keep the operation going until the last minute.

As Jake stepped into the large living room on the ground floor of the cottage, he saw that his men were all there. Irving, his tech guy, Curley and Leon, two lugs who were efficient muscle but not good for too much else, Martinez, a lanky, efficient killer and jack of all trades and finally Tucker, a 6'5" tall, brick shithouse built man with bone crushing hands and a thick head. It was Tucker who had become enamored of the two large, blond, work ponies, Dora and Flora. He had already indicated that once the Maddy rescue effort had been made, he was staying in Kalikastan to take care of them. Jake had explained carefully that the weather might not be too good for anyone who had helped Maddy escape, but Tucker had been insistent. He would take his lumps and hope for the best. He would never leave his beloved ponies.

Irving was another problem. When they had overrun the Georgia farmhouse where Maddy had first been held prisoner after her kidnapping, a heavyset, kind of homely young girl had been a prisoner in the subterranean cells beneath the barn. Jake had wanted to leave her there, they were, after all, charged with saving Maddy and no one else. They couldn't just release the girl or the whole world would soon learn what was going on and their efforts to track down Maddy would be frustrated. The slaving operation would dry up and no one would ever be able to trace her. But Irving's humanity got the best of him and Jake agreed to force Burnham to put the girl up in a sanitarium somewhere until the Maddy operation was over.

At the time, Jake had thought that it was a matter of a few weeks, not months as it had turned out. Burnham made arrangements for an ambulance to pick up the girl, Maureen, at the farmhouse, but, unbeknownst to Jake, he had instructed the men he hired to drop her in a hole somewhere. The idea that she could be held incommunicado in some secret hospital for weeks without running the risk that somehow word of who she was and what had happened to her would get out, was too much. In turn, the men that Burnham had hired had betrayed him and, instead of silencing her forever, had shipped her off to a Mexican whorehouse for a tidy profit on both ends.

It was a good thing too. Chocolate needed every edge to beat Lightning in the match race and Jake needed Irving to design a sleeker, more efficient sulky cart for her to pull. By lightening her load and making the cart more aerodynamic a few seconds could be carved off of the 3000 meter race, perhaps the edge of victory. But Irving had refused to cooperate until Maureen's location and safety were assured. He had grown suspicious when Jake could not get Burnham to tell of her whereabouts. When brought to Kalikastan to design the new cart, Irving had flat out refused to do anything until Maureen had been produced. And, if not, he had threatened to expose the entire operation.

Burnham had scrambled to find out what had happened to Maureen. To his relief, once he offered the men who had taken her away enough money, they fessed up to their switch and Burnham was able to track Maureen down. In consideration of another huge bundle of cash and the pulling of a few strings, he was able to extract Maureen from her prison-like whorehouse and bring her to Kalikastan.

Everything would have been fine at that point except for Maureen herself. She had been brutally treated while in Mexico. The madam, having given up all hope that the unattractive, overweight girl would ever be a successful whore, had, after a customer refused her services saying that she "looked like a pig", shaved her head, attached a round, squat nose and a pair of pointed ears to her head and forced her to walk on her knees. In short, she turned her into a pig. A pig-whore. In her new guise, Maureen was a huge hit. The madam fattened her up even more by force feeding her high caloric food all day and used an injection into her voice box that tightened her vocal cords so that, when she moaned and cried out as the gleeful men fucked her, she squealed just like a real pig.

When Maureen arrived in Kalikastan, she weighed about two hundred and seventy five pounds. She was glad to be rescued from her fate as a pig, but found her new life, back to being a fat, homely girl, a gross disappointment. She watched while the slave girls were fucked willy nilly by the men, none of them giving her a simple look other than to marvel at her gross folds of fat. It had been like this all of her life. At least as a pig people paid attention to her. She had never had as much sex in her life. She had a purpose, a function at last. People wanted her. Something had broken in her while she was in the Mexican whorehouse and she would never be the same.

It was watching the nine pony landau team being hitched to their large carriage that gave her the idea. Here were former women, tall and broad shouldered like she was. Except they were not fat. They were strong, sleek and muscular. The men fucked them and groomed them. Unlike her, they had a purpose in life. At that moment Maureen decided that she wanted to be a ponygirl too. At her insistence, Irving had broached the idea with Burnham who, laughing at the very thought of it and the irony of the fact that the girl they had saved now wanted to be a animal again, talked to his head trainer, Irkut. Irkut, after some reluctance, agreed. But he made it crystal clear: Maureen could not play at being a ponygirl. Once she was dehumanized, that was it. She would be a ponygirl as long as anyone had a use for her. Jake didn't know what happened to ponygirls who went past their usefulness, but he had a feeling that he didn't want to know.

And so Maureen had been hooded, stripped, collared and her hands bound behind her back. Irkut had been working her ever since, building up her strength and trimming her body. At the Fall Tournament there was to be an exhibition of ponygirl strength and Irkut had entered Maureen into the unofficial contest. Jake saw her daily now pulling a huge sled loaded with bricks around the practice track. Irving saw her too and was not convinced that she had really known what she was getting into. He had demanded, as the price of his help in setting up their get away, that Maureen be given the opportunity to flee. His mind could not accept that anyone, once they discovered what being dehumanized really entailed, would want that as a life. Jake, and only because he had, after all, promised that Maureen would be all right back in Georgia, reluctantly agreed.

But that was where he drew the line. Leon and Curley had their favorite slave girls that they initially wanted to liberate as well, but Jake nixed it. Martinez, to whom the slave girls flocked like pretty little teddy bears to honey, hadn't committed himself, but Jake had the feeling that he had made a side deal with one of the local gangs and that he would be, like Turner, staying too. But all his men were loyal and Jake had no reason to doubt their word that they would help in the getaway regardless of their personal preferences.

The ubiquitous slave girls had all been sent away on one errand or another and Irving had swept the cottage for bugs so that Jake knew that he could speak freely. He addressed Irving first.

"Are we all set?" he asked.

Irving, who had never forgiven Jake for what had happened to Maureen, looked up. He was sitting in one of the easy chairs and had a drink in his hand. He had been a virtual teetotaler before he came to Kalikastan, but the country had a way of changing people. He was short and thin and looked like a cartoonist's version of a nerd. But he was brilliant and efficient. His cart had, on the first test of it, shaved seven seconds off of Chocolate's best time in the 3000. She was doing even better now that she had gotten used to it. The cart would be kept under wraps until the match race.

"Of course, Jake. I told you I had it all figured out didn't I."

"Well, run it by me again anyway, Irving." Jake replied, annoyed.

"Okay," Irving spat back. "I've prepared a switch that will disable all the phones on the estate. No calls will go in or out during the escape. I've obtained a canister of gas for Leon and Curley to release into the guards' bunkhouse at lunch time that will disable anyone in there for more than an hour. The van we'll be using is all set to be hotwired. And I've given Martinez the gizmo that he will need to fly in and out of the country undetected."

"It sounds good," Jake responded. He turned to Martinez. "Well?" he asked.

"I've made arrangements for a large Sikorsky across the border. It'll hold eight people plus the pilot, even if one of them is a little overweight."

All the men laughed at Martinez's joke, except Irving. The scientist's enamoration for the fat girl was a source of constant mirth among them.

"Okay! Okay!" Jake was finally able to get out when he stopped laughing. "But did you test the gizmo?"

"It works like a charm. It'll make the chopper practically invisible to local radar. I had it tested by the guy I made the deal for the chopper with in Odessa. It blanks out everything for a mile around. No one will know what is happening until we're across the border."

Kalikastan, although backwards in practically everything else, had a quite efficient security apparatus which included a fledgling air force. All unauthorized flights in the country were strictly banned. Intruders or unscheduled flying objects would be shot down, no questions asked. Besides, the plan was to leave Burnham holding the bag. He would have to explain what happened to Chocolate and Lightning. By disguising their escape, Jake hoped to reduce the chances that the long arm of Russian gangsterism would reach out and touch them once they got back to the States.

Jake turned to Tucker. The heavyset man was of few words. But he knew his business and was as strong as an ox.

"No problem, Jake. I'll be able to round up all the grooms and trainers. They'll be hogtied and gagged. There will be no trouble."

"Then we're set," Jake stated flatly. "All that needs to happen now is for Chocolate to win her race."

CHAPTER FOUR

Elsewhere on the Burnham estate, the ponygirl who was once Maureen Donaldson of Bayleysville, Georgia, was dragging a large, flat, unwheeled sled piled with bricks along the dirt practice track. It was her third time around the 1500 meter oval and sweat was pouring off of her oversized, naked frame in rivulets. The rough, leather harness dug deep into her shoulders and across her belly and chest, leaving deep red marks. Her head was encapsulated by the standard, black, neoprene pony hood particular to the Burnham estate and her vision was limited to two tiny, dime sized holes over her eyes. A thick, leather covered bit was in her mouth and she chomped down on it fiercely with her jaws as she strained to move the load behind her.

A thin youth sat atop of the pony's load, shouting encouragement to her and striking her bare back occasionally with a long, thin dressage whip that made a loud cracking sound each time that it bit into her flesh. You could hear her grunts of effort and her little squeals of pain each time the whip kissed her bulky form as she passed by.

Irkut, the pony's trainer, stood by the rail at the finish line watching with admiration. He had trained many a ponygirl, and had, in fact, been in on the resurrection of this gentleman's sport some twelve years ago. He had never trained a ponygirl like this one. He didn't know much about the tall, big boned American female. She had volunteered to become a ponygirl some weeks back, a thing unheard of, and had since thrown herself into her new role with enthusiasm.

He had not formally given her new ponygirl name yet. She had been immensely overweight and out of shape when she donned her ponygirl collar and he had at first thought of giving her a name commensurate with her obesity, like

Beluga. Not the caviar, but the whale. The other trainers and grooms had mocked him when he began to work with her and suggested names like Jellyroll or Cream Puff. But there was something about the heavyset, former woman that made him feel that she deserved better than that. He had given it much thought and had finally come up with one that he thought suitable.

It was the large pony's sexual voraciousness and proud, almost regal bearing that had finally given him the inspiration for her new name. When she orgasmed as he plowed her rear opening while she stood fixed at the rail in her stall, her whole body shook, and she strained at her confinements like someone gone mad. Irkut had ordered the grooms to reinforce the bar that ran across her stall for fear she would pull it from its moorings.

Despite her freshness to her bit, she had thrown herself into her new role with apparent relish. She gave head with an astounding alacrity, although not necessarily skill. Irkut, who, despite his slender, almost diminutive frame, was enamored of big women anyway, liked to ride her belly as she lay prone on the ground, passing his rampant cock between her elephantine breasts, using his hands to squeeze the mammoth mammaries together to make a tunnel for his cock. The pony seemed to like it too as she puffed and grunted in the dirt lying on her now eternally imprisoned arms. Despite her freshness to her bit, she had thrown herself into her new role with apparent relish. It was like the former woman looked upon her conversion to bestial status as an escape from an alternative, unpleasant reality.

As far as the name went, Irkut had been reminded of the infamous Czarina, Catherine the Great, who ruled Russia despotically back in the eighteenth century and had been known for her huge sexual appetite. She had grown to be of gargantuan proportions in her later years, but always retained her royal prerogatives and governed her empire with an iron fist. So, he had decided that today he would finally name her, not Catherine, but Czarina.

As soon as this practice session was done, he intended to take her to the markings hut and have the name emblazoned on her chest. The other trainers would laugh at his presumption, but Irkut knew what he was doing.

The young groom who had been driving the new pony girl finally brought her to a stop and leapt down from his perch on the bricks. It was a bright fall afternoon, the air slightly crisp. No one else was using the track, most of the other ponygirls were still in the process of returning from the fall racing season and the few yearlings were locked in their stalls in the ponygirl barn after their noon workouts, undoubtedly receiving the pointed end of a few cocks. The young man looked almost emaciated next to the tall, naked, wide bodied pony. He was smiling broadly when Irkut, squeezing himself under the rail, entered the track and approached him.

"She's like a bullock," the youth said in Russian, laughing. "She could go on forever."

Irkut nodded. "It may seem that way, but we've got to make sure she doesn't pull any muscles. The tournament is less than a week away and I want her in tiptop form."

Andreyev was a local youth who had aspirations to become ponygirl trainer. He was just a little over 19 and eager as hell. Irkut saw some of himself in the lad. He had had to prove his mettle as a ponygirl trainer when he started out. They boy was progressing nicely and it was good to have an assistant he could trust.

The slender young man took a large, plastic bottle with a long, thin nozzle from the sled and brought it to where the ponygirl stood mutely. Her chest was still heaving from her exertions and sweat coursed over her body as if she had just taken a dip in a pond. Her fat breasts jiggled pleasantly with each labored breath and her skin glistened. The ponygirl collar forced her chin upwards, tilting her black hooded, featureless head back slightly as if she were disdainful of her surroundings. Standing there, straight and proud, in her shin high, thick heeled, black ponygirl boots, she was about 5'11" tall. The boy came up to her chin. Like Irkut, he was a comparative runt. Ponygirl trainers were supposed to be big, strapping fellows so that it would be easier to handle the dehumanized females. But Irkut had always found that a will of steel and skill with a whip were more important. He had trained many a ponygirl in his day, coming out of retirement at the behest of the rich American, Mr. Burnham.

When Andreyev placed the bottle to the ponygirl's lips, Irkut could hear the glugging of the water down her wide, round throat. Some of it spilled across her as yet unmarked chest and between her large, spongy breasts.

"Not too much," Irkut warned his apprentice. "You'll make her puke." The slender youth withdrew the bottle from the pony's bit and put it back on the sled.

"Now give her reward," Irkut told him.

Smiling, the young man came back to the ponygirl's front. He hesitated at first, as if he needed permission from the pony to touch her. He knew that wasn't necessary, but it was hard get over the cultural prohibition against touching women without their at least tacit consent. But then again, this wasn't a woman any more. Her hooded head atop her huge, naked form made her seem like one of those Egyptian statues with the body of a human and the head of a beast. And she wasn't a god either.

He placed his hands on her round, heavy breasts and began to rub them lovingly. The boy's hands almost disappeared into her flesh. The pony, soon to be named Czarina, spread her thick thighs and jutted her chest out. As his caresses began to stoke her passions, she gave out a loud, pleased moan.

It was a fact that the former Maureen Donaldson reveled in her relatively new status as a beast of burden. Life had been hard for the homely, big boned girl. Growing up, she had been mocked and ostracized by all the other girls, especially the shapely, good looking ones. But a bizarre set of events had enabled her, finally, to find her true calling.

She had been kidnapped, quite inadvertently, one spring night with her friend, Peggy Ann. It was her attractive, fair featured friend that the kidnappers had been after, but Maureen had been in the wrong place at the wrong time and they had to take her too. Her kidnappers, an old, married, redneck couple named Herman and Louise, had sold off her friend a few days later. But Maureen, big boned and heavy set, though not yet the immense creature that she became later, was not considered nearly as prime enough material for the buyers and had been rejected. So she had been kept a prisoner in the dungeon under the couple's barn on their isolated farmstead for many weeks and used and abused by them cruelly. She had been rescued only to find herself shipped off to Mexico where she sold to a whorehouse in a city far in the south.

It was there that Maureen realized it was her destiny to be a beast. Her head had been shaved and she had been forced to crawl around on all fours with a plastic pig nose glued to her face and fake pig ears attached to her head. She had been fattened and brought out at all the parties to squeal and bleat as the amused patrons used her. It was the first time that she had been good at anything. She hated being made into a pig, but came to believe that it was merely a case of her fulfilling her destiny. Wasn't that what the boys had called her when she was younger?

And then, inexplicably, she had been hauled away from the Mexican whorehouse and flown here, where one of her original rescuers, a man she knew as Irving, met her and tried to help her recover from her ordeal. But she had not been able to get over the trauma of being dehumanized, never really felt like she had recovered her human status. When she saw the ponygirls running proudly ahead of their carts, their bodies strong and well toned, given daily, intense attention by their trainers and the grooms, she had known immediately that that was what she wanted.

Being made into a ponygirl was everything that she had hoped. She no longer had to assuage her feelings at being a fat, humiliated, young woman, for she wasn't a woman anymore. She was a beast and responded as one. Every morning a man came and shaved her loins and her head bald once more. Her hair had not grown much since she had been rescued from the Mexican whorehouse and so, when her hood was reinstalled, a ponytail was attached to the back of it. Maureen didn't know it, but Irkut had taken it from one of the pretty, shapely and delectable slave girls from the mansion. The girl had cried uncontrollably when he lopped off her long, flowing, brown hair. Irkut had been so pissed at her reaction that he had had her assigned to the ponygirl barn for two weeks where the randy grooms, deprived of their usual source of carnal delight for the term of the racing season, used her quite well.

Maureen had benefited from the men's unsatisfied lusts. Each morning, of course, as was the custom with ponygirls, her groom would, after he had finished attending to her personal needs, bring her to orgasm with his hand, his lips or his cock. She always woke early and would spend her time, lying bound and blinded on her pallet in her stall, wondering which it would be today. Not that it mattered. But she did particularly enjoy it when the handsome, fit, young man placed his mouth on her sex and brought her to completion with his tongue. Nobody had ever done that for her before, not even when she was the pig-whore in Mexico. Her mind beclouded by ecstasy, she would writhe and moan on the floor of her stall her legs spread widely. In order to prevent her from injuring the groom by bringing her powerful thighs together when she came, her ankles were always chained off to rings in the floor.

Many times every evening, after she had been stood up at the rail in her stall, her legs splayed wide apart, her nose ring tied off to the hook in the wall in front of her, men had come and plowed her twin portals. Her pussy and ass delighted in the coursing of their hot, hard wands in her proffered passageways. When she climaxed, her body shook and she gave out deep, joyful moans into her gag. Being a woman, for her, could never compare to this.

During the day, the men often had her kneel on the ground and spread her thick lips for their meat. She relished the feel of the hard tubes of flesh as they brushed over her lips and tongue and found the entrance to her throat. It made her pussy convulse with passion when they came. She did all she could to facilitate their pleasure, certain in their right to use her and happy to bring them the pleasure they deserved in return for her now joyful life.

The training too was thrilling to her. She had never been good at sports and had been left out of most of the other kids' games when she was a young girl. Homely and growing quickly to fat, she had traveled inwards. It was just happenstance that she had been in the company of Peggy Anne the night she had been kidnapped. While a prisoner in the Mexican whorehouse, she often wondered what had happened to the svelte young girl who had taken pity and befriended her.

That was all in the past now. All that was in her mind was to be a good ponygirl, the best that she could be. So when she was brought out of the ponygirl barn and made to run, run, run, until she literally dropped and, at the behest of an angry whip, made to run some more, she celebrated in her mind the tightening she felt in her thighs, the strength that was building up in her body, the sloughing off of her accumulation of fat.

She realized, when she was first harnessed to her sled, that she was being given an opportunity to star in a class all her own. She knew about the ponygirl tournaments. Irving had told her all about them when he was trying to talk her out of her decision to give up human status. She knew that she would never be able to run like the other ponygirls; she was just too big boned and slow of movement. But hauling a sled full of bricks around the track was something she could do with aplomb. None of the other ponygirls on the estate could do what she did. Thus, having been provided with a chance to excel where others could not, she poured herself into her new role with all the enthusiasm she could muster.

She was whipped, it was true. The scouring of her body by the long, leather lashes or the thin, leather encased reeds was excruciating. The former Maureen took each painful kiss of her flesh as a sign that she had to try harder, dig down deeper within herself and give more than she ever thought she could.

Today's weight had been the heaviest she had pulled yet. She had no idea how many bricks were on the sled. Nobody talked to her and through her tiny holes in her head and face encompassing, black hood, she had no way to count them. But it had been heavy. Nonetheless, she had pulled it with all of her might, egged on by the whip of the small, young man who drove her. Now she would receive her reward.

Still standing in her traces, the powerful ponygirl let the small hands of her driver deliver a soothing, lust inspiring massage to her huge breasts. His lips seized hold of her fat, stiffened nipples and began a delicious suckling on them, sending a thrill to her plump, hairless slit. First one and then the other received the benefit of the young man's lips and tongue. He sucked hard at them until the pony groaned with delight. When his hand slid over her now flatter belly and delved between her outspread thighs, her knees felt weakened with the passion that flowed through her. Her mind exploded with delight when the hand encompassed her fleshy mons and then slid its fingers deep inside of her.

Irkut watched the ponygirl take her pleasure. Although he could not see them, he could imagine her eyes rolling back in her head. Her whole, large body seemed to melt before him. What a ponygirl she was! If anyone had told him how pleased he would be with her when he first draped a black hood over her face and applied her ponygirl collar, he would have been incredulous. But now, he considered her the pinnacle of his long career.

The ponygirl's body began to shake and her hips began a needy thrust at the hand between her thighs. She was making a lustful, "Orrrrrrrrmmmmm! Orrrrrrummmmmm!" sound as her crisis approached. Her head tilted back and her bound hands behind her tightened into a clench. Andreyev, her driver, lifted his lips from her billowing breasts and smiled at his mentor. His fingers were rubbing the hardened nubbin at the apex of the pony's sex. Her juices were flowing over his hand. Suddenly, with a deep throated moan that sounded more like a bellow, the pony's lusts crested. Great snorts of passion emerged from her dilated nostrils. Her breasts shook. It was almost a frightful sight to take in. All of the pony's considerable power was unleashed in uncontrolled reaction to the explosion of pleasure in her loins.

The former human female who had been called Maureen took a while to recover from the hard, intense contractions of her womb. Andreyev caressed and petted her breasts as she regained her breath. He looked over at Irkut who nodded back at him. Andreyev, bowing to his teacher's prerogatives backed away from the pony as Irkut assumed a position in front of her. The slender ponygirl trainer clapped his hands in front of the panting, still shuddering female and then pointed to the ground. Slowly, but obediently, the giant sank to her knees.

Irkut reached behind her head and released the buckle that kept her bit drawn deep into her mouth. The pony looked up at him through her tiny eye holes expectantly. The ponygirl trainer lowered the fly to his pants and fished out his flaccid, rubbery cock. She spread her lips as he moved closer to her and when the appendage was in reach, subsumed it into her mouth.

Irkut sighed as the soft, warm cavern enveloped him. He placed his hands on the sides of the pony's black hooded head. He was determined to teach the pony the proper way to suck a cock. When his piece had entered her, the pony had begun to eagerly suckle on it. Irkut pushed her head back until his cock popped out. The pony gave a little squeal of disappointment. "Slowly, slowly," he said to her in Russian. It was a word she had been taught when learning to run at the training ring. His cock was stiffening and he placed it between the pony's lips with his right hand, keeping his left resting on her head. When the pony's lips again circumscribed his pole, the pony let them close softly together over his meat and began a slow, deliberate motion of her head.

Maureen loved to suck her trainer's cock most of all. He was the one who had allowed her to become a ponygirl. If he had refused to train her, she did not know what she would have done. He taught her how to run, massaged her aching muscles, taught her through the use of his whip the right and wrong things to do. He had brought her to a new level of existence and she was appropriately grateful for it.

As a matter of fact, the oversized pony's reactions to her training were different from the typical ponygirl's only by degree. Ponies learned quickly that failure to succeed brought painful punishments and so they became appreciative of the efforts of the trainers who showed them how to reach inside themselves and draw on their inner strengths. Sucking her trainer's cock was the only opportunity for a ponygirl to find expression for her ironic gratitude for the rigors of her training.

Moreover, since it was virtually the only time a pony's mouth was free, other than to eat or for grooming purposes, many ponies found themselves grateful for the opportunity to taste something other than their gruelish food or the harsh leather in their mouths. A ponygirl left to her own devices would prolong her oral attentions to a master's meat for as long as she could, reveling in the ability to feel sensations on her tongue and inside her mouth. Using only her lips and tongue, she would tease and caress the manhood proffered to her, bringing the master repeatedly to the edge of his climax and then back again from the abyss. A blow job from a ponygirl was a thing to relish.

If subservience was your lot in life, you too would want to think of your master as all powerful, if only to justify your surrender to him. And so, when the master's cock began its dance within her mouth, its convulsions throbbing against her lips, his spume jetting into her, a ponygirl experienced the powerful ejaculations as confirmation of the wisdom of surrender. Sucking a cock was an easier and more pleasant way for her to reinforce her commitment to her new life than a whip.

Heeding her trainer's command, the muscular ponygirl let her lips soften and her motions slow. She let her tongue circle around the shaft as it slid across her lips. She let her master's hands on her head be her guide. Her efforts brought fruition as she heard her trainer's soft moans of pleasure. His cock was hard now and Maureen cherished the feel of its rigid strength. She moaned as her already pleasured pussy began to yearn for a return of attention to it.

Irkut delighted in the pony's mouth. He felt the blood surging in his loins. There was nothing better for him than being serviced by a naked and bound ponygirl, kneeling in the dust. What better proof was there of his mastery over them?

Their faceless, hooded heads bobbed in supplication to the power that he held. Devoid of features, they could have been anything in their young, prior lives, waitresses or secretaries, teachers or students, artists, musicians, or mall rats. That was all far behind them. From the neck up, they all looked the same.

Deep down, Irkut knew that it was a fiction that the females became other than human once they were collared and hooded. He knew that inside each and every ponygirl hood was a woman who remembered, even if ever so faintly, what it was like to be free and to have self determination. On the other hand, their strange appearance, their lack of speech, their inability to care for themselves, all served as a kind of justification for what they had become. If you looked and walked and acted like a pony, then you must be one. Their demeaned existence served as its own justification. It was as if you had cracked a young woman open and, lo and behold, found that a ponygirl had been living inside her all along.

The ponygirl trainer felt his juices begin to rise. He was moving the pony's head faster now, pushing his cock hard into the soft mass of flesh that surrounded it. Needing no encouragement to accelerate her efforts, she moaned as she slurped at his cock, accenting each retreat of her head with a long, hard suck.

When his cock began to convulse with pleasure, Irving began to rock his hips against the covered face of the ponygirl. He pierced the back of her mouth, lodging himself in her throat. The pony's huge breasts pressed against his knees. He could hear her gurgling as she struggled to encompass all that he had to offer her. "A-a-a-a-aughhhhhhh!" he called out as his climax overtook him. "Aaaaaaughhhhh! Aaaaaaaaaughhhhhh!!"

The ponygirl was ecstatic to hear the proof of her growing skills in her master's voice. Her pussy contracted as his warm discharge flooded her mouth. She gave out a groan at each throb of her pussy's walls. Coming for her was like being in a rocket and climbing to the highest altitude you could attain, spending a few, delirious moments there and then tumbling back to earth. If only those moments could last forever. She pined for it again and again. And she knew that later this afternoon, tonight and tomorrow, she would experience it again and again.

A wave of pleased relaxation spread over the man as he let the pony slurp over his cock, drawing the last drop of his cum from him. After a moment or two, he forced her head back and, retrieving her leather covered bit from Andreyev, pushed it back into her mouth. She accepted it willingly and made no protest as he reattached the belt behind her head. He gave her a motion with his hand to stand and she dutifully rose from her knees, first raising one powerful leg and then the other. Andreyev gave him a conspiratorial, gleeful nod and then hopped back up on the sled. He cracked the reins, gave a command and the huge, powerful ponygirl obediently began to tow her heavy burden away.

The sled had to be brought back to the storage shed near the ponygirl barn, the pony had to be cleaned and rubbed down, and then they would be off to the marking hut. Andreyev could handle the cleaning and the massaging of her firm, expansive muscles. Irkut would handle taking her for her tattoos. He had not yet had the mark of the estate put on her, Burnham's fierce mastiff. Her stomach had been so large that once she lost weight, the tattoo would have shriveled up until it looked like a mastiff puppy. Now that her belly was firmer, that mark could be applied as well.

Irkut watched her circle her sled around the edge of the track and toward the storage hut. It was open at both ends so that all she had to do was enter it from one side and then pull her load in. It would be difficult indeed to back up 250 pounds of bricks.

The fall racing season was over and the ponygirl racing teams were arriving back at the estate. They tried to stagger the readmission of the 30 or so ponies that made up Burnham's teams into the ponygirl barn. It was a dramatic shift in a pony's life style to be racing one day and then back in the barn another. During the season, of course, only the drivers and their assistants had the right to use them. In the ponygirl barn, however, they were all fair game.

Most of the returning trailers and their pseudo-equine occupants were laagered out in the park adjacent to the racing track. While some, like Chocolate, would be staying, spending the next day or so relaxing, resting sore muscles and feet in preparation for the Fall Tournament, most of them, unfortunately, would be heading back to the barn. There would be some nasty whippings tonight for the ponies who had failed to excel. Burnham would insist on it. Only Chocolate and his cabriolet team, the six pony carriage, had made it into the tournament. The others, as Irkut had expected, were a bust.

Irkut wondered whether Giorgi, the diminutive driver of the estate's chocolate skinned, 1500 meter sulky had gotten back yet. He decided to kill the three quarters of an hour it would take to wash and massage Czarina by making the dwarf a visit.

He had done the initial training on the appropriately named ponygirl, Chocolate. Irkut knew ponygirls well and there was something about her that just didn't seem to fit. As he strolled over the dirt pathways to the ponygirl park, as they called it, he recalled her lack of vigor during her early training, almost as if she thought that she would someday be able to resume her former identity. He had taken care of that, bringing such torment down on the newly minted pony that she abandoned thoughts of her former self and began to think only of how she could please him and avoid the lash.

Jake Barnes, Burnham's American fixer, had come up with the idea of challenging Lightning to a match race. He was the one who arranged for the tawny skinned Chocolate to be brought to Kalikastan. How well did he really know the lean, wiry American? If Irkut knew ponygirls, he knew men too and Barnes was too sure of himself, too confident and poised to be a mere lackey of the crass billionaire Burnham. Irkut had detected a mind of sharp steel and an absence of any kind of fear in the man.

No, something was up. Why was Burnham so hell bent on getting ownership of Lightning, Grobgy's American 3000 meter sulky runner, that he would make such an effort to set up and win a claiming race between them? A whole new cart had been designed, one that Irkut, even with his many years of ponygirl training, was surprised at. The darn thing really worked and gave the pony a distinct advantage. Why go to all that trouble? What was up with that?

Irkut was more than just an aficionado of the sport of ponygirl racing. He believed that the sport was an idealization of not only the human female form, but of its spirit as well. Freed of all responsibilities, liberated from archaic notions of sexual morality, the former women were at a pinnacle of existence. What creature was cared for better than a ponygirl? Their diets were carefully controlled, their medical needs seen to, and their bodies were trained to a level of fitness that the females who had been transformed would never have achieved in their former lives. To be cared for, to have all need to make decisions taken away, to be fucked or otherwise brought to several mighty crescendos of sexual completion a day, what more could a woman want? And there was the chance to achieve what Irkut considered immortality by becoming a champion as Lightning had and like he believed Chocolate would soon do too. The world would have taken little notice of the women they had been. All of Kalikastan knew the names of Chocolate and Lightning!

Anything that challenged the integrity of the sport was anathema to Irkut. He liked Jake and would not want to do anything to hurt him. But if he was contemplating something that was not in the best interest of the sport, that was something else entirely. He decided that he would try to get some insight from Giorgi as to what was going on if he could.

He identified Giorgi's distinctive RV and pony trailer easily. When he arrived at the camp, he saw that Giorgi was busy. The tall, broad backed but pleasantly formed pony was on her knees, her black hooded forehead touching the ground between her outstretched thighs. Her four foot tall driver was behind her. His cock was buried in her rear aperture and he was stroking himself back and forth slowly. He had hold of the pony's otherwise useless, bound arms and was using them for leverage. Irkut could see that the Velcro tabs over the small eyelets in the pony's hood were down, depriving the pony of sight.

Chocolate was obviously enjoying her ass fucking. He could hear her deep, almost mournful voice moaning from behind her gag. Irkut did not want to interrupt and so he stood at the edge of the small clearing and watched.

It was a perfect example of what he had just been thinking about. The pony was seemingly lost in a haze of low burning passion. He knew Giorgi's training methods and he knew that this pony, besides being driven hard during her practice runs, was subjected to six or seven passionate interludes per day either at the hands of her tiny driver or that of his pretty, blond slave girl.

Except for race day, that is. On race days, the pony would be driven into paroxysms of sexual need without fruition. She would have to win her race or face the rest of the day deprived. It was an effective form of encouragement, although Chocolate hardly needed that. She was a gamer all right, a real competitor. Her practice runs were almost always good, but unimpressive. Put another pony on the track running next to her, however, and she was all fight. She had won eleven of her fourteen races this season, no mean feat for a pony which only learned to run with a bit a few months ago. Her victories easily put her into the top tier in her division at the tournament. Irkut smiled as he remembered plowing the same path that Giorgi was favoring with his man sized cock right now. When the season was over Irkut would make sure that he did it again.

If Irkut had been able to read the lust driven pony's mind that moment, he would have found clear confirmation of his theories. Chocolate was lost in a world of pleasure. Not the mind thrilling, body shaking, lustful outbursts that she was sometimes subject to, but a low burn that went on and on as the dwarf's thick meat slowly and rhythmically crossed the tender membranes of her anal ring and passed in and out of her bowels.

When she had been known as Jackie, a high class hooker from Chicago, she had never let any of the johns fuck her there. Since being dehumanized, she had learned the pleasures of that alternative route to coitus. Her driver fucked her there at least once a day. Usually, he drove her past her passionate endurance and her body would quiver and shake as she came. Today, for the last twenty minutes or so, he had been leisurely running his cock over her anal ring, slowing each time he felt the ponygirl's body shudder with a mild, trance inducing climax, careful not to launch it into a full fledged orgasm.

Chocolate was thinking about how much like bliss this part of her new life was. Although, as a whore, sex had been her life, and she had enjoyed a stiff cock as much as any woman, she had never experienced the obsessive need that she had for it now, had never come like she had as a ponygirl, had never relished with such sublime pleasure the feel of a thick, hot prick as it passed across her lips and filled her eager mouth. When tied up alone in her pony trailer as they traveled from estate to estate over the last several weeks, it had been all that she had been able to think about: when were they going to stop so she could get fucked? It was a whole new angle to the, "Are we there yet?" that she and her siblings used to torment their parents with when they were on vacation.

Her body had never felt as alive and vibrant. She had kept herself fit as an expensive call girl in Chicago and, before that, when she was a track star in high school, she had trained every day, but she had never been in such good shape as she was now. The air smelled cleaner, her body felt better, her mind was focused and relaxed.

But contrary to Irkut's vision of happy, contented ponygirls a frolicking in the sun, there were many dark and lonely hours that Chocolate pined for freedom, the use of her hands, the ability to speak, even the ability to see more of what went on around her than the two little circles that served as her windows on the world. Imagine living in a land where almost everything that went on around you was hidden. You knew that something was happening, could catch a glance of some inexplicable event and no more. The men around her all spoke a guttural, harsh tongue. Only because Jake had briefed her on what Kalikastan was like did she know the language was Russian. It was indecipherable nonetheless. Like a dog or a real pony, she knew how to respond to certain sounds the men made. She only assumed they were words for 'faster', 'slower', or 'kneel and spread your lips", for example.

It had been this way for Chocolate for many months. Jake had told her it would be five months that she had to spend as a ponygirl. She had lost the ability to count the days. Somehow, though, she sensed that the end was coming soon. The prolonged, deliriously pleasurable fucking she was receiving this afternoon was quite unlike her driver, and she assumed it was a reward for her successful season. Before her driver had ordered her to her knees and closed the eyelets to her hood, she had seen various of the other ponygirls being led over to the mansion area, something that did not happen during the racing season. She had assumed, correctly, that they were being led back to the barn where she had spent so many nights bemoaning her agreement to be the centerpiece of Jake's plan to save Maddy.

All that was outside of her mind right now. The only thing in the world was her driver's hot cock as it brought her soothing waves of pleasure. She felt her blood begin to rise once more. Her breath began to become heavy and she uttered a low moan from behind her gag. Sensing her teetering on the precipice of a mind numbing explosion of delight, her dwarf lover slowed his movements gradually until he was at a stop. The enraptured pony felt a wave of comforting warmth spread through her as her pussy trilled with pleasurable quivers. "Uuuuuuuuuuummmmmmmm," she moaned again lazily. When the mini-orgasm had passed, her driver began his assault on her sphincter once again.

Irkut, although he enjoyed watching the ponygirl in passion, didn't have all day. He stepped into the camp. Giorgi's slave girl, wearing a shield gag across her lower face, naked but for her collar and slave wrist and ankle bracelets, jumped up and made a bowing gesture to the ponygirl trainer. She had been gazing with jealousy at the fucking the ponygirl was getting, wishing that it was her. Now she hurried to get her master's guest a chair.

The dwarf looked up and saw his friend. "I'll be done in a minute, Irkut," he called out in Russian. "Have a drink."

"I will, I will," Irkut responded, laughing.

The slave girl produced a chair and a small table. After setting them down where Irkut could have a good view of the copulating couple, she ran into the RV and returned with a bottle of clear, cool vodka, two small glasses and a pepper grinder. Irkut sat down in the chair. When the glasses and vodka arrived, he ground a small spritz of pepper into the glass and then poured the vodka into it until it rose two fingers high. He then tossed it back in one gulp.

Giorgi had picked up his pace in his ponygirl's ass. He was going to give her one more, earth moving climax and then he would be through. The ponygirl's moans were coming staccato now, emerging at each fierce thrust of his hips. "Uummm! Uummm! Uummm! Uummm!" she moaned, like a steam engine climbing a tall hill. She ground her forehead into the soft grass beneath her and she bit down hard on the thick, leather probe that filled her mouth.

Giorgi's own lusts were about to overboil. He grasped the slender, bound arms of the pony fiercely with his powerful hands and his eyes rolled back in their sockets. He had built up a large head of steam as well and, when his cock exploded, he issued a loud groan and then a series of deep, throaty grunts as his manhood pulsed and jerked within the pony's bowels.

Chocolate felt the dwarf's cock as it spasmed against her sphincter. All the residue of her many partial orgasms now came rolling home. She moaned loudly too. Her firm, ample breasts were swaying beneath her chest. Her pussy, though empty, convulsed and gave off a series of hard, exquisite contractions. She didn't know how it worked, but her pussy liked a cock up her ass as much as her ass did. She groaned and her body jerked again and again until finally, mercifully, her orgasm slowed to a mere echo of its former self.

Giorgi withdrew his shrinking rod from the exhausted pony's rear hole, giving a great sigh of satisfaction. The pony would remain as she was until someone told her to move. Volitional activity was discouraged in ponygirls.

Chocolate sensed that someone had entered the camp. She had heard a voice and her driver say something back to it. But she cared not who had been a witness to her ravishment. A fog of contentedness had passed over her. She was happy to remain where she was, her rear proffered to any and all comers, her twin love lips peaking out underneath.

Without putting away his tool, Giorgi strolled over to where Irkut was sitting, waiting for him. The chair that the slave girl had put out for him was small in its dimensions and the dwarfish ponygirl driver would be sitting at a level below that of his guest. But what other choice was there? If he used a regular chair, his legs would dangle over the sides like a little kid at family dinner. It was better to have his feet firmly on the ground. After all, there was no use trying to hide the fact that he was short.

"So what brings you out here, Irkut," he said once he got himself comfortable. When he had finished his task with the ponygirl, his blond slave girl had jumped up and ran to the small fire that was burning in the middle of the encampment. She returned now with a small, steel bowl of soapy, hot water and a cloth. She knelt between the thighs of her diminutive owner and began to wash his long, thick cock. Irkut had often been amazed by the fact of its girth and length. It seemed so incongruous on such a small frame.

Giorgi leaned back in his chair and enjoyed the application of the moist heat to his now softened pole. The slave girl made a good job of swaddling it with the cloth and removing all traces of the pony's waste from it. When she was done, she put the cloth back in the bowl and leaned forwards, presenting the back of her neck to her master. He unbuckled her gag behind her head and, when she raised her head again, removed it from her mouth. The girl then leaned forwards and took the dwarf's cock in her mouth, washing it with her lips and tongue. Making her check her work with her mouth was an efficient way of making sure the slave girl did a good job in cleaning it.

Irkut responded to Giorgi's friendly question. "I had some time to kill and I wanted to see how Chocolate was doing." He tilted his head towards the dwarf and added, "I wanted to talk to you, too." His gaze went to the slave girl. While most of the slave girls knew no Russian, Ilona, Giorgi's property and chief assistant, was Latvian. She knew Russian well. Giorgi knew at once that Irkut wanted to talk to him about something private. Although they spent much of their time gagged and verbal discourse between them was actively discouraged, slave girls were incorrigible gossips. It often seemed that what happened at one end of a pony camp found its way to the other end in less time than it would have taken to dial a telephone and call it in.

"Go get your hood," Giorgi ordered the girl. A faint shadow of unhappiness crossed her face and she stood up like a shot. She brought her bowl and washcloth back near the fire and ran into the trailer.

While she was off on her errand, Giorgi ground some pepper into both their glasses and poured out some vodka. The men both lifted their glasses and, tilting them and their heads at the same time, poured the fierce liquor down their throats. This was no 80 proof store bought concoction. It was the real thing with a kick like a horse. The eyes of both men watered and they engaged in a mutual smile.

Ilona had emerged from the RV and had a leather hood in her hands. She knelt in the grass a few feet away from her master, directly in front of both of the men. She bowed her neck and proffered the hood to Giorgi.

The dwarf got up from his chair and drew the leather hood over her head. The hood fit the girl tightly, as if it had been designed for her specifically, which it had. It followed the contours of her face and left her mouth free. He then reinserted her gag, its leather shield overlapping slightly with her hood. In this way, if someone wanted to use the slave's mouth, the hood did not have to be removed.

There were no eye holes in the hood, just two indentations which would press the slave girl's eyelids closed. At each ear was a plug that fit inside. A tiny speaker was in each plug and, once activated, would send a hum of steady static to the girl's brain. She would hear nothing of the men's conversation, or anything else, until the hood was removed. Giorgi stepped behind the now isolated girl. He grabbed her wrists and, bringing them behind her, locked them together.

Ilona hated her hood. Her master often made her spend hours in it when they were on the road. It didn't do to have slave girls know too much about the road systems of the small former republic. They were feckless creatures and you never knew when one might plan an escape. Especially Ilona, whose knowledge of Russian would get her far. But unescorted women in Kalikastan traveled at their own risk and all it would take was for some man to order her to open the top of any blouse she managed to find to see her slave name tattooed there. And then there would be hell to pay.

She swooned when Giorgi activated the tiny speakers in her ears. The loss of all visual and aural sensation was disorienting. She had no idea how long she would be left in sensory deprivation. It could be minutes or hours. The whole encampment could move away and she wouldn't know it. Time would stand still until then. Being a slave girl was a lonely life. You had no real friends. You had no one to convey your inner thoughts and fears to. You lived day to day and tried to forestall any thoughts about your fate, how long you would be held captive, if you would ever escape. But when she wore the hood, those thoughts just ran into her head. She began to recall her former life, her family, her lovers, her friends. There was nothing else to do. Except, maybe, ruminate about her future.

Ilona had been Giorgi's slave now for about two years. She loved taking care of the ponygirls for him. But something had changed in his attitude towards her. He was a little colder than usual, a little more aloof. She had begun to fear that he was going to sell her. Change was never a good thing for a slave girl. No matter what your situation, it could almost always be made worse. Her master, although strict and ready with a whip when she displeased him, was not really cruel, not like his depraved brother Jerzi, the one who drove Lightning. If she were sold, she might be bought by someone like him. And now, being hooded and deprived of hearing while the men talked, made her fear that they were discussing her fate. Her body shivered and a lump formed in her belly.

Giorgi sat himself back down in his chair. Irkut had poured two more shots and they finished them off quickly.

"So, what's the big secret?" Giorgi asked.

Irkut was admiring the delicious form of the long haired blonde slave girl kneeling a few feet away from him, her thighs widespread as befitted her station in life. Her nipples were two small, pinkish circles with tiny dots in the middle. Her breasts were large and fluffy, still holding the upward curve of youth. Her belly was marked by a tattoo of a snarling, black boar, its fangs a gruesome yellow, its eyes red. It was the emblem of her training house, one of the finest and harshest in Kalikastan. Her thighs were graceful and well toned, her sexual slit revealed between them, hairless and smooth. If he recalled correctly, her facial lips were thick and pouty. Not a bad slut.

"Irkut, are you there?" Giorgi asked, bemused by the ponygirl trainer's fascination with his slave girl. "She's for sale, you know," he continued. "Twenty thousand zlotskis, five thousand dollars."

Irkut shook himself from his lustful examination of Ilona's charms. "No, no thanks, but I might like to come back and fuck her later if it's all right with you."

"No problem," Giorgi returned. "And if you have her suck your prick, you might change your mind."

Irkut waved his hand as if dismissing the dwarf's suggestion. Like a used car, one had to be careful about buying a used slave girl. The first question would be, if there was nothing wrong with her, why was she being sold?

"I wanted to ask you about the Americans, Mr. Burnham and his assistant, Jake Barnes," he said. "What do you think of them?"

"Oh, they're typical Americans," Giorgi replied. "Everything is about dollars and they want everything right away. They're like children who have gotten hold of their daddy's cash."

"Yes, that's true," Irkut replied. "But what about this match race between Chocolate and Lightning. Burnham has spent a lot of money on it and gone to a lot of trouble. Don't you think that that is unusual?"

Giorgi was busy pouring another round of shots. "Nah," he answered. "That's just the way they are. I knew a rich American once, back in St. Petersburg. He wanted the best looking broads, the fastest car, the best food, everything the best. And if anyone was a few seconds late, well, he raised hell. There was a car that he wanted, a 1927 Bugatti Royale, a wonderful car. He practically drooled over the pictures that the seller was sending him. He was willing to pay anything the seller demanded. He had to have that car."

"Did he get it" Irkut asked.

"Unfortunately, no. The sellers were Russian mafioso types. They took his money and blew his brains out. It was all a big con. But you get what I mean."

"I'm not so sure that that's all there is to it," Irkut said. He and Giorgi lifted their shot glasses, little specks of ground pepper floating at the top, and poured them back.

Irkut took a moment to let the fire in his throat and esophagus relent before speaking again. "It just smells fishy to me."

"Listen, Irkut, the Americans are paying you very well. Now don't deny it. Me too! Just take their money and enjoy it. Don't be such a worry wart."

Irkut smiled at his friend's suggestion. Yes, he was a cautious man. And yes, Burnham had paid him lot of money with a huge, promised bonus if Chocolate pulled off winning the championship and defeating Lightning. But there were things more important than money and ponygirl racing was one of them. He hadn't gone into it for the money, after all. It was the pureness of the sport, the total commitment of the ponies to the race, the long training hours in which their personalities were transformed, the thrill of possessing them. No, he would put aside the money if he found out that something was going to happen that threatened the sport, you could be sure of that.

"Have another shot, Irkut and relax," Giorgi demanded.

"No, I've go work to do," Irkut responded. "I'll come by around 8 o'clock tonight and sample your whore. In the meantime, stay well."

The men rose and shook hands. Irkut took a glance at the kneeling, bound and hooded, naked, blond slave girl as he left the camp. "Twenty thousand zlotskis," he thought. "Mmmmmm...."

CHAPTER FIVE

The next day, around noon, Drabik was hustling along the paved pathway on the Grobgy estate to their own ponygirl park. Just when he was getting his ducks in a line for his coup against his boss, he seemed to be faced with crisis after crisis. Lightning, he had been told, had come down with an injury and might have to forgo the Fall Tournament.

He had already sent for the estate physician. Word, too, had been sent out to the boss. Drabik didn't know what he would do when he got to Lightning's encampment, but someone was going to get it in the neck for damaging the estate's premier ponygirl.

At the encampment, he found Lightning kneeling on the grass. She saw him too as was reflected by the tilt she made with her head. Her thighs were spread wide, revealing her hairless cleft, and she was sitting on her haunches. Like Suki, she sported a rampant, yellow wolf on her belly. Oddly, one of her tall, black ponygirl boots was off of her feet.

The sight of the naked ponygirl made his stomach tighten. She had cast a spell over him to be sure. Even now, although it would violate all protocol, he wanted to take her full, thick nipples in his mouth and give them a long, passionate suckle. He longed to have her lips around his tool, or to be able to bury it in her deep recesses.

Love? He could not call it love. One did not love a ponygirl, who was a mere step above a horse or a cow. But each time he saw her, every inch of his body began to crave her.

Drabik had tried everything to dissolve his obsession with the pony. He had beaten her to within an inch of her life. He had ignored her. He had some of the grooms fuck her in his presence. He had gone away for several weeks, hoping that the fierce attraction he felt for her would fade. But everything he did seemed only to make it worse.

And then he had committed a grave error. Like Irkut, Drabik was suspicious of the Americans. When he found out that they planned to challenge Grobgy to race her against one of their ponies, winner take all, he had bristled with rage at the thought of losing her. He needed to see what the capitalist dogs were really up to. He had them investigated through some connections he had in the States. Barnes came up, as he had suspected, as a notorious fixer who operated outside of the law. He was a freelancer and his pose as Burnham's sidekick was a sham. And then he found out something more interesting. It seems that Burnham's niece, Madeline, had been kidnapped. She disappeared just about four or five weeks before the Americans showed up in Kalikastan.

In an attempt to learn more about what Barnes and his crew were doing, he engineered the theft of his slave girl, Klara. She was down now in a secret dungeon in Grobgy's mansion, a dismal prisoner to Drabik's angry lusts. She had known little but suffered grievously before she gave up what she did know. Jake's men had talked about someone named Maddy. Maddy? Madeline? It was too much of a coincidence to ignore. He asked his connection to send him a picture of the girl. He was sent one of her in a bikini, posing by some lake. It was the picture the police had used when they were searching for her. Although he had never seen her face, when he saw the photograph he knew immediately that the girl Madeline was known throughout Kalikastan as Lightning. The shape of her body, the swell of her breasts and, as if that were not enough, a mole on her right hip, all told him that the famous sulky pony and the kidnapped girl were one.

As soon as he made that discovery, he was sorry he had ever seen the picture. Now the object of his obsession had a face, a smiling, youthful, happy face. She was more than a mere ponygirl now. If there was one constant in the handling of ponygirls it was that no one ever took a look at their faces. When their hoods were removed for cleaning and grooming, their faces were turned away in some confined space so their visages would remain unknown. It was essential to the loss of their human status that they never be thought of as people. As long as they were anonymous, faceless beasts, almost any agony could be inflicted on them in the name of training or discipline. They had no innate value other than their ability to pull a carriage and to fuck.

Drabik had experienced a good example of that necessity just yesterday. His Arabian customer, Ali, had shown up about three that afternoon to examine the ponygirl Suki. Drabik had spent about an hour fucking her before he came.

It had not been his intent to copulate with the new pony when he entered the barn just after lunch. There was another new pony that had come in a few days before he wanted to give a workout to see how she would run. As he passed Suki's stall, he heard the distinct sound of her intense sobs through the door. Even her shield like gag could not suppress the noise. He became angry at her foolishness and entered her stall intending to apply some discipline to her.

When he saw her, her booted feet widespread and lashed to the floor, her soft, plump derriere angled up as a result of her being forced to lean across the bar that ran across her stall, her nose ring tied off to the wall in front of her, his resolve to punish her faded. Her little hands were squirming in her confinements behind her back, her wrists pulling futilely against their confinements. Her long, brown ponytail shook and trembled with each of her sobs. Her wailing rose as she reacted to the sound of him entering her stall.

Drabik could not help but think of the pretty, shapely girl who had been dehumanized before his eyes a few weeks ago. She had pleaded to be spared and wept and sobbed as the men stripped her, shaved her head and installed a ponygirl collar and hood on her. Then Grobgy had raped her, as was the custom for a new ponygirl, while she lay on her back in the dust, her hands bound behind her, her protests stifled by a cruel, mouth filling gag.

There was no doubt about it; something had changed in him since he had seen the face of the girl named Madeline in that picture about a month ago. He was softening. He had let three prostitutes live after watching him commit homicide on four men, although he had ensured by enslaving them that they would not go to the police. They were probably serving some Turkish or Arab master by now. But to let them live at all was not like him. He had killed dozens of men since becoming Grobgy's enforcer and hundreds, maybe thousands of men, women and children when he commanded a regiment in Afghanistan. What were three lowly whores after that? But he had let them live.

Taking pity on the frantically distraught pony, Drabik approached her from behind. He pressed his body up against her back and began to rub her bare shoulders. He leaned his head forwards and began to whisper in her ear, "Poor, Suki, good Suki," again and again in an attempt to comfort her. After about a minute of his affectionate attentions, the crying of the pony began to abate. He leaned away from her and ran his hands across the upper portion of her naked back, massaging the muscles there, letting the warmth of his large hands communicate itself to the pitiable ponygirl. It was hard to adjust, he knew that. And so much harder when you could believe that someone might find you and save you if they just knew where to look, that maybe her conversion to non-human status had just been a cruel joke meant to punish her for her transgression, to teach her a lesson. The idea that she had lost her life, the one she had been leading until then, as the result of a few moments of carelessness was hard to bear.

The pony reacted to the administration of Drabik's hands to her body. He had been pressing his loins against her rear and his cock had grown hard as a result. He ran his hands down her soft arms as he kissed her graceful shoulders. Taking a small step away from her, he caressed the smooth, bare, soft haunches that jutted out so deliciously at him. He slid his hands over her hourglass like hips and down the outside of her slim, elegant thighs. Her skin was like hot silk. When his hands rose again, over her rump, up her arms and once more across her shoulders, the pony emitted a low moan, incipient to passion. Drabik stepped back closer to the pony so that his thighs pressed against her bottom cheeks, her bound hands against his hard, taut belly and his chest against her back. He circled his hands to the pony's front where her plump, round breasts hung freely from her chest and captured them. When he began to massage them, the pony gave out another distinctive moan as she took in the sensation of his hot hands on her tender, soft projections.

Drabik took his time in massaging the firm, spongy orbs. He pulled at her nipples, which had grown hard with her growing desire. He pinched and massaged them. He kissed her shoulders up to where her ponygirl collar began and then down and across her back.

His prick was expressing his own needs. The pony had begun to sway her rear cheeks back and forth over his loins. Keeping one hand busy at her breasts, he dropped the other along her side, over her soft hip and then between her legs from behind. He took possession of her mons with his whole hand and began to rub it gently. His finger traced a line along the divide between her engorging love lips to find that her crevasse had grown slippery and wet. Putting his largest two fingers together, he pressed them inside the bound pony, making her sigh and her body shudder.

Drabik needed no better signal than that. He lowered his fly and eased his stiff prick from its enclosure. Before impaling the helpless but impassioned pony, he let the hardened prong lay between the soft cheeks of her rear and pressed himself against her body. His free hand had rejoined its mate and he gave her breasts a squeeze, gentle at first and then harder and harder until the pony gave a deep, enraptured moan from within her chest.

When he eased his cock between the pony's dilated labia, the pony's knees gave out and her belly pressed more heavily against the beam that crossed her stall. Her slit parted easily and he sank himself within her to his hilt.

The pony's cunt was tight and hot. Drabik let go a groan of his own as the pleasure of being sunk into her soft depths passed through him. He began to stroke his meat along her passageway, his hands holding her full, hard breasts, his mouth pressed against her back. Slowly, but surely, his lusts began to rise. The pony he had named Suki was breathing heavily and her moans had turned to grunts as she tried to thrust her hips back at her assailant.

Having her head fastened firmly in a forward looking pose by the ring through her nose, the pony could not know which of the masters was using her so. It did not seem to matter as her lusts were rising far higher than Drabik had seen to date. "This is how a ponygirl fucks," he thought to himself as he continued to scrape his cock along the walls of her moist, soft, cleft. The pony's exertions in her bonds were becoming more and more frantic. Suddenly, she gave out a scream and her pussy began to convulse and contract around his cock. The added pressure and the thrill of feeling and seeing the pony's exuberant orgasm set Drabik off. His cock began to pump his spume deep within her as it jerked and throbbed. He groaned loudly. His hands twisted and pulled at the pony's breasts.

When his forces became exhausted, Drabik, breathing heavily, could feel the still shuddering body of the pony pressed up against him. She had finally given into her lusts, a milestone in her progress towards her new life. Drabik decided to take full advantage of her passions. After pulling shut the Velcro tabs on the pony's hood to assure his continued anonymity, he let his cock slide from the pony's quim and began to release her from her bonds. It was easy to remove the chain that held her nose ring fast and to release her booted ankles from the rings in the floor. He pulled her back off of the rail and, placing his hands on her shoulders, urged her to the floor. He kept pushing until the pony was laying on her back, her graceful legs spread widely, her chest heaving with passion.

The pony's smooth, delicate, hairless entranceway between her thighs glistened with the combination of her own passionate emissions and his. Kneeling between her thighs, he let his hand slide along their soft interior surfaces and then pressed them wider apart so that her sexual divide was free to his attentions. He leaned over and, after drifting his hot tongue along the inside of her thighs, placed his mouth upon her leaky sex and began to lavish it with his tongue and lips.

The pony gave out a deep sigh of pleasure. Her hips bucked and her legs quivered. Drabik draped them over his shoulders as he licked the length of her gash and then probed her hardened clit with the tip of his tongue. His attentions drove the pony into an ecstatic rapture. She came almost at once, her blind, blue hooded, featureless head twisting from side to side, deep moans and sighs escaping from behind her gagged lips. Her breasts swayed and shuddered as her body quaked.

Drabik let his attentions wane and then resumed them. Twice more he led the naked, hooded creature past the point of endurance. After the third orgiastic climax, he relented and let the slender, diminutive pony come to rest.

The ponygirl trainer brought his body up until he was laying side by side with the pony. He drifted his hand over her tattooed belly, with its fierce, rampant, yellow wolf, over her breasts and the tops of her thighs, easing her letdown from her passionate heights. When her body had calmed and her chest resumed a more rhythmic rise and fall, he rose from the floor. He reached down and, taking hold of the ring in her collar, pulled the pony to its knees. There was one more thing to do.

As a result of his oral caresses to the pony, his cock had grown hard and full once again. It jutted out from his loins like a soldier on parade. Reaching down behind he pony's head, he released its gag and eased the long, thick prong of leather from her mouth. "If she tries to talk now," Drabik thought, "I will beat her senseless." But she did not try and speak. She licked her lips and posed her head upwards, cognizant, as she should be, of her master's need. When Drabik presented his rigid wand to its mouth, the pony eagerly took it within and began her caresses.

Suki's blow jobs to date had been forced affairs. She moaned and cried as the cocks passed over her lips, sobbed when the heavy jism was spurted against the back of her mouth or down her throat to her belly. This was different. Slowly, but eagerly, she was bringing pleasure to her master, whoever he was. For to a ponygirl all men were her masters. When not training or racing, it was her whole purpose to serve and pleasure them. A good pony accepted that and Suki's delicate, skilled delivery of oral pleasure to Drabik's cock demonstrated that she was beginning to learn and accept it too.

The pony took her time in sucking her master's prick. She circled her lips around the knob and let her tongue run underneath it. She pressed her head forwards slowly, her lips gripping the shaft firmly, her tongue washing it. When she pulled back, she flicked her tongue along the underside, making Drabik moan with delight. Drabik let his hand fall lightly on the faceless, blue hooded head, urging the pony to completion of her task. She responded by quickening her movements, and began rapidly pushing her lips down the length of Drabik's prick and then back up again, slurping and sucking at his meat. Drabik felt his balls tighten and his cock began to glow with the imminence of his climax. He reached it suddenly, shooting a torrent of his viscous, white juice into the ponygirl's mouth.

She continued a pleasant, gentle, oral caress of Drabik's prick long after his spasms came to a halt. Drabik swayed on his feet, enjoying the interregnum between orgasm and full consciousness. When he came to his senses, he drew his softened cock from the pony's mouth and lifted her to her feet. He picked up the gag that he had tossed onto a shelf on the wall of the stall and reinserted it between the pony's lips. She spread them widely to accept it. He refastened her to her mount against the rail, attached her nose ring to the chain that led from the wall in front of her, and rechained her ankles wide apart. He gave her ass one last, affectionate caress and exited the stall, leaving the pony to contemplate her lustful responses to her ravishment.

When the Arabs arrived about a half hour later, Drabik was in a quandary. He was sure that he had achieved a major breakthrough with Suki and was now regretful of his haste in wanting to sell her. On the other hand, he hoped to develop a steady market with the Arabs for trained ponygirls and did not want to be guilty of having brought them all they way out to the estate for nothing. They arrived in two vehicles. One was a flashy, black Mercedes, the other was a much used, dusty, light blue van that had its back portion converted into a pony trailer. Out of the Mercedes came two bearded men with short hair and finely tailored suits. They looked to be in their late thirties. They both wore wraparound sunglasses. From the van came two younger looking men wearing blue jeans and t-shirts. Their beards and hair, as compared to the older men, were scraggly and unkempt. They were both lean and even somewhat gaunt. The older men, while not fat, certainly looked well fed.

Tea was served on the veranda of the mansion by two of Grobgy's naked slave girls. The young men waited outside. Drabik engaged in desultory conversation with the men, exchanging pleasantries and listening to their complements on the slave girls, the mansion, the wonderful countryside. Most of all, they expressed their happiness to be in partnership with the Kalikastani government. He kept thinking about the carnal session with the pony he had just had and wondering if he could get out of selling her to these men. He could offer them another one, but, so close to his goal of launching a coup against his leader, he did not want to cause a breach now. Grobgy would go ballistic if he sold off one of the other ponies without his consent. He was riled enough when he learned that Drabik had made arrangements to sell Suki without his permission.

Knowing that he could not prolong the inevitable any longer, Drabik offered to show the men the goods. They were happy to come along with him to the ponybarn. Drabik had left instructions for the pony to be mounted in a harness from a davit that extended from one of the thick, wooden columns sunk into the ground outside the barn and she was standing there when the five men, the younger men having joined the group, arrived.

The harness was designed so that a ponygirl could stand secured in one location and allow a master access all around her, whether to administer a whip to her back and front, or to assess her, as was going to happen today. It ran across the chest and back and under the pony's arms. Two strong but thin straps ran down between the pony's legs and up again, resting on either side of her slit. Thus, if a master wanted to torment the pony's sex, his blows would not be blocked. Another set of straps ran under the pony's breasts and across her back. After a while, it became dangerous to hang a ponygirl from her arms since the muscles quickly withered to ineffectiveness. A pony with a wrenched shoulder or aching arm could not pull a cart efficiently. A harness held her in place more than adequately as a substitute.

Suki's eye ports were still closed as per his instructions. She looked beautiful and vulnerable in the harness. The blue Cyrillic letters on her chest spelled out her name proudly and the yellow, tattooed wolf on her belly proclaimed her as a product of the Grobgy estate. Her heavy breasts, soft and white as cream, swayed slightly as she tried to adjust her weight in the harness. A slight breeze had caused her long ponytail to waft slightly away from her head. She stood only 5'5" or so with her boots on, a good 5 inches shorter than most ponygirls. Her shoulders were not broad and strong, but rounded and graceful. Her thighs had not developed the strength that would grow there later after weeks and weeks of exercise. Even a show pony, like a dancer, needed strength in her legs.

Drabik recalled their recent passionate interlude. This was not what he expected when he had called the Arabs and told them she was for sale. The shorter of the two well dressed Arabs, Ali, spoke first, in English. "She's wonderful. Just what we were looking for."

The second man, who had been introduced to Drabik as Hassan, nodded silently.

"May I," Ali said, holding his hands out towards the pony.

"Be my guest," Drabik replied. The two men proceeded to inspect every inch of Suki's flesh. Drabik sensed the pony's nervousness. He wondered if she understood English.

It just happened that she had taken three years of it in high school and the man's statement that she was just what they were looking for conveyed to her the fact that the men intended to buy her. The hands that wandered her body, poking and prodding, caressing a muscle here and there, pushing open the cheeks of her ass, testing and weighing her breasts, all confirmed her fear. She felt the men running their hands through the long ponytail that jutted out from the rear of her hood. She tried to shake it free, but one of the men held on to it, uttering a small laugh.

The men's hands were like foul creatures devouring her body. She had no power to keep any portion of it from them. A hot, soft hand ran up the inside of her thigh close to her sex and made her jump. Fingers seized her nipples and pinched them until she moaned with pain.

Being blinded made her fears more intense, made the experience of being assessed like a farm animal more humiliating, more unreal. Was her trainer really going to sell her? She trembled as she thought of it. "Please let it not be true. Please! Please! Please!" she thought fearfully. She nervously pulled at the bindings to her wrists, bindings that gripped them remorselessly. She waved and jerked her head futilely to try and open the eyelets to her hood. She whined and moaned. Her belly was tense with her apprehensive imaginings of what could happen to her. "Please! Please!" she thought. "Please let me go, please!"

Life here was hard enough, but there was always the remote chance that her family would find her and she could be saved. Her father, maybe, could borrow some money and buy her. But if she was taken to a remote estate, she would be lost forever.

And then Ali spoke to Hassan in Arabic. The sound was distinctive, with the guttural accents and the fluid movement of the tongue. Hearing the unmistakable Middle Eastern tongue, the unfortunate and unlucky girl who had become Suki began to panic. Her legs began to tremble and she emitted an audible whine. Being sold to another estate here in Kalikastan was one thing; she might manage an escape somehow. But to be brought to some remote Arabian country meant she would never, ever, be seen again by anyone who knew her, not even by the remotest chance. She was torn between protesting her sale to these foreigners and her fear of punishment for breaking the rules. It was when the men removed her gag to take a look at her teeth that her opportunity came. Her lips trembled and she struggled mightily to restrain the words that threatened to pour out of her. "P, p, p, p, ..." was all that came out when the men released her cheeks after their inspection.

The first Arab looked up at Drabik, surprised. "She speaks?"

"No," was all Drabik said in reply. He pushed the business end of the gag back into the pony's mouth harshly and buckled it tightly against the back of her head.

"You are too soft on your ponies here, Mr. Drabik," the Arab said. "In my country, once a woman becomes a pony, we insure that she never speaks again."

"And how's that?" Drabik asked.

The man took hold of his tongue, pulled it out of his mouth and drew a line across its base with a finger of his other hand. "You see," he continued, "one cut and no more talking."

At this, Suki released a long stream of her urine. She didn't mean to, it just happened. Fear had pierced her like a knife. Her golden discharge dribbled down the inside of her widespread thighs, down her shins and onto the ground. "They're going to cut out my tongue!" she thought desperately. "Oh my god! They can't buy me they just can't." She whined a desperate protest through her gag.

The four Arab men laughed. This morning, Drabik probably would have too. It was always funny when a pony expressed close to human reactions.

Drabik noticed that the men had only inspected the pony's sex cursorily. "Don't you want to see her responsiveness?" he asked.

"Oh, no," the man replied. "We're not concerned with that. Our ponies are not given pleasure. In fact, once they're collared...," he said as he swiped one palm across the other. "Clean off."

"Off?" Drabik asked, horrified. To deface a pony was anathema to local training customs. Cutting out her tongue was one thing, although he didn't agree with it, after all, he enjoyed a pony's tongue on his cock. But to slice off her clitoris was something else! A life of intense sexual pleasure was considered one of the consolations of being dehumanized.

"The whole thing," the man replied.

"You mean...." was all Drabik got out.

"The labia too, the whole thing," the Arab continued. Drabik could see his astounded face in the reflection on the man's sunglasses. "The hole is sewed up nice and tight, just the circumference of a cock left open for penetration from the rear. It's called the harem cut. Very popular. It feels wonderful. I recommend it. You can still induce a pony's moisture by tickling her inside or sucking on her breasts, but the pleasure belongs to her master not to her."

"I don't think we would ever do anything like that here, Mr. Ali," Drabik said. "Does the Commission know your customs?

"Of course! Your High Commissioner was our guest for a few weeks last year. He enjoyed himself immensely."

Drabik pondered his options. He could not see condemning the pony to that kind of a life, but what could he do? He could jack up the price so high they wouldn't pay it. That's what he would do.

In the meantime, Suki was trembling and shaking like she was having a fit. Her piss had puddled on the ground between her boots. During these inspections, ponies often reacted unhappily to the prospect of being sold. When you had no rights, security was everything. The devil you knew against the devil you didn't. So it was customary to fix the pony's boots to pegs in the ground, her legs spread wide to accommodate her inspection. This way she couldn't put up too much of a fuss or kick one of her potential buyers with one of her powerful legs.

Suki was trying desperately to pull her ankles free of their confines. She didn't know what she would do if she managed it, but running away was the first thing on her mind. It was better than nothing. Just a half hour or so ago, she had begun to feel that she had to accept the fact that she was a ponygirl and make the best of things until she could be freed. Whoever had fucked her, and she suspected it was the same cruel man who was proffering her for sale now, he had given her extreme pleasure. Her sexual responses had startled her. It was the beginning of what people had talked about, the wild, sexual cravings of ponygirls. Now, her world was being turned topsy-turvy once again. She recoiled at the idea of her prospective sexual mutilation and instinctively tried to press her thighs together to protect her loins. The men could hear her moaning and sobbing behind her gag. Unfortunately for Suki, she had not heard the worst of it.

"I don't understand," Ali asked offhandedly. "Why do you keep the arms on?"

"What?" Drabik replied. "The arms?"

"Yes. Ponies don't need arms. They are just surplusage and get in the way of the reins. Don't you have that problem?"

"Sometimes," Drabik answered, "but we live with it."

"There is no need," the Arab stated. "You cut the arms off here," he said running his straightened hand edgewise across Suki's arm about five inches down from her shoulder, "and here." He made the same motion on her other arm. "That leaves enough leverage under the arm for a harness like you have her in now but eliminates the problem of tangling in the reins. It is also helpful in the area of escapes. If one of our ponies slipped her confinements during the night, a very unlikely thing, well, she would be unable to open the door to the barn. And if she did, where could she go? She couldn't put on any clothes since she has no hands, and, again, even if by some magic she did, she has no arms. She would be recognized for what she is right away, an escaped pony. Then, when she was questioned and couldn't talk, she would indeed be sunk. So you see no arms and no tongue is really the more efficient way to handle a ponygirl."

Suki's demonstration of her unhappiness became more than exuberant at this point. She had lost all semblance of obeying the rules. Her muffled voice could be heard pleading from behind her gag. She shook her hooded head violently.

The lead Arab stepped closer to her and took one of her breasts in his hand. He squeezed it gently and then lifted it playfully in his palm. "She is a beauty," he said. "She'll match one of our American ponies very nicely. And her hips are made for breeding. I'll take her. How much do you want?"

It was the moment of truth. Suki's sobbing had gotten louder. She was thrashing in her harness, pulling violently against the bonds on her ankles, howling wildly behind her gag. She bit down fiercely on the long, thick, leather prong in her mouth. The men paid her no mind.

Drabik had been intending to ask for $50,000 and settle for much less. He had to keep from insulting the man. He had come all this way. And he had friends on the Commission. Big friends. So the price had to be high enough that the man wouldn't take it but not too high so that he would think that he was being made a fool of.

"$95,000," Drabik blurted out. "I've had an offer for her for that much already. I probably should honor it since it was first. I'm sorry I didn't call. It just came in this morning."

"No problem," the Arab said. "$100,000. I really like her. And she has good spirit. It will be fun to break her."

Drabik was backed into a corner. He couldn't very well refuse to take their money because he thought they were scumbags due to the way they treated ponygirls. He would be a laughingstock. Besides, who cared how anyone treated a ponygirl. Well, he did, for one. He tried to imagine his reaction if Lightning was sold off to one of the Arabs. With pressure from the Commission and the right price, Grobgy would have to sell. "Shit!" was all he could say to himself.

"Okay, Mr. Ali," he said unhappily. "You've got a deal."

Suki screamed a violent protest from behind the leather shield that covered her lower face even as Ali signaled his workers to go get the pony van. They ran off as per instructions. Hassan had said practically nothing but smiled at Drabik in a way that was sickening to him.

"By the way, Mr. Drabik," Ali said. "I am aware of the market value for ponygirls. I know that you set a very high price. What your reason is, I don't know or care. But I hope that you take account of my generosity in our future dealings. I understand that your estate sells a few trained ponies every year. Please let me know when one is available and we will meet again."

Drabik knew that he was fucked. All he needed was the man complaining to the Commission that he had tried to rip the Arab off. While the men waited for the pony van to be brought around, they continued their chat. "Have you ever had a Persian girl, Mr. Drabik?"

"I can't say that I have," Drabik replied.

"You will get the chance soon. Mr. Burnham has made arrangements for regular shipments. These are beautiful girls, dark hair, dark, almond shaped eyes, sultry, with honey colored skin. Like the wife of Alexander the Great, what was her name? Roxanne, that's it. Women of stunning beauty."

There were the Americans again. Drabik hated them. He had watched his men slaughtered by mujahedeen armed with automatic rifles and rocket launchers paid for with American money. They had brought down the system that had nurtured and taken care of him for almost thirty years.

"And how do you convince the Iranians to give up these beauties," Drabik asked churlishly.

"They are heretics, of course. Non-believers or young women who have committed crimes of disloyalty to their Muslim faith. There are many of them, more than you would suspect."

"I get the feeling that there are as many as you can sell, Mr. Ali," Drabik returned.

"Of course," Ali answered with a smile.

The van pulled around the corner of the barn. It drove past where they were standing and then backed up so that the pony could be more easily loaded in the portable stall behind the passenger compartment.

Suki had collapsed in despair. "How could these men be so cruel? Why is this happening to me?" she asked herself dismally. She heard her trainer and the man he called Ali, the man who had bought her, talking, but the meaning of their words did not pierce the thick fog of her unhappiness and fear. When she heard the sound of the van being pulled up, doors to its sides opening and closing, she realized that she would be soon loaded on to it and driven away to a horrible fate. "I've got to escape! I've got to! I couldn't bear it! I'll be just like an animal! Oh god! Oh god!" She tried to shout her supplications through her gagged mouth. "Please don't do this to me, please! Please!" Her words emerged merely as muted noise.

The workers emerged from the van and advanced towards the pony.

"I'll have the cash brought to you tomorrow. That will be sufficient won't it?" Ali asked.

"Certainly," Drabik answered. He felt sick inside. He still saw the dismal face of the attractive, young, Russian girl just before she was hooded a couple of weeks ago. It would haunt him, he knew it.

"I'd like to take possession of my pony now, if you don't mind," Ali said. "My men have to prepare her for her journey. We'll be leaving after the tournament so we'll need all the proper paperwork by then."

"Okay," Drabik mumbled. He had never felt so powerless in his life. The workers approached Suki and one began to unbuckle her gag while the other removed the golden disks that decorated her loins declaring her as the property of the Grobgy estate and tossed them aside. When her gag was pulled out, she began to scream.

"No! Please don't sell me to them, please! I'll do anything you want! I'll be good I prom....."

That was all she got out. One of the workers had grabbed her face by her cheeks and was squeezing it hard. The other presented a silver ball to her mouth which sat on the end of a long prong. The ball slipped in easily. Drabik knew what it was. When the prong was turned, sharp spikes would emerge from the ball, sealing it in the pony's mouth. It was extremely painful and used only for punishment, never for travel. By the time they got to their destination, the pony's mouth would be painfully torn as she recorded every bump in the road. It would keep her quiet though.

Once the ball was in Suki's mouth, the man twisted the end of the device. Her whole body stiffened as she felt the sharp needles pierce her delicate membranes. "Ouuuuuuuu! Ouuuuuuuuuuuu!" she whined desperately. Her voice was low and restrained by the terrible instrument. The one worker looked at the other and nodded. He gave he prong another turn. Suki's back turned rigid and there was a slight, high pitched whine from her mouth. Her knees were shaking. Her breasts quivered, her knees turned weak and she collapsed despondently in her harness, her blue hooded head and featureless face swaying listlessly.

Satisfied that they pony would make no appreciable sound, the worker released the prong from the ball and put it in his pocket while the other man freed the pony's ankles from the posts in the ground. He quickly pulled her ankles together and connected them by the hooks embedded in her boots.

The pony's whole body was shaking as she realized that there was no way she could stop the men from taking her, that the cruel, heinous future she had heard described would be hers. Her stomach was roiling. The pain in her mouth was excruciating. Her heart was beating wildly. Tears poured down her face inside her hood. It was like some horrible dream come true. "Oh god! Please help me, please!" she prayed.

The men released the distraught ponygirl from her harness and pulled her to the ground, laying her on her back. They acted quickly, not giving the pony any time to marshal her forces for resistance. They were obviously professionals despite their scraggly appearance. One of the men took hold of her joined ankles and drew them up. The other man had positioned himself at the pony's hooded head. Placing his knees on her shoulders, holding her in place, he took the pony's feet from the other man. The first man produced a bag from his belt and took out a long, thick needle. It already was attached to a heavy, leather thread.

Suki's position exposed her delicate love slit between her pressed together thighs. The man who had her feet pushed down on them, spreading her knees to make it more available. Drabik cringed as he watched the first man take hold of the bottom of Suki's soft, tender labia and push them together. When they were joined, he ran the needle through them and pulled the leather thread through.

The pony gave out a wild scream despite the brank in her mouth. She tried to move her hips so that the man could not proceed with his work, but the other man was holding her firmly in place. She tried to move her feet and push her thighs together to bar access to he loins, but the man's grip was solid. The man with the needle pulled the thread tight until the knot in its end was firm against the skin of the pony's sex. Holding her labia tight with his left hand, he ran the needle through it the other way about half an inch away.

Suki continued to scream and struggle as her sex was sewn shut. Blood dribbled out of the punctures as the man heartlessly made one after the other. Her efforts were fruitless.

"They never like to be closed," Ali said to Drabik nonchalantly. He had forgotten that the Arab was still next to him. He was transfixed by what the men were doing to the pony. And he thought that he had a heart of stone! He would rather put a bullet in her head than do that to her, he thought.

When the man was finished sewing the labia together by running stitches up the sides, he looped the thread under the stitch at the top of the pony's sex and pulled it tight. Suki's wails of pain increased as her damaged flesh was forced together. The man ran the thread back down the length of her sex and looped it through the first stitch at the other end, pulling tightly once more. He tied it off there.

Drabik hoped that the man was finished with the torture of the ponygirl. He remembered the kisses he had bestowed on her sex less than an hour ago. She had a sweet, tight pussy. And she screamed in pleasure when she came. Well, she had come for the last time in her life.

The Arab worker was not finished. Having tied the thread off at the bottom of Suki's squashed sex, he began to drive the needle through her labial walls once more. This time, going left to right, once he pulled the needle through, he brought the needle back to the other side and, pulling it tight, ran the needle in the same direction again. Each time, he captured the strand that ran lengthwise down the pony's tortured slit, making it tighter and tighter. While the first run had left an alternating stitchwork up each side of the pony's sex, this time the threadwork ran over her love lips in a kind of upward spiral not unlike a barber pole. Drabik could see her abused flesh trying to poke through. But the stitches were too tight and too close together for that to happen. Suki had stopped struggling by this time, but Drabik could still hear her piteous sobs.

When the man was done with his sewing, he ran the needle through several times at the joinder of the pony's labia near the top of her slit, tying it off. There was a small, almost imperceptible gap left at the bottom of the pony's sex so that air could get in and liquids flow out. The man had pushed the needle several times through a hole in the top of a shiny, square, golden medallion. When he was finished, the medallion lay flat against the tortured sex of the pony just below the yellow, rampant wolf tattooed on her lower belly. It was about three inches by three inches and was engraved with a coat of arms.

"My escutcheon," Ali said proudly. "The men can fuck her ass all they want, but her cunt belongs to me."

"I see," Drabik replied unenthusiastically. All he wanted from the men was that they leave. Several of the grooms and trainers had gathered around. One or two were shaking their heads in disgust. A few gave him dirty looks.

All that was left was to load the pony on the van. The men released her legs and, grabbing her by the ring in her nose, "encouraged" her to her feet. Blood was trickling from the corners of her downturned mouth and dribbling down her thighs. She was moaning forlornly. One of the men bent over and, placing his shoulder in the pony's midsection, raised himself until she was lifted in the air. He carried her struggling form to the van and placed her in the rear. Quickly they fastened her waist to a bar across the middle with a long, leather strap and locked her boots on the floor. A chain that ran from the wall of the stall was connected to her nose ring and pulled tight.

Suki groaned at the pressure to her nose from the attachment to its ring. She dared not shout or plead for mercy, lest the razor sharp points of the needles in her mouth increase her agony. Her loins burned with a pain that she could not have imagined. All hope of avoiding the terrible fate the men had planned for her was gone. Her heart went empty and dead inside her as she realized that she was totally powerless to resist anything that the strange, foreign men wanted to impose on her. She could not put from her mind the horrific image of what her stitched up, compressed love lips must look like. It sickened her and made her yearn for the ability to tear the offensive bindings out. But she knew that even if she were able to free her imprisoned hands and liberate her tortured mons, the men would punish her and then just sew her back up again.

The weight of the square medallion on her raw, tortured labia caused a new stab of pain every time she moved. The thought that she carried the mark of her abuser affixed to her body revolted her. It made the men's ownership of her and her reduction to a piece of property seem all too complete. She was a prisoner in her own body, that was clear. Her mind was overwhelmed with the thoughts of what they had planned for her. It seemed impossible to believe that one human being would impose that kind of torture on another. And then she remembered. She was not a human being any more. She was a ponygirl and had lost all rights to humane consideration.

Drabik could see Suki's hands writhing in her bonds behind her back, hands that she would soon no longer have. She was making a high pitched whining sound. She could no longer shake her blue hooded head. Her legs had been fastened a few feet apart and, since she was fastened to the bar across the stall in a leaning forwards position, Drabik could see the stitches in her sex. He knew that her sufferings had just begun. Men who could do this to an animal, human or not, were capable of the most extreme, excruciating punishments. Suki would be subject to an ironclad discipline where disobedience or failure to perform adequately would produce horrific consequences. His heart was heavy from the fact that he was the one responsible for her predicament.

There was one more torture for the unhappy pony. The worker who had sewn up her pussy produced a jar of ointment. He stepped behind the pony and, after taking out a large glop, placed his hands between her spread thighs and covered her tortured mons with it. Suki stood as straight up as she could, tied off as she was, and screamed.

Drabik looked at Ali, appalled at this senseless torture. The bearded, sunglassed Arab looked back at him and shrugged his shoulders. "It's a salve to prevent infection. It hurts like hell, but it's effective, I assure you. We do not inflict unnecessary cruelties on our animals."

Drabik just gave the man a stupefied nod. Ali and Hassan shook hands with Drabik and thanked him again for his hospitality. "Come visit with us someday soon, Mr. Drabik. Your eyes will not believe what you see," he said.

Drabik thought to himself that there was nothing less that he would rather do.

As Hassan and Ali made their departure towards their Mercedes, the workers hopped in the front of the van, started the engine up and put it in motion. Suki groaned in pain as her body shifted inside the van. As it turned the corner of the ponygirl barn, Drabik watched the poor, tortured ponygirl disappear forever.

* * * * * * * * * * * * *

That was yesterday. He had been unable since then to shake the vision of the poor pony as she was taken away. He could not stop wondering where she was and what they were doing to her. But, for now, another problem was taking all of his attention.

"So what the fuck is going on?" he asked. Drabik was feared by anyone with sense enough to preserve their life force. His fiercely spoken words pierced the small crowd that had assembled.

"Great!" Drabik thought. Whatever injury the pony had would be known to all the world in about fifteen minutes.

"Get the fuck out of here!" he yelled at the onlookers. The crowd quickly melted away.

Jerzi, Lightning's dwarf driver was pacing up and down the small camp holding a long, leather quirt. Standing near his caravan was his slave girl Natasha, who cared for his ponygirl. She was balanced on her tip toes, her hands held high above her head by a chain to her slave bracelets and attached to a pole that swung out from the long, tall vehicle. She was gagged and wore a series of fresh, dark red stripes over her breasts, belly and thighs. She was crying and had a look of terror in her eyes.

"It was her, that cunt!" Jerzi yelled. Jerzi, the younger of the two brother ponygirl drivers was bearded like Giorgi and stood a whole ¾ of an inch taller, something he never let his older brother forget. There had always been an intense rivalry between them. Jerzi's face was drawn a little narrower than Giorgi's, a feature that aptly reflected his crueler nature.

One aspect of his cruelty was to deny his ponygirls any sexual completion unless they had won a race and for that day only. On the other days, either he or his slavegirl would tease and caress the ponygirl into passion only to leave her constantly unfulfilled. It was a devious torture given that ponygirls were used to a series of sexual releases every day. Lightning had suffered his insidious torture and his readiness with a whip at even the smallest transgression or failure for two racing seasons now. She knew his temperament well and she feared him intently.

Drabik was frustrated on not getting a clear answer to his question. "I want to know what's happening here. I was told that Lightning was injured!"

"She is! She is! That cunt did it! I'll whip her skin right off of her scrawny little body!"

Jerzi reared his arm back and gave the black haired, dark eyed slavegirl a vicious blow of the quirt across her breasts. She howled behind her gag and her feet did a little dance of agony. Jerzi brought his arm back two more times and landed blows of the stiff leather across her belly and her thighs. Long red welts appeared, matching ones that were already there. Natasha screamed, "Ohhhhhhhhhhhh! Ohhhhhhhhhhhh!" sounds that could be heard through the leather shield over the lower portion of her face. Tears ran down her cheeks like rivers.

"Hold on! Hold on!" Drabik screamed. "What did she do? Lightning looks well enough to me."

"Look at her foot," Jerzi screamed back. "Her right foot! It's all over I tell you. The season's ruined. I'll kill that whore!" He stepped up and issued two more cracks of his whip across Natasha's body. It looked like he was running out of new places to hit and his blows raised welts that criss-crossed others on her breasts and thighs. Natasha's screams continued.

"Stop it!" Drabik yelled. "Stop for one fucking minute, will you!" Jerzi stood still finally. Drabik paused to rein in his temper.

"I'm going to look and see what's wrong with the pony. Okay? And then calmly, and without, for now, any more whipping of your slave girl, you'll tell me what happened. If she's responsible for an injury to Lightning, believe me, she'll suffer plenty."

Natasha, who had, for the moment, ceased her screams of pain, cringed when she heard Drabik's words. She knew that he was not a man who would hesitate to inflict suffering if he thought it was deserved.

Drabik walked over to where Lightning knelt calmly on the grass. His heart began to thump in his chest at his proximity to her naked form. She shifted her weight slightly and her plump, heavy breasts swayed enticingly. Ignoring his excitement at being near her, he stepped behind her and, crouching down, took a look at her foot.

In the middle of the top portion of the bottom of her right foot was a nasty abrasion. Something had worn right through the sole of her foot. The wound was bright red and about the size of a half dollar.

"Oh my god!" Drabik exclaimed. "How did this happen?"

"That cunt put a stone in her boot, that's how!" Jerzi went to raise his whip again. Drabik leapt up and snatched the evil instrument from his hands.

"Enough for now!" he shouted. And more calmly, the tension still evident in his voice, he said, "Why would she do a thing like that?"

"She hates her, that's why!" Jerzi returned. "I should have gotten rid of the scrawny bitch a long time ago! She's a nasty piece of work!"

"Calm down, calm down," Drabik tried to soothe him. "Let's wait until the doctor gets here before we decide the season is over. Maybe he can do something. Go get me some vodka."

Since his slave girl was tied up at the moment, Jerzi had to get the vodka himself. He stepped into his caravan and rummaged around a while before emerging with a bottle of vodka and two glasses. Jerzi liked to take his with a little squeeze of lemon, but he hadn't cut up a lemon in years, having relied for such menial tasks on a slave girl. He didn't even know where the lemons were kept, so he forgot about it for now.

Drabik had pulled two chairs over to the side of the caravan in a position where they could watch both Natasha, who was still moaning and dangling by her hands, and Lightning, who was watching them back with her unseen eyes beneath her hood, her arms folded behind her, a broad leather shield across her mouth.

There are certainly times when being able to evaluate a facial expression would be helpful, as well as receiving communication on how bad something hurt. This was one of those times. But, such things were not possible for ponygirls since they had no face and could not speak.

Lightning looked over at the men. She hadn't understood what the men were saying, but she certainly knew what they were talking about. As much as she wanted to be removed from the custody of her cruel driver, she wanted to win another championship more. She had moved up from a shorter to a longer race this season. She didn't know why, nor what the exact distance was that she was running. No one told her anything. All she knew was that it was longer and harder.

She had beaten almost all comers this season despite her change in division. Her record was not as good as Chocolate's. While Chocolate had won 11 of 14 races, Lightning had won 10. Most of her losses were in the beginning of the season though, when she was getting used to the longer distance she had to run. Of course, while Chocolate knew all about Lightning, Lightning knew nothing about her. She knew nothing about the rescue effort, Jake, or the fact that her uncle had found a new home in Kalikastan. She had no idea that if she won the 3000 meter championship and Chocolate won the 1500 there would be a winner take all match race between them and that her future happiness, her freedom, her only chance to become a person once again, depended on her losing the race, not winning it. All she knew was that her foot was hurt and it was painful to run.

The unhappy pony was warmed by the sight of her trainer. She didn't know his name, but she knew well his face, his touch and his cock. She yearned for all three. While at times he had treated her quite badly, horribly in fact, she felt from him the closest thing to affection that she had felt from any of the masters. She returned the affection many fold.

There had been only one other creature who had given her warmth since she had been kidnapped and turned into a beast. That was Persephone, the pony she had been matched with when she first learned to race. Lightning had never seen the pony's face, but she would know her breasts and other bodily features anywhere. They had spent an idyllic ponygirl summer together before Persephone was sold away.

It was the cruel daughter of her owner that did it. Lightning didn't know her name either, but she recognized her on sight and had been whipped severely by her. Lightning knew that the svelte, young, dark haired woman was her rival for her trainer's affections and attentions. However, while the black haired woman was able to do something about it, beat and impose cruelties on her, Lightning was powerless to do anything in return. She could only hope that when she returned to the ponygirl barn after the tournament, her trainer would welcome her back with open arms and a ready cock, and that the dark haired woman would leave her alone.

But that was after the tournament. Lightning had been in one before, the Spring Tournament, and had won the 1500 meter championship that year. She was a ponygirl champion and had been awarded a gold medal that she wore proudly from her collar all summer. Long ago, Lightning had decided that if she had to be a ponygirl, and there didn't seem to be any reasonable prospect that she would ever be anything else, she would be the best one that she could be. She ran with all her body and soul. She had amazed everyone. No yearling, the Kalikastani name for a first season pony, had ever won a sulky championship. It was considered too early in a pony's training to be able to compete with the more experienced, longer trained ponies. But Lightning had done it.

At the beginning of this season, her driver had taken her medal away. It was the closest thing to a piece of property that Lightning had. Technically, since she was considered by Kalikastani law and practice an animal, she didn't even own her own body. She had been devastated by its loss, but her driver's meaning was clear. That was then and this was now. If she wanted to wear a gold medal, a mark that distinguished her from the bulk of all other ponygirls, she had to earn it again and again.

Lightning cast a glance at the dangling slave girl, Natasha. She had seen the devilish slave girl put the stone in her shoe. It wasn't the first time. For some reason that Lightning couldn't fathom, the slave girl hated her. What Lightning didn't know was that, immediately following her enslavement and training, Natasha, who had been a beautiful, young woman with delicate features and a thin, attractive body, had been selected by one of the finest whorehouses in Dlitski, the nation's capital. It was still slavery, and she had to work as a whore, but her surroundings were lavish and she was able to enjoy the best lotions and soaps to keep her body beautiful, good food, gentlemanly company and was relatively free from the whip.

One night the dwarf came in. He selected her at once and savagely abused her all night long. In the morning, having developed a perverse attraction to her, he bought her.

That was five years ago. Since then, Natasha had lived under his cruel regime constantly. He had bought her to fuck and abuse, but also to take care of his ponygirls. In Natasha's eyes, it was the ponygirls who had caused her to be taken from her relatively idyllic existence and be thrown into hell. Five years down the road, her beauty was gone. Her body was thin and scraggly and she bore the scars of many a beating. For in the winter, when there were no ponygirls to torment, Natasha received the full brunt of her master's evil disposition. Natasha hated ponygirls and did everything she could, short of being detected by her master, to abuse and torment them. She had put the stone in Lightning's boot and had done so before so that the pony would suffer. It had caused her nothing more than pain before. This time, however, she had been injudicious in her choice of stones. This one had a sharp edge to it and when it landed in the bottom of the boot, sharp side up, it had torn the flesh of Lightning's sole and practically disabled her.

There was no way for Lightning to tell her driver that she had a stone in her shoe. Ponygirls didn't speak and if she had exhibited any reticence at running, she would have suffered severely for it. It was after her practice run was over, an unusually intense workout since they would have several days off before the tournament, that her driver noticed something wrong. Absent the adrenalin of running, the stone and the cut that it caused started to hurt like the devil. Lightning could not help limping her way back to the encampment. When they got there, her driver had pulled off her boot and found both the stone and the injury. He had put two and two together and thereby hung the tale.

Drabik gulped down his shot of vodka and poured another. Jerzi had explained what happened. "If she was such a cunt, why did you keep her around, you stupid ass!" he told the dwarf.

"She was good with the ponies," Jerzi answered.

"Good with the ponies? Are you mad? She put stones in her boot! She might have ruined the best sulky runner in the last ten years! If she's ruined, you will pay with your life my friend. That's for sure." Drabik poured and downed another shot of vodka. There was no way Grobgy would keep a disabled ponygirl around for long, she would be sent on and all that would remain of her would be a picture on the wall of the clubhouse. But, of course, Drabik had his own plans for Grobgy and that would take care of that problem.

But what would he do with her? He knew her now both as an attractive young woman and as a ponygirl. Which one would he choose to live with? No ponygirl had ever been freed, as far as he knew. When no one could find a use for them, well, they were gone, that's all. Now a man might have a favorite ponygirl, but a ponygirl who couldn't run, well no one in his right mind would keep a pony like that.

Right mind? When had he been in his right mind since his obsession with the pony had erupted? Well, those things would work out, he thought.

There was another issue that was not so simple to put aside. If Lightning ran the match race with Burnham's sulky and lost, she would become Burnham's property. He would own his own niece. But would he free her? He better not. Drabik didn't care how wealthy the man was, if the Commission found out, his body would probably never be found. But if he didn't free her he would have to keep her as a ponygirl. The only way that he could get her back from Burnham would be to blackmail him with the information he had obtained about the charade Burnham and Barnes had launched to try and rescue her. But, Burnham, by keeping Lightning as a pony, could easily refute that argument. Intending to commit a crime is not the same as committing one. Whatever his intentions in coming to Kalikastan, he was in with both feet now and no one could contest his earnest commitment to the country's peculiar institutions.

He could act against Grobgy before the tournament. He had been warned by the Commission, however, that he was not to do so. Any disruption to the Fall Tournament was to be avoided at all cost. Drabik had to wait until the ponies stopped running to make his move.

The best solution was for Lightning not to race at all. Maybe her injury was all for the best, a blessing in disguise. If the doctor couldn't fix her up, she wouldn't be able to run the match race and he could deal with what would happen between them once he got her.

A team of ponies came running down the dirt pathway of the ponygirl park. It was two of the estate's work ponies, Diamond and Ruby. They were sturdy, black haired ponies retired from racing. They had been cabriolet ponies, part of a six pony team that had championed twice. They wore their medals on their collars now, next to two silver and one bronze one. The medals jangled together as the ponies ran, giving their passing a musical charm.

Sitting on the speeding two pony trap were the doctor and Axmail Grobgy.

Grobgy leapt from the cart as soon as it slowed. "How is she?" he yelled as he entered the camp. "What's wrong with her?"

Drabik explained the whole thing. Grobgy gave out two of his standard issue death looks. One to Jerzi and one to his dangling slave girl.

Meanwhile, the doctor, who had pulled the pony team to a halt and stepped calmly off of the trap, was crouched behind Lightning examining her foot. The other men crowded around him. He dabbed at the wound with a sanitized, wooden probe and looked closely at it with a magnifying glass. If Lightning had not been wearing a hood, you would have since her wince with pain as the probe entered the wound. As it was, everyone noticed her body flinch. No one but Drabik paid that any mind.

The doctor released Lightning's foot. "You want the bad news or the good news first?" he asked.

"The good news," Grobgy answered immediately.

"The good news is that the tendons have not been ripped. She'll recover."

That brought smiles all around.

"The bad news is that it's a serious injury and will take at least three weeks to heal properly." The faces turned to frowns, except Drabik's of course.

"You mean she can't run in the tournament? Grobgy asked demandingly.

"I'm afraid not," the doctor replied. "It would be risking a much more serious injury. The tendons aren't torn, but they are weakened. Too much strain on them before they heal and they could tear. They could be repaired surgically, but they would not be the same. The pony would always be prone to injury. She'd be finished as a racer."

There was glum silence from Lightning's driver and her owner. Drabik was celebrating inside. At last, he had gotten a break!

"There's nothing you can do to patch her up so she can race in the tournament?" Grobgy asked.

"Well, if she rested for a couple of days, received proper care, she might be free from significant pain, but the danger would be still there."

"What else?" Grobgy demanded. "How about taping her foot? Would that help?"

"It would help," the doctor replied. His face reflected a growing anxiety. He didn't want to tell the gangster/ponygirl owner that Lightning would be okay. There was a high risk of additional injury no matter how he taped her foot or how much she rested before the beginning of the tournament in three days. "But I couldn't be held responsible for the results," he continued. "I've given you my medical opinion and I have to stand by it."

"But wrapping it would reduce the risk, wouldn't it, Doctor?"

It was Jerzi speaking. It might, to the uninitiated, seem a simple matter. A ponygirl was injured. There was always next year. But there wasn't next year. There was only this year. Ponygirl champions in the sulky races rarely repeated from year to year. All the stars had to be in the right configuration: the pony's competitive spirit ran high, her driver made no significant mistakes, she suffered no significant injuries. And there was always the chance that some promising sulky runner from this year, or even a dark horse, so to speak, could have a career season and put you out of the running.

No. Lightning couldn't count on next year. This was her year. She was poised to champion in both the 1500 meter and 3000 meter sulky in one year, something that had never been done, and by a pony that had been a yearling at the beginning of the spring season! Before Lightning, no yearling had ever won a sulky championship. So, it was this year or probably nothing.

After a few moment's hesitation, the ponygirl specialist replied, "The answer is 'yes', it would help reduce the risk but not significantly enough to risk the chance of a more serious injury."

"That's my decision, Doctor," Grobgy growled. He paused for a moment. "I need a drink!" he announced.

Since there was no slave girl, Jerzi ran to get two more chairs and two more glasses. Drabik had to suppress a chuckle as he watched the little man shuffle back across he encampment lugging chairs bigger than he was. The men sat in a little semi-circle around the two females that were of concern right now, one to determine whether to risk her health on what was essentially a throw of the dice, and the other, what form of excruciating punishment would be appropriate for her. The subject of punishment of Jerzi for his negligent role in letting Natasha within a mile of any of the ponygirls was not brought up. But all knew that if she didn't run in the tournament this year, or, if she ran and didn't win both the championship and the subsequent match race, he would inherit a world of shit.

Technically, Grobgy had not yet agreed to the match race. But the Americans had done such a good job of touting it that to refuse it would seem a coward's way out. After all, if he had the 3000 meter champion, it should be able to beat any pony at that distance, especially a pony that had never run one. Grobgy had no doubt that the chocolate pony was training in the longer race. Only a fool would offer that kind of a bet, winner take all, without giving their pony some training. But Chocolate had never run a legitimate 3000 meter race. And no matter how good a driver Giorgi was, Jerzi was better as was shown by his record. No, the bet had to go forward.

If Lightning was injured, maybe the race could be cancelled, but not if she won the championship. How injured could she be if she did that? If they pulled her out altogether, people would say that he had crapped out because he was afraid to risk his pony and would scoff at the seriousness of Lightning's injury. It would look all made up or as if Grobgy had ordered the stone be put in her boot himself.

The four men all shot back a glass of vodka. Jerzi poured them all another and they shot that back too. Grobgy's head was down, an uncharacteristic pose for him. He was not a deep thinker, but a man of action. Finally, he raised his head. "Do it," he snarled. "Treat her here today and tomorrow and the next day while she takes the trip to the tournament. I know that it's a day later than usual, but she'll have to forgo her usual workouts. That would only put more pressure on her foot. When you get there, you can take her out for a slow run or two around the track so that she gets familiar with it and with running with her foot all taped up. But no more. Understand?"

He was speaking to Jerzi, whose life was on the line.

"Yes, Mr. Grobgy," he answered.

Drabik was not happy with the decision for reasons of his own. "Aren't you taking too big a risk, Axmail?" he asked, ashamed to be acting so obsequious to a man he hoped to kill in a week.

Grobgy turned on him angrily. "Don't call me that! You haven't the right. And she's my ponygirl, not yours, remember that too! Just get back to the ponybarn and fuck one of your little pets there!"

Grobgy was not done. "And what was with the pony yesterday? Are you trying to make a fool out of me? I got a call from the High Commissioner. $100,000 dollars? You know as well as I do that that pony was worth 30, 35 thousand at the most. We had agreed on a price. Why did you tell the Arabs $100,000?"

Drabik was taken aback by his boss's verbal assault. He rose to his defense. "Since when does getting more money than you thought possible mean a bad thing? I thought I could get more than $35,000 from them, that's all. I said $95,000 and they upped it to $100,000. That's how it went."

"In other words, you tried to cheat our guests. The Commission has placed a great deal of importance in dealing with our Arab friends. We are in a position to be the major conduit of Western slave girls to the world and from east to west as well. Everyone will benefit. I've purchased a training center in Dlitski. And the Arabs will be one of our best markets. They can operate the girls from Libya, Morocco, Tunisia, Egypt, all a stone's throw from Europe. The Europeans and the Americans will pay a fortune to whip a real, authentic slave girl. So don't go trying to think for yourself. From now on, I will be doing all the negotiating both for ponies and slave girls. You go back to teaching them how to take a cock up their ass. It's what you're good for!"

Drabik's ire rose. Nobody talked to him that way! Nobody! Especially this fucking former sergeant for State Security! Only the knowledge that the gang leader would soon be eating dirt enabled him to check his anger. "Yes, Mr. Grobgy," was all he said. But his anger from his treatment was readily apparent in his voice.

Grobgy looked his killer in the eye. "Right after the tournament, he's a dead man" he thought. "He's gotten too big for his britches. And now that I've insulted him in front of this dwarf and the doctor, he has to kill me."

"Okay," was all Grobgy said in reply. And then to Jerzi, he said, "You fucking stupid runt! If my ponygirl suffers any kind of permanent injury because you were too lazy to train another slave girl, you better find a hole to hide in. Do you understand?"

"Yes, Mr. Grobgy," he answered.

"And she better win! You got that too!"

"Yes, Mr. Grobgy," Jerzi replied.

Grobgy decided that he would wait until after the tournament and the match race to decide whether the dwarf should die, even if Lightning took all of her races. In Grobgy's world, lazy, incompetent people met death.

"I've got to get her iced down right away," the doctor said. He was cowed by so much anger and the heavy threat of violence. When bullets started flying, it was often the bystanders who suffered.

"I'll get you some ice from the caravan," Jerzi said, glad too to get away from Grobgy. He ran off immediately. He knew that Grobgy meant every word that he said.

During all of this, two pairs of concerned female eyes had been attending to the conference between the men. Lightning knew they were talking about her and whether she should race or not. When you are in a land where you can't understand the language, you develop other skills, such as reading people's emotions from their faces, picking up those words that you are familiar with. She had witnessed the argument between her trainer and her owner and she knew that it did not bode well. Both men exhibited an intense hatred of each other. There would be a showdown between them soon, she knew that. She could only hope that her trainer would win.

And she heard her name mentioned several times, 'Molnya', Russian for 'Lightning'.

She saw the doctor's concern on his face and knew that there was some risk if she ran in the tournament. She saw from the relieved face of her driver that the decision had been made to go forwards. "Good," she thought. It was the same decision she would have made.

Natasha was not quite so satisfied with the results of the men's arguments. She could sense the underlying anger in each one of them. She would be its target. Her master had already whipped her severely. Would she get off with another whipping? She doubted it. She had been present when Jerzi slit the throat of that young man who had merely fucked Lightning. No, something else was in store for her.

Maybe it was time for her to go, she thought. Gone forever were the days of her youth in Romania. She had been stolen when she was a pretty, naïve, 19 year old girl. People there would have long written her off as dead. And what did she have to look forward to here? Her beauty had been destroyed. Her master would have kept her maybe another season, maybe not even that. All she had to look forward to was life as a 20 zlitski whore down in the capital. Or maybe some run down old tavern would buy her to attract customers. A few drinks and she might look fine to the peasants and workers who would come in. At least her master knew how to fuck, even if he was cruel and often hurt her. No, it was time to go.

Maybe she had known that all along. She couldn't commit suicide, that was a mortal sin, as if God was even present in this horrible land. Maybe she put the stone in the ponygirl's boot so they would kill her and relieve her of her misery. She was sorry she hurt the ponygirl. She realized that she had been wrong to torment her. It wasn't her fault that she was what she was. She looked over at the naked, blue hooded creature and smiled gently. She couldn't tell if she smiled back or not.

Natasha jumped when she heard the men getting up from their chairs. "Maybe they'll make it quick," she thought frantically.

Grobgy had no such thing in mind. Jerzi offered to whip the slave girl to death.

"No," Grobgy answered. "You fucked up your chance to get rid of her and prevent this. I'll deal with her. There's a house in Dlitski that caters to men of a special taste, experts in their avocations. I have a truck going to the capital tomorrow. That's where I'll send her. They'll send back a video of the whole thing. She'll suffer, believe me. Until then I have a good idea what I'm going to do to her."

Drabik had dropped Jerzi's quirt to the ground. Grobgy picked it up. He was so angry he needed an outlet right away or he would burst. Natasha saw him coming and started to cry even before he raised his arm. He gave her five fierce strokes across her front. Jerzi's blows had hurt. Grobgy was a much bigger and stronger man than Jerzi. His lashes drove deep into her skin and were exquisitely painful.

"Aaaaaaaaaaauuuuuurrrgh!" the slave girl yelled from behind her gag at each devilish stroke of the whip. "Aaaaaaaaaauuuuuuurgh!"

Drabik was standing, watching. "She's getting what she deserves," he thought. From now on, anyone who hurt Lightning was on his death list.

"Turn her around," Grobgy ordered.

Drabik stepped forward to the girl and swung her on her chain so that her back was now facing her torturer. A peg had been driven into the ground with hooks on each side of it. This is where the pony would normally be mounted during the day to be washed or to receive punishment. The hooks would fasten her boots in place. They did the same thing for Natasha's ankle bracelets now as Drabik affixed the hooks to rings in their sides.

Natasha's back was already covered with welts from Jerzi's assault on her. Grobgy cared nothing for that. He unleashed a flurry of hard, cruel strokes of he whip against the slave girl's back, her ass and the backs of her thighs and shins. Natasha was, at first, in too much shock to react. By the third one, she was howling.

When he had given the screaming, writhing slave girl five in the back to match the five in the front, Grobgy relented. "Do you have a hood for this cunt?" Grobgy asked Jerzi.

The small driver nodded and ran into the caravan. He came out a moment later with the same type of leather hood that Ilona, Giorgi's slave girl, had worn the day before. When

Giorgi had gotten the one for Ilona, Jerzi had seen it and ordered one for Natasha.

Grobgy grabbed the leather head covering from Jerzi and placed it over Natasha's head. He pulled the straps tight so that it was firmly seated. Then he turned on the speakers that produced the static. The slave girl would know of nothing that was going on around her except what she could directly feel.

"Drop her in the back of the trap," Grobgy commanded.

The doctor was icing Lightning's foot. He had washed the deep abrasion with an antiseptic and applied a salve that contained an antibiotic. The ice was to keep down the swelling on the damaged tissue.

"You stay here until I send someone up to help him," Grobgy ordered. The doctor nodded his assent.

Drabik had released Natasha's hands from the overhead pole and confined them behind her back. She was listless from her beating and did not resist or otherwise acknowledge his handling of her except when he brushed against one of her bright red lacerations. He unhooked her ankles and dragged her over to the trap. After hooking her ankles to each other, he lifted her and threw her on the floor of the small cart. There was a gate on the back and he slammed it shut so that the slave girl would not fall out during the ride. That might spoil their fun. Drabik didn't know what Grobgy had in mind, but he didn't want to miss it. Although he hated his gang leader boss, right now, he hated the slave girl more.

Grobgy gave the two ponies in front of the cart a snap of the reins and they took off immediately. Drabik had joined him on the seat. The dirt path made a loop and returned to the mansion and the ponies followed it unquestioningly. Their large breasts bobbed while they ran and their fit bodies were soon covered with sweat.

It only took about ten minutes to reach the mansion's environs. Grobgy grabbed one of the grooms and told him to get two shovels and a chair with arms on it from the bunkhouse. He told another groom to help him and to meet him near the back door to the mansion as soon as they could. "And bring a ring gag," he yelled after them.

Drabik nodded with appreciation. He knew what Grobgy was going to do.

The two young grooms came back within a few minutes. For the moment, the slave girl was left to lie in the back of the cart. She could hear nothing and see nothing. All she knew was that the cart had stopped and that she was a helpless prisoner.

Grobgy had chosen a well worn area of the estate grounds. He pointed to a spot just beside the macadam walkway that led from the mansion to the ponybarn and ordered the men to dig a four by four by four foot hole. He held one of the shovels and placed it next to the chair. He pointed to where the long shovel handle matched the top of the back of the chair. "This deep," he said.

Drabik and Grobgy watched while the two young men worked. It took them about twenty minutes, working together to get the hole wide and deep enough as per Grobgy's instructions. "Go get the cunt," Grobgy told Drabik. It was an order he was glad to obey.

Drabik went to the back of the cart and, after lowering the gate, dragged the slave girl out by her heels. He was careful not to let her head bang against the ground, because he wanted her fully conscious for her upcoming ordeal. Grobgy helped put the girl in the chair. There were straps in the back of the cart and Drabik brought them around. They strapped the slave girl's body in tightly, running straps across her belly and chest and around her thighs and ankles. Her wrists had been released from behind her back and they strapped them to the arms of the chair. She was transfixed.

Natasha had no idea what was happening, but she knew that she would not like it. The straps bit into her flesh they were so tight. She prayed that her suffering would be short although she knew that it would last at least until tomorrow when she was to be given a ride to her ultimate destination. "Maybe I'll die first," she hoped. She could not envision what a man like Grobgy would describe as "special tastes", as if whatever was to be done to her was beyond even his cruelty. Inside her hood, tears ran down her face. She knew that being tied to the chair was prefatory to something awful. She did not try and speak when her gag was removed and replaced by the ring gag, although she knew what ring gags were used for. Someone was going to use her mouth.

Suddenly the chair was lifted into the air. Natasha felt herself being moved a short distance and then lowered again. She sensed that she was lower than when she started out. Then she felt what seemed like a clod of earth being dumped on her. Then another, then another. "Oh my god!" she screamed inside, "They're going to bury me alive!"

Panic rose up in her as she struggled to free herself from her straps. But if there was one thing the men of Kalikastan knew it was how to tie knots. She was going nowhere. Unable to form words, she screamed out "Gaaaaaa! Gaaaaaaaa!" in the forlorn hope that someone would take mercy on her.

The dirt kept coming and coming. It covered her ankles, then her shins, then her knees and started to creep into her naked lap. Natasha was moaning, crazed with the prospect of being covered with the dirt and left to suffocate.

The shoveling of the dirt continued until it reached just above her breasts, a couple of inches from her collar bone. She could feel the weight of the men as they stomped on the dirt to compact it over her. It felt heavy on her body and she thought of all the bugs and worms crawling around in it and shivered. A wave of relief passed over her as she realized that she would live at least another twenty four hours. What happened next demonstrated the exact nature of what would be her abuse.

Grobgy looked with satisfaction at the mostly buried slave girl. Her leather covered head bobbed back and forth and swayed side to side. He would start the party.

Grobgy lowered his fly and pulled out his cock. A small crowd of grooms, trainers, security guards and slave girls had stopped to see what was going on. Once his cock was freed, he stepped closer to the bobbing head and sank to his knees. His estimations were just right. His cock was, when he spread his legs, at the perfect angle to enter her forcibly distended mouth.

Natasha had sensed someone close to her. Her first realization of what was happening, however, was when Grobgy's stiff, thick cock pressed across her lips. It pushed her tongue aside and entered her throat. A heavy hand covered the back of her head. Then the man started to thrust himself back and forth, seeking his pleasure.

A chorus of male laughter resounded from the crowd. The feminine sounds were gasps of dismay. This was a whole new way to torment a slave girl. She would feel nothing, know nothing, except when a cock was shoved into her mouth. Then she would have to endure the rape of her mouth and throat until the man had his pleasure. His spunk, if not jetted down into her belly, would linger in her mouth since, with the ring gag in place, it was almost impossible to swallow. Two of the slave girls who had been watching ran back into the mansion, unable to witness the cruel abuse of the girl, whoever she was.

Grobgy took a long time to come. He pushed himself to the back of the girl's throat until she began to cough and choke and then withdrew. He forced the head back and forth so that his cock could revel in the warm interior of the girl's mouth. Finally, after at least ten minutes, his cock began to dance and jerk. He pulled it from the girl's throat and let it splash against the back of her mouth. When he was finished, it dribbled down to the bottom of her mouth and accumulated in a pool. He drew himself out and rose to his feet.

Natasha was frantic with horror of what had been done to her. She had been throat fucked before; any slave girl could bear that. But she understood now what would happen. Her readily available mouth would be a target of opportunity for every male who walked by. It would be a unique experience for them. How many times did you see a woman's head sticking out of he ground ready to accept your cock. The fact that she could do nothing to speed the men's pleasure and that she had to lap up their spunk with her tongue and bring it to the back of her mouth in the hopes that she could swallow it, made things all the worse. She began to sob when the second cock found a home between her circled lips.

Drabik was next. He was quick. He grabbed the back of the slave girl's head and just sawed his cock in and out of her mouth. He finished in little over a minute. He wanted all of the men to get their chance.

Back at Jerzi's trailer, the doctor had finished applying the ice to Lightning's foot for now. There was a pony with a sprained ankle who he was intending to see and he told Jerzi he would be back in twenty minutes or so.

Suddenly, the campsite, which had been crowded with onlookers and then the scene of a test of wills between two mighty men, was silent and peaceful. It was just Jerzi and Lightning.

The pony had remained kneeling while the doctor administered to her wound, her bare foot stuck out behind her. She looked up at her driver and saw the worry and concern on his face. She shared it. No matter how cruel he had been to her, no matter what torments he inflicted, their fates were tied together.

Jerzi was realizing the same thing. There was only one way for him to express his concern for her needs, to return her to a semblance of normalcy. He stepped over to her and lowered his fly, pulling his thick, long cock out. He went to the naked, kneeling pony, unbuckled her gag behind her head and pulled the long, fat, leather prong from her mouth. The blue hooded pony looked up at him through her small windows on the world, spread her lips and took him in.

One might think that it was Lightning doing Jerzi a favor and in one sense that was true. But in another, the strength and hardness of his male member gave relief to the disconcerted ponygirl. She had seen the slave girl hauled away and knew that something terrible would happen to her. This was the second time in a couple of weeks where someone suffered because of something they did to her. That young man was murdered and the pretty girl was turned into a ponygirl right before her eyes. Now the slave girl, who she should have no love for, had been taken to a certain, unhappy fate. Lightning hated the idea that she was the cause of so much misery. All she wanted was to run and be with her trainer. Anyone could do anything they wanted to her if they gave her that.

Jerzi's cock quickly grew to its full length and width. Lightning suckled the heavy meat readily. Its heat was comforting, its strength reassuring. She was a ponygirl and didn't want to know anything about the lives of real people. She wanted to live in her little world so that tormenting memories of her prior life and her unhappiness at being dehumanized would stay away. Sucking her driver's cock was a return to her role, one she felt safe in now. It wasn't often that she got the chance. Usually he had the slave girl suck him to the point of orgasm and then he would jerk himself off into her mouth, giving her the product, but not the pleasure of his lust. Today she was blessed with his full attention. She would not disappoint him.

Lightning brought all of her skills to the stiff wand. She only let her master and driver come after about twenty minutes of tortuous pleasure. As he spilled himself into her mouth, she rejoiced in the warmth and the piquant taste, reassured now of what she was.

The next morning, a little before noon, two grooms dug up the listless form of Natasha. She was barely conscious. She probably had had a hundred cocks in her mouth over the last 20 hours or so, many of them repeats. During the night, someone set up torches behind her in small semi-circle so that she could be used all night long. You couldn't miss the leather covered head poking up out of the ground when you walked out of the back steps of the mansion. The men stopped and joked, even if they did not avail themselves of her services. The slave girls hurried by overwhelmed with the fear that someone would decide that they should take the unknown slave girl's place. Natasha had no conception anyone was there unless they knelt before her and shoved their manhood between her lips.

Twice, during her torment, a slave girl was detailed to wash out Natasha's mouth and give her some water to drink. But that was all the relief from her torments she was given.

When the grooms had Natasha fully freed from her partial entombment, they brought her to the side of the ponybarn and washed her body down with a hose. She was not able to stand by herself and so one of them had to hold her up. Her ring gag was removed and the spout of a ponygirl watering bottle was shoved into her mouth.

Natasha was happy to receive the cool sustenance. She was happy to have her body cleaned of the dirt that had covered her so remorselessly. She had no idea what time it was, but knew that she was due to be put on a truck to travel to a whole new, worse travail that afternoon.

When they were finished with her, the grooms inserted a standard shield gag into her mouth and bound her arms behind her. Not removing the terrible, isolating hood from her head, they escorted her to the back of a truck that was waiting nearby. They lifted her up and the driver, who was inside the back, received her from their hands. Next to him was a large, empty crate with quarter sized air holes drilled into it. It was open at the top.

The truck driver pushed the slave girl into it. It was just large enough for her to fit if she drew her legs up to her chest. Once he saw that the female was settled, the driver placed the lid on the crate and locked it shut. He jumped off the back of the truck and rolled the corrugated steel door down. It too was locked.

Once he started the engine to the truck, he took it down the long, curving driveway that led from the front of the mansion and entered the open road heading east. In ten hours, he would be in Dlitski.

Ten days later, the tape of Natasha's demise was delivered to the mansion. All of the slave girls were assembled in the ballroom and forced to watch it.

CHAPTER SIX

The small nation of Kalikastan, though unfortunate to be surrounded by such large, voracious neighbors, (it has been conquered many times by Russians, Poles, Ukrainians, Germans (twice), Mongols and even Swedes), it's geography had granted it one special blessing. The days of late October and early November are almost uniformly graced by warm temperatures. While the areas to their east and west are growing colder by the day, the configuration of the Carpathian Mountains to the west and the Urals to the east act as a kind of funnel, bringing the country a steady stream of warm, Black Sea air. Usually, after November 15, or so, the process is reversed and the Arctic cold sweeps down upon it with a vengeance, as if to make up for nature's mistake. During the cold, long winter, the snow sometimes piles four or five feet high.

So it was not unusual for the 28th of October to be a warm, sunny day, still fit for slave girls to run about their tasks dressed in only their confinements, or for tall, strong ponygirls to prance about without anything covering their statuesque, fit bodies. This was the day before the opening of the Fall Tournament and the grounds were filling up with eager, excited racing fans. The ponies had mostly arrived the day before. Their encampment was spread out over about twenty acres west of the race track. The public camp grounds lay to the north. South of the track were the camping areas reserved for owners and dignitaries.

There were no hotels or other amenities in this part of Kalikastan. Other than during the Fall Tournament, the area was essentially a backwater. It was a backwater of a backwater, being one of the poorest areas of a poor country. As a result,

everyone brought their RV's, their caravans or their trailers
and camping gear and roughed it.

Of course, there was roughing it and roughing it. No one
would call the spread put out by Michael Burnham roughing
it. He had brought a trailer full of cooks and food. This
morning, he had sponsored a breakfast for the other owners.
Slabs of bacon and breakfast sausages cooked over open fires,
rich, buttery American style flapjacks, pure maple syrup, spicy
Cajun style scrambled eggs, home fries, barrels of coffee and
several large bowls of fresh fruit. All morning his slave girls
scurried around the eating area he had staked out, delivering
trays of hot food, cleaning tables and, occasionally, spreading
their lips or thighs to receive the cock of a guest. Tonight
there was to be a Texas style barbecue and a floor show.
Burnham did nothing small.

Jake had nothing to do with the management of
Burnham's fetes, and so he and Irkut were wandering the
fairgrounds to the east of the large clubhouse and finely
manicured track. The fairgrounds were teeming with people,
eager to catch the stylish side shows, eat native delicacies and
mingle with their countrymen and women. It was customary
for there to be several entrepreneurs selling ponygirl rides.
They were expensive, but for many, it was the thrill of a
lifetime.

There were to be some ponygirl exhibitions: a series of
show pony contests and, for the grand finale of the day, the
weight pulling contest that Maureen had been training for.
Andreyev was warming the giant ponygirl up at the
encampment and Irkut felt free to spend some time enjoying
the sights.

There were a few tents close to the perimeter of the
fairgrounds where squadrons of excited men were lined up
outside. These were the itinerant whorehouses that followed
the racing circuit. The third or fourth level slave girls that
staffed them would take on upwards of fifty cocks per day, a

significant workout by anyone's standards. During the times when there were no races, the girls would be parceled out to various taverns and inns or assigned to mobile whorehouses in trailers or vans and driven about the hinterland servicing the yokels.

The two men chatted amiably as they passed by several tents selling the accouterments of female slavery: collars, bracelets, special confining apparatus. One small tent had a collection of hand painted collars which had various designs and illustrations on them. Another tent was selling various clamps and jewelry. As an added service, the operator provided piercing services right on the spot.

When Jake and Irkut walked in, a slight slave girl with long, black hair and delicate teacup breasts was having a series of rings attached to her labia. Her owner explained to Jake that the girl had been caught sneaking out and fucking one of the local lads in their village at night. Once the rings were installed, he would be able to run a chain through them and connect its ends with a lock, closing off the girl's principal avenue of delight. He would then place a lock on her gag every night. This way, if she snuck out, she would only be able to satisfy her lover with her rear entrance. The man figured that after ass fucking her a couple of times, the lad would lose interest in her, or she in him. Jake and Irkut had a little laugh over the man's ribald tale. The girl, however, didn't think it was funny at all as she squirmed and sobbed each time a puncture was made to her love lips. She was securely mounted in the piercing chair and gagged so that her squeals of pain would not disturb the other customers. Jake thought of his slave girl, Dana, who he had caught in the midst of self abuse several times. Chaining up her pussy would certainly break her of that habit.

The next tent was large, about 30'x 40'. In it there were seven tattoo artists at work. Jake was amazed at the speed and alacrity with which they worked while still maintaining their artistry and fineness of line. One of the artists was working on a blond haired girl with large round breasts. He had colored her chest and breasts a light blue. He was now working on a series of bright yellow stars that swirled up from each breast, crossed the slave girl's chest and disappeared over her shoulders.

Irkut struck up a conversation with one of the men. He was thinking of decorating Maureen's big, broad body with a series of tattoos. The young artist showed Irkut a book of his designs.

While Irkut looked at the book, Jake wandered over to where some of the slave girls were kneeling, their collars chained to a pipe that led along each side of the tent. On the left were young women whose work was completed and were being held pending pick up by their owners. On the other were girls waiting their turn. Neither side looked particularly happy to Jake. While a finely designed and executed tattoo could add significant value to a slave girl, it was a stark reminder to them that their bodies were not their own to dispose of. A master's idea of an appropriate beautification of the female's body might not match her own.

Jake saw a good example of that in a girl whose tattooing had just been completed and was having her collar connected to the four foot high pipe. The artist noted Jake's interest in the girl and held her up so that she could pose for him. The girl looked disconsolate and it was not hard to wonder why. On her face, surrounding her mouth, the artist had etched an exquisitely detailed and expertly rendered depiction of an oversized, dilated, love ready vagina. The sexual opening was positioned around the girl's mouth and the minor and major labia extended over her cheeks, forehead and chin. The clit was depicted between her eyes. A smattering of etched in, curly, black pubic hair surrounded it. Jake was taken aback. Then the artist had the slave girl sit on the ground, lean back and spread her legs. Around her sex the man had tattooed a pair of luscious red lips pursed so that the opening between them circled the girl's slit. The lips were drawn upside down and horizontally with their edges running up the inside of the slave girl's thighs. There were tears in the girl's eyes. She had been shown her new decorations in a full length mirror a few moments ago. It certainly, in Jake's opinion, marred the natural beauty of the girl. However he could see the logic in the work. Every time you fucked her pussy, you would also be fucking a mouth. When you kissed her, it would be like laying your lips on her cunt. When you were reversed, her lower mouth would kiss yours while you fucked the pussy on her face.

Jake felt Irkut nudge his elbow and he tore himself away from the strange apparition.

Irkut wanted to watch some of the show ponies at work. They drifted over to the performance area. At the Spring Tournament, Jake had watched some of the show ponies dance. There had been a decent crowd then. Today, by the measure of the people watching the naked ponygirls prance and maneuver, he would have said that interest in the sport had grown. Two sets of bleachers had been set up on each side of the grassy square within which the naked ponygirls were performing. There was a long judges' table with five older men and women wearing badges denoting their status sitting at it. At the end of each performance, they held up cards denoting the score they had given the show ponies and the scores would be tallied up and then posted for all to see.

Jake and Irkut, after securing tall cups of the potent, bitter, local ale from a vendor, sat in one of the bleachers to watch the show. Irkut explained to him that it was the two pony mandatories. Each team of two ponies had to maneuver themselves through a kind of obstacle course while maintaining their gracefulness of step and unity of action. The two ponies in the square now were slender and had matching, moderately endowed breasts and long, brown ponytails. They seemed an exact mirror of each other, right down to their hairless slits, something easier to do when you didn't have to match their faces as well. Their hoods were lavender with tall, fluffy, white plumes at the top. They wore harnesses of lavender dyed leather and lavender ponygirl boots. White flowers were intertwined in their collars and their trim waists were surrounded by circles of fine, white lace.

The ponies were pretty to behold. Their movements were graceful and sure. When they entered the square, they had to perform a series of high stepping prances toward the first obstacle, a white plinth jutting out of the ground about four feet high. They approached it, their knees jumping high, their slim arms confined behind their rigidly straightened backs, and did three steps in front of it. The pony on the right then took the lead and pranced around the plinth, keeping her face turned towards the judges at all times. The other pony followed her in the same manner.

The goal was to reform after circling the plinth in perfect order. Jake thought they had done all right, but Irkut pointed out that the one on the right had not raised her knees sufficiently on one or two steps and the other pony's back was, at times, not straight enough. There were a number of similar challenges for the ponies as well. Their steps varied. At one point they were required to move to their right, lifting each foot as they moved so that their thigh was parallel to the ground. It was accomplished in a series of hopping steps. When they had made four steps to the right, they returned to their original positions and then made four steps to the left and returned again. Jake thought that they had done poorly, but Irkut was excited by the style that he observed. At the end of the exercise, the naked, hooded ponies bowed gracefully to the crowd on all four sides of the square and then, just as gracefully, departed. They were rewarded with enthusiastic applause.

They watched four more teams compete before moving on. To Jake it was exciting to watch the perfectly formed, naked females stroll sublimely through their routines. Their breasts bobbed and swayed gracefully. Their hips tended to be narrow so as to accentuate the straightness of their posture. Their bellies all curved nicely downwards to their hairless slits. Jake got a hard on watching them. Their names were etched into their upper chests and each pair wore the same tattoos on their bellies. Instead of the frightening beasts and serpents common to the racing ponies, many of the show ponies had tattoos of elegant flowers or brilliant, multicolored, abstract designs. Jake determined then and there that he would try and fuck one of them later. He would pull professional courtesy and promise a fuck with one of the Burnham estate six pony cabriolet team in exchange. They were not expected to make it past the first round anyway and so would be available for fucking once they were out.

As he and Irkut strolled over to the area where the four pony teams competed, he was contemplating the fact that all of this would very soon be behind him. Here he was thinking about chaining up Dana's pussy when, within a few days, he would never see her again. And then too, there was the fact that he had become the kind of a man who would believe that he had the right to deny a woman access to her own body, never mind deprive her of the right to choose when and where and who she would fuck. Living in Kalikastan for eight months had certainly changed him.

This morning, while the communal breakfast was being set up, Burnham had held a war council regarding the upcoming races. Jake had traveled with Burnham in his large, double wide caravan. They had arrived the day before. It had taken most of twelve hours over the winding, roughly paved roads. For the last five miles, they had crawled along in the massive traffic jam that had formed. But the caravan came with all the most modern conveniences, including four specially chosen slave girls locked into small cages for their amusement. Jake had found ample means to wile away the time.

One of the slave girls chosen to travel with them was Burnham's former secretary, Elizabeth, or Libby, as she had been known then. Burnham had enticed the attractive and elegant brunette to Kalikastan when he had first decided to move his headquarters there. She had known too much about his nefarious business dealings back in the States to be left behind. A surreptitious search of her apartment had produced a sheaf of documents memorializing Burnham's deviations from lawful business practices. Elizabeth, when confronted with this find on her arrival in Kalikastan under the impression that she was going to stay a month or so to help Burnham get set up, claimed that she had the documents for self protection in case the Feds ever lowered the boom on Burnham. Burnham didn't believe her and gave her the option of accepting a life of sexual slavery or having a bullet put in her brain. Holding a pistol that he kept in his desk to her head, he offered her life or death. Elizabeth chose life.

Burnham had the forty two year old secretary strip right on the spot and initiated her career as a sexual thrall on the carpet of his office. Jake, who had been there, joined in, much to his later regret. He knew her from before Maddy's kidnapping from when he had done other jobs for her boss. He was ashamed that he had so easily cooperated in her degradation. He was even more sorry when he saw how Burnham treated her.

Elizabeth, despite encroaching on middle age, was a beautiful woman. She had kept a nice figure and had a set of tits that produced yearning stares wherever she went. But she was no match for the young, beautiful girls who were standard fare on Burnham's estate. That and the fact that Burnham wanted to punish her for her perceived disloyalty motivated him to impose a crueler regimen on the tall, brown haired woman than the other slave girls. He had her new slave name, Betty, etched onto her chest and his emblem, the fierce, black mastiff's head tattooed on her belly. That was not unusual since it was what all his slave girls wore.

But Burnham went further than that. He had all the woman's hair above her waist shaved and permanently depilated from her body. He then had a series of interlocking red, green, yellow and blue tattoos placed all over her body above her waist, including her breasts, head, face and arms. They were designed to look like feathers. She was forced to wear a chain through the ring in the front of her slave collar and her hands were kept constantly chained to it up about the level of her breasts. This made her elbows jut out to her sides like wings. Her legs he left to turn pale white. Most of the slave girls had their pudenda shaved either wholly or partially, leaving a tuft of hair over their love lips, or perhaps a fine trim along their edges. Betty's he left on. It was ironic that at home, most women would be disconcerted to be forced to shave their pubic hair and be paraded around so that everyone could see their soft, smooth mons. But if you lived in a land where hairlessness was more or less di rigueur, appearing with your mature growth intact would single you out from the crowd. All eyes would be directed towards it.

The effect was that she now appeared as an exotic, bird-like creature. Her pale legs and bushy sex were a stark contrast to her brightly colored, hairless body above her waist. Burnham usually had her sit outside his office at an elegant, polished oak table as a kind of gate keeper for him, her ankles affixed to the legs of the desk on either side of her. Since his office was on the second floor just opposite the main stairway, when you walked up, the first thing you saw as you approached the second floor would be Betty's spread legs and her hairy loins. Since she was gagged, and her hands were confined, all she could do when you arrived was to bend over and push a button to let Burnham know that someone was there. Her gaudy breasts would drag on the table as she leaned forwards. He would look out into the hallway on his closed circuit TV and tell her whether or not to buzz the person in. There was another button that the bird-like secretary would strain to push that opened the locked door.

The strange creature was a favorite of the guards of the mansion to torment. Burnham, too, enjoyed making her life miserable. Sometimes he would send her out in the morning with instructions to give fifteen blow jobs or get ten ass fuckings before five o'clock or suffer a severe beating. Betty would have to scurry around the mansion begging men to let her suck them off or proffering her ass to them for rogering. Burnham had developed a system where slave girls would receive a token from each sexual partner during the day, for a blow job or a vaginal or rectal fucking. This way, his slave master could keep track of which girls were pulling (or, rather, fucking) their weight and which were not. The ones who were not received punishments. If they consistently failed, they were sent up to the dismal workingmen's brothels at one of the construction sites for the pipeline to serve out their days there. There were so many slave girls at the mansion/offices that it was considered adequate if a girl returned from her shift with four or five tokens. Less than that was the basis for discipline.

Betty would return to Burnham's office and he would take the tokens from the little bag he had installed around her neck and count them. If she fell short, he would whip her himself or send her down to the steward for her punishment. If she succeeded, he would congratulate her on being such a good whore and either fuck her or send her down to the guards' barracks for more exercise.

Burnham was proud of the work he had done on Betty and he brought her out on all major occasions. It had initiated a series of tattooed girls at the mansion and slaves with exotic designs all over their bodies could be seen scurrying around.

Jake felt sorry for the woman and, every once in a while, selected her as his bedmate just so that she could get a little bit of kindness and a proper, pleasurable fuck. Betty enjoyed the times she spent with Jake. It was the only time she smiled. After she sucked his cock, a task she had become quite an expert in, she would crawl up next to him and whisper in his ear, "I know that you're leaving some day, Jake. Please take me with you, please. I can't stand this life, please help me escape too!"

Jake would demure, but the woman's plight was constantly on his mind. He separated her in his mind from the hundreds of other slave girls he came into contact with because he had known her before she was enslaved.

Betty occupied one of the four cages in the caravan. The afternoon of their voyage to the tournament grounds, Jake had brought Betty into his bedroom on the caravan and spent about an hour and a half fucking her. It was thrilling to see the strangely painted body underneath him as he fucked her from behind, or the exotic, tattooed head as she sucked his cock.

During one of their resting intervals, Betty had snuggled up to Jake and whispered lowly in his ear. "I know that you're planning an escape, Jake. Burnham knows it too. You've got to be careful."

Jake was not shocked to hear that Burnham suspected he would try and save Maddy in spite of Burnham's apparent desire to keep her as a ponygirl, but he was surprised that he had spoken so openly that Betty would have heard about it. It is a common fault to believe that those of a lower social caste than you are deaf and dumb and pay no attention to what goes on around them. Burnham apparently suffered from this defect and had talked to someone in Betty's presence.

"Take me with you, Jake, please," the bird-woman begged. "I can help. I'll let you know what Burnham's plans are. I'll let you know if he has discovered the details of your plan and what countermeasures he takes. Please Jake, please! You're my only chance to get out of here!"

Jake wondered what life on the outside would be like for the exotically tattooed woman. The whole point was to escape and to lay low so that maybe, just maybe, the Kalikastanis wouldn't come after them. Betty would stick out like a parrot in a field of sparrows. What explanation could she give for her appearance? It would take a year for a doctor to laser out the colorful markings on her body.

On the other hand, it would be good to know what Burnham was up to. An inside ally would be very helpful. There was room on the helicopter for at least one more.

Jake knew that if he gave his word to Betty, he would have to keep it or spend the rest of his life regretting it. He paused in thought before he answered.

Finally, he said, "Okay, Betty. I'll let you come with us if I can. You've got to understand that getting Maddy and Jackie out are my first priorities. If getting you out jeopardizes that, I'll have to leave you behind. I won't tell you when or how we're going. You'll just have to be ready at all times. And keep your eyes and ears open. Okay?"

Betty smiled. Her teeth were a field of white amongst a sea of yellows, reds, green and blues. "Okay Jake," she said. "Thank you. I can't ask for more." She slid one of her confined hands over his chest and added, "How about I give you a real special blowjob, Jake?" She didn't wait for him to say yes.

Betty was at the little breakfast that he, Irkut, Giorgi and Burnham had in the caravan early that morning. She had served them coffee. Her bright white eyes kept flickering over Jake's face as if seeking to confirm their deal. "She's not much of a conspirator," Jake thought nervously.

"Well," Burnham said. "Here's the news. I've been told that Lightning has suffered an injury." All heads popped up.

Obviously if the pony could not race, all they had done would have been for naught.

"I don't know how serious it is. It has something to do with her foot. The Grobgy people are being very closed vest about it, but my source is very good."

"Fuck!" Giorgi spat out. He was counting on being able to defeat his brother in the match race after the tournament.

Jake felt his heart sink. Irkut shrugged his shoulders. He was used to such happenings in the pony racing business.

"Maybe it's all a front," he said. "You know, to get the odds to go up."

"That's possible," Burnham answered. "But she didn't arrive yesterday as would be expected. She's to arrive later today. They've set up an encampment on the other side of the ponypark to keep prying eyes away from her. She'll have to work out a least once to get used to the track. My people will have their eyes on her. Irkut, I want you to watch her when she works out. Got it?"

"Okay, okay," Irkut answered. But nothing was going to stop him from watching Maureen's match.

"Jake, you nose around and find out what you can. Talk to some of the touts and see what the scuttlebutt is. Other than that, we'll just have to sit tight and see what develops."

Rescuing Maddy had fallen way down on Burnham's list. He was more interested in acquiring the premier 3000 meter sulky ponygirl she had become. If the match race didn't come off, he still had probably the best 1500 meter pony, Chocolate. He didn't care what Jake had promised the whore. There was no way he was letting a pony like that go. As to Maddy, or Lightning as he now thought of her, if he didn't get her this year, there was always the spring. And if not then, well, at least he could tell himself that he tried. He would have run her for another year or two at least before even thinking of liberating her anyway.

All of these developments were on Jake's mind as he drifted along with Irkut through the fairgrounds. They stopped and watched the four pony shows for a while. The ponies pranced along in formation, breaking and reforming in groups of two. They ran together over steeple chase like obstacles in unison and then one after the other. The display of horsemanship was impressive, but it was nothing, in Jake's mind to compare to the two pony shows. They just didn't seem as graceful and vulnerable.

Irkut espied a large tent up ahead and a smile crossed his face. He slapped Jake on the back and said, "Lunch is on me, Jake. Come on!"

They walked briskly over to the bright orange, canvas tent. Unlike most of the other tents, its sides were down. There was a sign outside with a ponygirl's head wearing a white hood. Irkut opened the flap to the door and invited Jake in. There were a series of small tables strewn throughout the tent. A divider hung down, separating the back part of the tent from the front. Pairs of men sat at some of the tables. They were drinking from small, elegant, porcelain cups. Jake was led by Irkut over to a table in the back and they sat down. Shortly afterwards, a tall, heavyset, big breasted, young girl came out of the back. She had mid-length, straight, black hair and a kerchief over her head. She wore a long, colorful, striped skirt with a white apron over it that tied behind her neck. Her face was ruddy and had a wide grin on it.

"How can I help you, gentlemen?" she said in Russian.

Irkut explained to her that Jake was American and she readily shifted into English.

"What can I get for you? Two cups?"

"No, no!" Irkut exclaimed. "We're here for lunch."

The girl smiled. "Of course. Would you like to come in the back and make your selection?"

Jake gave Irkut a quizzical look. Irkut just smiled and gave him a "just do what I do," look.

The men followed the girl into the back of the tent. She held the flap open and let the men precede her. What Jake saw, even after his long time 'in country' so to speak, astounded him.

Along the sides of the tent were two rows of naked, white hooded ponygirls. They seemed to be sitting on some kind of bicycles. Straps held their torsos in place. An older man and woman were administering to them. The woman had one of the ponygirls leaning forwards and she was stroking her breast. After a few tugs, a creamy, white substance started to jet out into a small stainless steel pail. Milk! The woman was milking the ponygirl. Jake looked around and saw that almost all of the ponygirls had breasts that seemed set to burst. A couple of them had heir heads up and were sucking at nozzles that hung from a large tank that hung over them. A few were moving the pedals of the bicycles and seemed to be swooning as they did.

The man, dressed all in white like a dairy farmer and wearing a narrow white cap came over to them. He was about 5'10" tall and barrel-chested. His face was covered with a full, black beard. Like the waitress, his cheeks were rosy colored as if he spent a lot of time outdoors. He was grinning.

The waitress said something to him and his grin grew broader. "My daughter tells me that you are an American, yes?"

"Yes," Jake replied hesitatingly. He was still taken aback at the sight of the twenty or so ponygirls lined up on the sides of the tent.

"Is this your first time?" the man asked him.

"Y,yes," Jake answered. He didn't now what was going to happen, but whatever it was it certainly was his first time.

"Come and take a look. Pick out the one you want," the man said. "My name is Gregor and this is my wife Anastasia. You have met my daughter, Katrina."

"His name is Jake and mine is Irkut," Jake's companion told him. "He really has no idea what this is all about. Why don't you give him the 50 kopek tour."

The man laughed. "Okay!" he answered.

He led Jake over to the end of one of the rows. "Above you are the feeding tanks. We mix grains and greens and some beans into a puree, add water and pour it into the tubs above the ponygirls. We put in my own special formula of herbs. It encourages the flow of the ponies' milk and keeps them quite content throughout the day. It also increases their sexual desire." He walked Jake over to one of the ponygirls. Jake saw that the bicycle had a very special seat. A wide, penis like object rose out of the seat into the pussy of the ponygirl. When the pony moved the pedals, it moved up and down in a stroking motion. This one was pedaling at about half speed and the faux penis was sliding in and out of her quim at a nice, easy pace. Her chest was rising and falling and her skin was flush with her lust.

"It's self lubricating so there no problem with a dry passageway," Gregor pointed out. "With it going in and out of their pussies most of the day, that could be a real problem. We give them a half hour break every two hours. The lubricant is a special formula I developed that actually makes the nerve endings inside them more sensitive. Thus, the longer they are a milking pony, the greater the satisfaction they get out of it."

Jake watched as one of the ponies started to tremble and moan in her seat. Gregor leaned over and turned a dial on the side of the bicycle. The wheels and the intruder in the pony's sex slowed. "We don't want them to come too often so the speed of the bicycle is regulated by a little meter on the side. It's not the orgasms of the ponies that we want, it's their arousal. It helps generate the milk."

They stepped over to where Gregor's wife was milking the pony girl. She was now working on the pony's other breast.

As she squeezed and massaged the breast, small jets of thick, human milk spurted out. The brown tailed pony was moaning with what seemed to Jake to be exquisite pleasure. Anastasia smiled at Jake. "Have you ever had mother's milk?" she asked. "I mean since you were a baby?" She was even heavier than her daughter and had a bright, gold tooth in the front of her mouth. She wore a calico kerchief over her short, brown hair. "Here, have a taste," she offered without waiting for an answer from Jake.

Jake was unsure of what to do. Drinking human milk was not high on his list of things to do before he died. "I don't think so," he muttered, holding up his hand.

"Come on, Jake," Irkut bellowed. "When in Rome, do as the Romans do. Ponymilk is considered quite a delicacy here. Don't be bashful. You've sucked on pony tits before. This one just has milk in it."

Jake looked around at the smiling faces. Katrina had joined them, for now ignoring her customers. He thought he detected a flash of electricity pass between her and Irkut.

"Okay," Jake conceded. "Just a taste."

He stepped closer to Anastasia who held the pony's tit out to him. He leaned over the rail that separated the ponygirl from the corridor down the middle of the tent. Her hand circled the taut, pale white globe so that the nipple was projected slightly outwards. It was fat and engorged. Jake leaned over and, capturing the stiff projection, started a gentle suck. Anastasia must have given the breast a squeeze since a stream of the pony's milk jetted into his mouth. He closed his lips and stepped back. Some of the milk squirted onto his shirt.

Jake took a minute to absorb the taste of the pony's product. It was warm, creamy and sweet. It had an unfamiliar accent to it that was not unpleasant. It was good! He smiled.

The men and women around him erupted into laughter. Irkut slapped him on the back. "See," Irkut exclaimed. "It's not poison!" The men and women all laughed again.

"You have tasted the barley line. The other three vats are rye, soy and wheat. I experiment with different mixtures to get different flavors. My wife and daughter help me."

Anastasia gave a big grin. "Would you like to see?" she asked. Before Jake could respond, she had released the pony's tit and untied the apron behind her neck. She unbuttoned her blouse down to her naval and removed a large, bulbous breast from inside a large, stretched out, soft bra. She circled her hand under it and proffered it to the astonished American. "Have a taste," she said happily.

"Come on, Jake," Irkut said. "It's a great honor. If you don't, Gregor will be displeased."

Jake gave a weak smile and bent his neck to get access to the big woman's teat. She grabbed the back of his head and mashed his face into her breast. "Don't be bashful, Amerikanski," she laughed.

Jake had to slide his lips around the massive mammary in order to find her nipple. Once he did, he started sucking on it. Nothing came out.

"You have to milk it, my little baby boy. Just like when you were at your mother's tit." Anastasia laughed heartily. Jake's head jumped up and down as her chest heaved.

Taking the big woman at her word, Jake started to suck at the teat in short, staccato bursts.

"Put your hands around it! Don't be shy," Gregor called out.

Responding to instructions, Jake moved closer to the large woman and placed his hands around her fluffy breast. He squeezed it gently and began to work it like he saw farmers do on a cow's udder.

"That's it," the woman said. Her voice was mellower and her hand on the back of his head softened. "Ohhhhhhhh," she moaned. "That's it! A little harder now!"

Jake gave the breast a hard squeeze. A dribble of slightly sour substance came out at first followed by a torrent of the woman's breast milk. When it filled his mouth he rose from her breast and swallowed. After he got it down, he took a gulp of air. "Strawberries!" he exclaimed.

The others laughed.

"I've been eating them like mad for the last two weeks," the woman said, laughing.

Katrina made eyes at Irkut and said, "I've been eating cherries. Would you like to try some?"

Irkut's eyes lit up. Katrina, although young, maybe 19 or 20, was his kind of woman, zaftig and brazen. "I'd love to," he answered.

Katrina pulled down her apron. She was wearing a bright yellow pullover underneath. She grabbed the hem and exposed two, large, delightful, firm orbs with long, thick nipples. Her areolas were bright pink and as wide as sand dollars. Irkut stepped up to her and put his arm around her back. He gave her a lecherous look and then leaned over and placed his mouth on her left teat. He put his free hand around it and started a firm massage of the bulky, spongy mound. Katrina gave out a long, pleasured sigh. Irkut worked his lips over her teat for a few moments and then his body seemed to sag as her milky fluid poured into his mouth. "Mmmmmmmmmmmmm!" he moaned. He took much longer than Jake did at the mother's teat. Finally, he brought his head up and smiled.

He looked the young girl in the eyes and said, "That was delicious!"

"Katrina!" Gregor yelled. "You've got customers!"

"Yes, Papa," the girl replied, smiling ear to ear. She pulled her shirt down and retied her apron. To Irkut she said, "Later, tonight, we have to milk all the ponygirls and Papa needs some help." And then, somewhat shyly she added. "I need to be milked at least three times a day."

"I'll be happy to help out," Irkut replied. With that, the girl spun and ran out into the public area.

Gregor smiled at Irkut and slapped him on the back. "Come back around ten tonight. I could use a hand."

Irkut nodded eagerly. He then turned to Jake. "Now, we could buy a cup or a pitcherfull. But my recommendation is that we buy what is called a lunch. Pick out your pony and she'll be brought out to you. You can drink her until you're full."

"Oh, I don't think..." Jake said.

Gregor interrupted. "Sure, pick out a pony. It'll be the best lunch you've had in a long while. Full of nutrition."

Jake did feel an urge to suck on a teat some more. It had been a delightful experience.

"So," Gregor asked, "which do you want? Barley, rye, wheat or soy?"

"I liked the barley so I guess I'll stick with that," Jake said somewhat sheepishly.

"Okay," Gregor replied. "Which pony do you want?"

Jake looked at the five ponies all lined up in a row, breasts swaying invitingly as they pedaled their way to bliss. "I don't know," he answered.

"Drindel here on the end was milked a little while ago, so I can't let you have her. Jana, she's a good producer. How about her?"

Jana had a black ponytail extruding from the back of her hood. Her name was spelled across her chest in blue, Cyrillic letters. On her belly, she wore the tattoo of a roaring bear's head with bloody, red teeth. Her body was trim, her legs were well muscled. Occasionally, without breaking stride on her bicycle, she rooted her head around until she found the nozzle opposite her mouth, seized it between her lips and started to suck.

Jake looked and saw that all of the ponygirls had their eyelets closed. "They don't even seem to notice that we're here," Jake observed.

"Oh, they do and they don't," Gregor answered. "After about three months at the nozzle, their awareness of what goes on around them kind of disappears. Jana we've had for three years. She'll probably produce adequately for two more and then we'll have to retire her. Now Irina, she's on the end of the wheat line. She's only been with us a few days. Her estate retired her from racing at the end of the fall season and we picked her up rather cheap." Jake and Gregor walked over to the end of the wheat line. Anastasia had gone back to her milking.

On the end of the group of five ponies under the wheat tub, a large breasted, blond haired, white hooded pony sat on a bicycle. Like all pony and slave girls in Kalikastan, her name was stenciled above her breasts. Her thin and seemingly fragile arms, desiccated from disuse, were bound behind her. On her stomach, above her hairless mons, was a fierce looking badger. The nozzle that the other ponies sought so eagerly was fixed into her mouth by a strap that went around her white hooded head. Her feet were strapped to the bicycle pedals and her body rested in a harness that kept her firmly in her seat, unlike the other ponies, whose harnesses seemed more intended to keep them from falling over. The penis like prong that emerged from the bicycle seat was slowly plunging back and forth in her leaking cleft, seemingly on automatic. When she heard their voices and sensed their nearness, she gave a little moan and squirmed.

"We look for big ponies with large, undamaged mammaries and thick nipples. They're the best milkers. Irina here was ideal, like she was made for it. She's been a little trouble and we've had to strap her in more securely than the others,"

Gregor explained. "Some of the ponies just don't take to becoming a milker. All that running and now just to sit on their stools day after day. It must be hard to adjust. But they all do. It's a kind of heaven for them. We never whip them. There's no need. Once they are acclimated, they live their lives in a blissful haze. In the mornings, some of them can't wait to get to their seats. And at night, sometimes we have to drag them off." He laughed. "Isn't that true Anushka," he called out to his wife. The woman just smiled and nodded.

The activity of the ponygirl Irina seemed to pick up as Gregor spoke. There was a faint murmuring from behind her sealed lips and her head swayed from side to side in an attempt to break free of its confines. The harness which encompassed her torso and her white hooded head kept her relatively still. Jake thought he heard the words 'please' and 'help' emerge from her mouth but he might have been mistaken. Suddenly the nozzle in her mouth rumbled and the hose attached to it shook. Jake heard the sound of the wheat mixture being transmitted to the pony's sealed mouth. She struggled in her bonds, whining, while the mixture sluiced down her throat. Her breath became agitated and her torso squirmed. She let out a squeal of helplessness.

"We have to force feed her every hour or so," Gregor continued. "It'll daze her after a few minutes and then she'll be all right for fifteen minutes or so. The formula has to build up in her body. Every day she'll stay dazed a little longer. Like I said, after a few months, she'll be no trouble at all."

"It must be difficult to get her up on her stool every day, if she's so reluctant," Irkut commented.

"It's a job," Gregor replied. "It's why we rarely break in more than one milker at a time. We can get her seated on her stool easily enough and fixed up in her harness, but it's getting the nozzle fixed in her mouth that's the real trick. And don't get in the way of those powerful legs." He laughed heartily. "Fortunately, we have a special tool that forces open the jaws so the nozzle can be inserted. Irina still gives us a terrible fight every morning, but we manage. It'll get easier as time goes on."

Jake wondered what it would be like to be condemned to a life as a cow. An active mind, no matter how conditioned to obedience as a racing ponygirl, would rebel. Irina looked, from her body, to be between 28 and 30 years old. That meant that she probably ran for at least six or seven years. Now she would spend the rest of her life producing milk and sitting in a daze, a false penis encouraging but rarely fully rewarding her lust.

The machine stopped its force feeding of the reluctant ponygirl and she gave out a maddened shriek from behind her gag and tried to rise from her seat. Jake concluded that she was an English speaking pony, maybe even a former American, and had understood everything they said. It didn't matter if she did or didn't. Whatever Gregor had planned for her would happen regardless of any protests she might make. Just as when she became a ponygirl, her will and her desires counted for nothing. "Well," he thought, "there are worse fates in life than this."

Gregor leaned over and squeezed one of her breasts. "She won't be in milk for a couple more days. Then she'll calm down a bit. Being milked is soothing and pleasurable for them. She'll enjoy it like the rest."

Jake hesitated for a moment before walking away. He knew that once this was an innocent young woman who had never heard of Kalikastan, ponygirl racing or any of this. One day she had been torn from her former life and thrown into a life of hell. It pleased him to think that her days of torment would soon be over, whether she wanted them to be or not.

Irkut picked one of the soy ponies and the men went back out into the public portion of the tent. Katrina was waiting on some customers. There was a long counter with refrigerators behind her. She went behind the counter, took out a covered pitcher and poured its contents into two small cups. After placing them on tiny saucers, she brought them back to the men. Jake noticed that a pair of matronly women had come in and wondered what their reaction was going to be when they saw him feeding at the breasts of a ponygirl.

He didn't have long to wait. Anastasia came out of the back leading two woozy ponygirls by leashes attached to their nose rings. She presented one to Irkut and the other to Jake. Before she did so, she carefully wiped their teats with a damp cloth.

"Just put her on your lap and enjoy yourself," Irkut said, smiling. "It helps if you caress their pussies."

The wiry ponygirl trainer guided his selection to his lap and had her lean against his shoulder. He put his mouth on her teat while he caressed and massaged her fat breast. He was soon rewarded and gave out a satisfied sigh. The pony, whose mouth had been covered with a shield gag, stiffened for just a moment and then, moaning, seemed to melt in Irkut's arms. Having started her milk, he placed his hand between her thighs.

Jake's pony was sitting on his lap expectantly. He placed his hand on her large, seemingly ready to burst breast and rubbed it gently. The pony started to squirm a little anxiously. Looking first over at Irkut to make sure he was doing it right, he let the pony sink into his shoulder. He then leaned forwards and placed his lips on her breast and began to suckle her. His hand wrapped itself around her mammary and he began to encourage the pony's production.

After about fifteen seconds, his efforts were rewarded. The pony moaned and a rush of its milk came into his mouth. It was creamy and sweet and tart all at the same time. He spread her strong, muscular thighs and began to stroke her hairless mons. Her slit quickly moistened and he slipped his fingers inside her, stroking her pussy's walls and then, moving his hand up, teasing her stiffened bud of pleasure. Her nipple was fat and engorged and she moaned every time that he drew hard on it, each time being rewarded with a squirt of her creamy sustenance.

Jake lost himself in a reverie as he took the pony's nectar. It was the most pleasant, most comforting thing he had ever done. After about ten minutes, when her tit went dry, he shifted her to the other side of his lap and began to suckle the other.

The pony came twice while he was stroking her. Her body shuddered and her legs quaked. But she never tried to pull her breast away from his lips. Rather just the opposite. She seemed to press it forwards so that he could better access it.

Jake's belly was full by the time the milk stopped flowing. He knew that he probably had not drunk more than a half a pint, but the richness of the liquid made him feel sated. He leaned back, his hand still in the pony's now messy quim. Irkut had guided his pony down between his knees and she was suckling at his meat dreamily.

"Have her suck you off," Irkut said. "It'll be one of the best orgasms you ever had."

Jake eased the pony off of his lap until she was kneeling on the floor between his knees. He looked over at the two women and realized that he had no need to concern himself with their sensibilities. They both had ponygirls on their laps and were sucking hungrily at their tits. Jake opened his fly and freed his cock. It was already hardening. After removing the pony's gag, he placed his hand on the pony's head and guided her forward. When she felt his cock brush up against her lips she opened them and pulled him in.

A wave of pleasure flowed over Jake as the pony ran her lips and tongue over his stiffened crank. After the delirium of feeding on the pony, it was blissful to have her now suckling him. He closed his eyes and leaned back in his chair, letting the pony take charge of his cock. She took her time, slowly ascending his pole with her lips and then lowering her head until he was fully subsumed within. From within his pleasured haze he wondered idly how the pony could regain enough of her mental acuteness to perform this task after the pleasure of having her breasts milked by his lips. The hungry mouth that worked his needy pole soon pushed all questioning from his mind. When he came, it was like he had never had an orgasm before. His whole body seemed to reverberate with the pumping of his spume down his lengthy rod. Each slow, lazy pulse of his cock made his body tremble and his mind cloud over. Irkut was right. This was one of the best.

When Anastasia came to collect the ponies, Jake was lying back with his eyes closed, reliving in his mind the delights of the last half hour. The pony was lazily suckling at his softened meat, her white forehead pressed down on his belly. He thought of the great chain of random events that led him and this feminine creature to this moment in time to share bliss together. He would never know who she was and she would never know him. It was odd when he thought about it. He would probably remember this moment for the rest of his life. She would not remember it for more than thirty seconds after she was remounted on her bicycle in the rear of the tent and took a mouthful of Gregor's stupefying concoction.

Anastasia shook him gently by the shoulder and Jake awoke from his sleepy haze with a start. He realized that his cock was laying limply outside his pants. He eased the pony's head off of his lap and, embarrassed before the 50 year old or so lady, tucked it away. Anastasia just laughed and Jake realized that she had probably seen a thousand cocks. After all, this was her business and he couldn't have been the first guy to fall asleep after a magnificent delivery of oral delight.

Irkut rose and thanked the woman for her hospitality. He paid her what Jake thought was a quite substantial sum. As they were getting ready to leave, Gregor came out to say goodbye.

"I hope you enjoyed your meal?" he said, smiling.

"Very much," Jake replied.

"I assume you work for Mr. Burnham, is this true," Gregor asked.

"Yes," Jake answered, a bit suspicious.

"If it is not too much of me to ask, I have been trying to get an investment in my business for a couple of years. There is a great demand for my product but I don't have adequate production facilities. I would like to have a farm where milk could be produced and sold under a special label and have sufficient transportation to get it to the city nice and fresh. There's good money in it and it does provide a good life for ponygirls who might otherwise be considered of no further use. I like to think that a few years of bliss as one of my milkers is a kind of reward for all their hard work and discipline. If you get the chance, would you speak to him about it?"

"Of course," Jake answered. But he knew he wouldn't. If Burnham got a hold of it, there would be soon a hundred milking barns throughout the country using thousands of females recruited for the sole purpose of producing milk. He would not mention it to Burnham at all.

The two men stepped out of the tent. The sun was high in the sky. It was a little after noon. Jake took a moment to adjust his vision to the bright light.

"You know, Jake," Irkut said, "you have to agree that there is a kind of beauty and purity in this world we have created here in Kalikastan. Yes?"

Jake, who was not one prone to philosophizing, replied, "What do you mean?"

"I mean that there is much cruelty in the lives we have devised for ourselves here. Innocent young women are stolen from their lives, all their rights are taken away and they are made to serve our baser instincts. On the other hand, a ponygirl is a thing of beauty to watch and a properly trained slave girl is like nothing else in the world. They are both totally devoted to their crafts. They live lives bracketed by extremes of pain and pleasure. They are more alive than they ever were as free women. Even the ponies we have just seen, where would they ever get the chance to experience the absolute bliss they do here. Kalikastan is like no other place on Earth. I'm not sure I agree with some of the changes we have had in the last few months with Mr. Burnham and all; it puts everything at risk. And that is something I would never let happen. No friendship would ever be strong enough for me not to take action if I thought someone was endangering our little paradise. Do you understand me?"

"Clearly," Jake answered.

"Then that's good. We will speak no more about it. And speaking about bliss, I have to get Czarina ready for her performance. I really think that she has a chance to medal. Where else but Kalikastan, eh? I will see you later. Come and watch Czarina if you can."

"I will," Jake answered. The two friends shook hands and parted.

CHAPTER SEVEN

Michael Burnham was leaning back in a chair in the lounge area of his large, luxurious caravan. A blond slave girl was between his knees servicing his cock. She had long, blond hair that was bunched up in a loose tie behind her head. She and three others had been brought down directly from the slave reception center in Dlitski. They were not marked and had yet to be adorned with their collars and bracelets. He needed the sluts for tonight's show. He had decided that he might as well try one of them out. She wasn't bad, but she had been nervous as a kitten when he had brought her into the caravan. The other three were lying in the grass outside, hooded, hogtied and gagged. The blond girl would join them as soon as she was finished with his dick. After the show tonight, he would hand them over to his security guards.

Burnham had come to rely more and more heavily on his Russian security team. He kept Jake and his boys around as kind of a counterweight to them but he knew that soon he would have to have Jake and the others dumped into a big pit somewhere. Jake would never stand for the continued enslavement of Maddy and Jackie. He couldn't let Jake's crew go back to the States knowing what they knew, especially that asshole Irving who had blackmailed him into bringing that pig whore back from Mexico. He was going to enjoy seeing that one eat dirt. He might even do it himself.

And as for the fat ponygirl, as far as he was concerned she was an embarrassment. She could lie in the same hole as Irving. They just had to make the whole a lot bigger.

The slave girl gave his cock a little thrill as she wrapped her tongue around it and slurped it up and down. He gave a moan of appreciation and placed his hand on her head. She wasn't bad. He couldn't remember her name. Maybe he had never learned it. She was just a sexual pleasure delivery system after all, so why did she need a name?

"I must own over 200 cunts by now," he mused. None of them needed names as far as he was concerned. "Maybe I should start giving them numbers instead." Numbers he had no trouble remembering, especially when they were preceded by dollar signs and followed by a bunch of zeros. There was one cunt whose name he wouldn't soon forget. She was outside his caravan right now, kneeling in the grass, the back of her slave collar affixed to a post.

He was running out of things to do to his former secretary. Maybe she should join Jake in his hole, he thought, they seemed to be great friends. On the other hand, he had been talking to one of the Arabs who had come over to sell and buy the other day, the one who had set up the deal for the Persian whores. He told Burnham what they did to their ponygirls over there. Maybe he would have Betty's cunt lips shaved off and her clit too, like they did. She could run around with her little hole and beg men to fuck it. But no, she wouldn't have a tongue either, or arms. He would have little prosthetic wings made up for her to complete her conversion into a fuck bird.

He had added something to her decorations today. It was a little, orange beak that sat above and below her mouth. It was attached to her face with studs through the skin in her cheeks above and below her mouth on both sides. It was made of soft rubber and when you wanted to fuck her mouth you could just lift the top up and push the bottom down. He had tried it out and it worked great. She had squeaked and complained because the posts in her cheeks still hurt. But that was the point, wasn't it. She had tried to double cross him and nobody got away with that.

After he had fucked her mouth, he had his guards take her outside and put a ring gag in it. She was kneeling out there now with her mouth wide open under her beak and a sign on her chest that said, "Complements of the House". Someone had been working his cock between her lips when he came back with the new whores. It had made him laugh. He chuckled now when he thought of it.

Burnham looked down at the blond haired head in his lap. She was a good cocksucker, but he had things to do. He grabbed her hair and started to pump her head up and down. She gurgled each time that his stiff piece jammed into the back of her throat. It only took a minute for his juices to over flow. He jetted his come down the cunt's throat as she struggled on his lap for air. "Uuuuuuuuugh!" he moaned as his cock danced for joy. He would never get tired of fucking a new girl's throat, that's for sure.

When he was satisfied that he had urged out every drop of his come, he pushed the girl's head back. She sputtered and coughed and gasped for air. He had to hand it to her. She was good, even if untrained. She would have suffocated before she did anything to interfere with his pleasure. Maybe he would remember her name after all.

He called out for one of the guards to hogtie, hood and gag the slut out on the grass like the other ones and got up from his chair. He needed to make a phone call.

Telephones were strictly rationed in Kalikastan, especially ones that could make international calls. Burnham guessed that he had one of the only ones within a hundred miles of the encampment. He had been waiting for the Fall Tournament to start so that he could draw Jake away from the telephones at the mansion. There was something that was going to happen that he didn't want Jake to know about until he was just about to tumble into his grave.

The jaded billionaire got up from his chair and walked back to his bedroom at the back of the caravan. He passed the cages containing the other slave girls he had brought with him. One of them was the Malaysian slut who had given them a hard time the other day. He had enjoyed her unhappiness so much that he had cut short her training so that he could enjoy her suffering more. She had been tattooed with her new name and his insignia. He decided that all the Malaysian girls would be named after flowers. He had her named Orchid. The Vietnamese girls, when they came in, would be named after birds, the Chinese after gems, etc. This way you could tell where a slut was from by her name. It was something that appealed to his sense of order.

Seeing the unhappy girl all scrunched up in her cage reminded him that he had not whipped her yet today. He would take care of that as soon as he made his call.

Once in the bedroom, Burnham pulled out his cell phone and dialed another cell phone back in the States. An urban accented, male voice answered. "Yeah?"

"It's me," Burnham said. "Everything is in order here. You may proceed."

"Okay," was all the voice said in response. Burnham smiled as he closed the phone. And then he looked for his whip.

* * * * * * * * * * * * * *

Youngstown, Ohio is one of those formerly vibrant cities in the eastern United States that had suffered from the migration of so many manufacturing jobs overseas. A few of the old tire and auto assembly plants had survived, some machine shops for auto parts were still left and a small electronics industry had sprung up struggling to compete with the cheaper labor rates of Mexico, China and, more recently, India. There were quite a few abandoned factory sites left by now bankrupt companies, or companies who had moved their operations elsewhere.

While it was just a little after noon in Kalikastan, it was a little past 4 a.m. in Youngstown. A large, brown delivery van was running along Poland Road, parallel to the railroad tracks that used to carry the industrial output of Youngstown to the world. On its side was written in large, yellow letters, "National Uniform Company". The driver, a tall, well built blonde, was yawning. It had been a twelve hour drive to Youngstown from Elizabeth, New Jersey. Her partner, an equally stunning, statuesque brunette was dozing in the passenger seat. They had shared the driving across the mountains of Pennsylvania. Once they picked up their cargo here in Youngstown, the brunette would take the first shift on the way back.

Carla, the blond and Yvonne, the brunette were part of Mary Ellen's crew who were running the US end of Burnham's slaving operation. Word had been passed down by Mary Ellen that this was probably their last run. The women, both in their late twenties, were looking forward to a long vacation together in the Keys. They had been lovers for a couple of years and tried to get away as often as they could to keep their relationship hot. With the slaving operation at full blast, they hadn't had much time.

Lesbian relationships, like heterosexual ones, are hard to generalize about, but in this relationship, Yvonne was definitely the top. They never went away without a dildo and a set of handcuffs.

About 2 miles down River Road was an abandoned tire factory. It had once employed about 1500 people but had been closed down now for over ten years. Where there once was a ten foot high security gate, there was now just the remnant of one. Every year or so there was a drive to clean out the addicts and other criminal types who hung out there, but the guys who did the real business in the abandoned buildings always got fair warning.

Carla pulled the van through the entrance and backed into what had once been a busy loading dock. It ran right into the abandoned building. No one outside would be able to see what was going to be loaded. It was a good thing too, because most people would have been appalled.

Santo Margolis, a tall, thin man in his mid thirties, was the proprietor of this decrepit kingdom. He had wavy, black hair and sported a thin moustache. He usually dressed to the nines and tonight was no different. He was wearing a sharply tailored silk suit, an expensive, flowered print shirt and a pair of hand sewn Italian loafers. He and his boys haled mostly from the Dominican Republic, although some of them were actually born here. They had carved themselves quite a niche here in Youngstown. With connections to their *hermanos* in the Bronx, they were able to deliver primo crack and smack to the eager youth of the area. They also served as a fence to the many junkies and other desperados of the city and its environs. Trucks would go east with goods where they could be unloaded easily in the Bronx and would return with narcotics.

Santo had developed a very lucrative sideline. It seems that Youngstown was one of those towns where nice suburban teenagers liked to run away to and to which, after graduation from high school, kids came to get their first real job and an apartment all their own. There were a couple of universities nearby and a thriving drug addict community. From this pool, Santo was able to cull maybe three or four pretty, young females every month. A few he kept around for the boys' amusement, but most of them were gathered monthly by the girls from Elizabeth. Santo used to do business with Feeney and his crew, but shifted over easily to Mary Ellen's when Feeney was eased out and shown the door to eternity.

Tonight was collection night and five pretty, young females were waiting in a special room he used for those purposes deep inside the abandoned factory. It was far from prying eyes and also served to keep his randy crew away from them. Their clubhouse was in another section of the factory where they kept their own playthings until they got tired of them and sold them to Dominican pimps in New York or Chicago. The girls meant for Mary Ellen's crew were kept clean and pure, or at least as clean and pure as they were when they came in.

Two of the girls were kids who had moved in from Neshannock Falls over the Pennsylvania line. They had gotten their own apartment down near the University. One of Santo's boys had chatted them up one night in a bar and had followed them home. They were picked up a few days ago in a late night raid personally directed by Santo, a terrible penalty for underage drinking.

One of the girls had been sold to them by a junkie way behind on his debts. Santo had made it clear to the hophead that he didn't deal in girls who were all cranked up. He was assured that this girl, a 19 year old brunette from Cornersburg, was not. She was a friend of a friend, he said, and the junkie produced her, as promised, last night. She had been very unhappy when she had been pulled from the trunk of the junkie's beat up, 1979 Chevy, but was easily quieted and installed, naked, bound and hooded in one of Santo's cages deep in the belly of the abandoned factory.

The other two were just a stroke of luck. They and a third girl had driven out to the former industrial park late at night to smoke a little weed and drink some beers. One of Santo's boys spotted them as they drove by the tire factory. Two of the girls, an 18 year old blond and a 20 year old redhead were prime specimens. The third was a little chunky and shopworn. Santo gave her to his boys as fresh meat and she had entertained them very well for the last week or so. He had the girls' car driven out to Cleveland and abandoned near the waterfront.

Santo watched the van pulling into the loading dock. This was a cash business and Santo always made sure he was there to collect the price on the girls. There was some negotiation involved too and he didn't trust any of his crew to hold up their end with the dykes from Elizabeth.

Once Carla had placed the van into park, she gave Yvonne a little nudge. It took a few moments for the brown haired woman to shake off her drowsiness. When she was fully awake, she and Carla hopped out of the van and walked up the stairs of the loading dock. They were wearing brown uniforms with thick cotton shirts and slacks and heavy work boots. The name National Uniform Company was stitched on the shirts just over their hearts. Santo and three of his crew were waiting for them.

"*Hola*, Santo," Yvonne said. "You all set?"

"As always, beautiful," Santo returned. "There's one more we got in last night. Come on down and take a look at her and see if we can agree on a price. She's clean and good looking with nice tits. Like you."

"Cut the shit, Santo," Yvonne spat back. "This is business, remember?"

Mary Ellen had looked over the photos of the other four girls Santo had sent her by email and the prices for them were already worked out, subject to a physical inspection, of course. The new girl they didn't know about and so Yvonne would set the price. It wasn't unusual for that to happen since potential slave girls didn't grow on trees but had to be harvested somewhat haphazardly as the opportunity arose.

It was also not unusual for Santo to have a couple of his gang with him when he greeted the "dykes from Elizabeth" as he called them. Two of them would stand by and watch the truck while Carla and Yvonne went down into the bowels of the factory to inspect the girls. First, though, they removed from the back of the truck a carton containing the bondage equipment that the girls would wear on their way to New Jersey. The efficient Santo always provided a hand truck to ease its transport to the secured room where the sluts to be were held.

Carla was not one to let men do her work when she could do it herself, so she placed the carton on the hand truck and, following Santo and Yvonne, descended the stairs that led to where the girls were housed. Santo led the way with a battery powered lantern. It was three levels down, along a long corridor and through a door that was usually hidden by a large tire rack that took two guys to move. Due to the laziness of the typical cop sent on sweeps, Santo had three times avoided the discovery of his secret room.

The immense rack had already been moved and the trio passed through the secret entrance easily. The doorway led to a long hall. About halfway down, on the left was another door. It had a small, yellowed, opaque window and was made of steel. It looked like it hadn't been opened in ten years. But that was just part of the camouflage. Santo always made sure that the passageway to his holding area was not unduly disturbed. Anyone who found the secret door, looking down the hallway, would not know that it was being used.

Santo knocked on the steel door three times and then twice again. The sound of a bolt sliding back behind the door was heard. A moment later, the door swung inwards.

The three stepped into a large room, about 40' x 20'. For a place way down in the dungeon of a deserted factory, it looked pretty good. There was a heavy, red and black, patterned rug on the floor, some easy chairs, a refrigerator, and a stove, all electric and powered by a line run from the streetlights a few blocks away from the factory. The cement walls had all been spackled and covered with a new coat of white paint. It had a drop ceiling and recessed lighting. Some guys from the electric company had been into Santo big for some drugs and he let them off the hook in exchange for electrifying the clubhouse and his hideaway.

The room had a dual exhaust fan that took stale air out and brought fresh air in. A small port-a-potty was set behind a screen. Along one wall was a wet bar with several stools in front of it. A long, leather couch divided the room in half. It was facing away from the bar and towards a series of small cages that lined the walls. Outside the cages, their arms tied off behind them and connected to ropes that ran down from the ceiling were five naked, young women. Their ankles were tied off to rings in the floor, spreading their legs widely.

Yvonne and Carla paused to take in the sight of the unhappy prisoners. Three had breasts that would satisfy any mammary aficionado and two had smaller, but ample tits. The fifth, one of the blond girls, was tall and thin and had small, conical, twin mounds. Except for the blond, the others were shapely and seemed fit. All of them still sported their pubic hair, except for the blond again, although two of them had trimmed theirs back to bikini cuts. Their mouths were covered by wide silvery tape. Blindfolds had been drawn across their eyes and tied off behind their heads. Three of Santo's men were lounging around the room. The one who had let them in made four. Usually there were only two of Santo's boys in the room when Carla and Yvonne stopped by to pick up merchandise, but neither woman took special note of it.

This was Santo's personal lounge which he used for meetings with his lieutenants and for relaxing after a hard day of committing crimes and mayhem. The gang's prohibition against using the merchandise did not extend to Santo himself and he often chased everybody out so he could have fun with one of the unlucky girls who struck his fancy. Although Mary Ellen had strict rules about this sort of thing, Santo's discretion was such that his activities were considered to be within the level of tolerance. None of the girls came to Mary Ellen any worse for wear.

Two of the displayed girls were sobbing mightily. The others were silent although you could see the wetness of their tears on the blindfolds across their eyes. Yvonne did not like to unnecessarily prolong the girls' agony and so she set down to business right away.

There was no need to make any kind of announcement to the girls about what was going to happen to them. They would find out soon enough. Talking to them only served to humanize them and nobody wanted that. They were just five pieces of merchandise being held for pickup.

Carla and Yvonne approached the first girl on the right. From her bodily shape, they pegged her as the one that Santo had received the night before. She was, in fact, the girl delivered by the junkie. She was a pretty brunette, about 5'6" tall, with large, round breasts. Her name was Paula Delaney. She attended Trumball County Community College and lived with her folks in Leavittsburg. Just 19, she hoped one day to be a journalist. She had been working on a class assignment for Journalism 101, an article about the local drug problem and she had decided to interview a real life junkie. He had promised to meet her out at Davidson Park, but she had to come alone and at night.

She struggled fiercely when the junkie overpowered her. He just managed to get her hands tied off behind her back and then her ankles tied together. He then stuffed her mouth with a rag and threw her in the trunk. Paula still couldn't believe what had happened to her and was sure that somehow it would all turn out all right. Her folks had a little money and she was awaiting the results of what she presumed would be a ransom demand. During her brief captivity she had been kept, for the most part, hooded and gagged. She knew there were other women in the room with her since the gags did not block out all sound, but she hadn't worked out in her mind yet what they were doing there.

Before untying her hands, Carla ran a wide leather belt around the girl's waist. Yvonne then undid her hands from the rope that led up to the ceiling and untied them from each other. The two women each took a wrist of the frightened girl and trapped them in the steel cuffs on the sides of the belt. Paula squealed with unhappiness as she was handled. Undoubtedly she was surprised and shocked to feel feminine hands on her body. She might even have caught a whiff of Carla's cologne.

The next thing to do was to inspect her for physical defects. This was Yvonne's bailiwick as she was the senior member of the crew and ultimately responsible for any errors or omissions. She ran her hands over the girl's body looking for hidden scars or tattoos that would devalue her. Seeing none, she felt her breasts, pushing them into the girl's chest to assure herself that they were real. She spread her rear cheeks to make sure that she was relatively intact there and had no rashes or polyps. Finally, she thrust her hands between the girls' legs and assessed her sex. She rubbed it until the slit produced lubrication and then worked two fingers inside, feeling the walls of the vagina for sores or any growths. She then bent down and, spreading the girl's thick pubic hair, made a visual assessment of her loins and the surfaces of the girl's inner and outer labia.

The girl, who moaned and whined throughout her inspection, checked out okay. While Yvonne removed the girl's blindfold, Carla went back to the large carton and retrieved a thick, leather hood. Yvonne peered into the frightened eyes of the girl. She took hold of her nipples with two fingers of each hand and gave them a little squeeze. She spoke to the girl for the first time.

"Listen carefully to me. I'm going to remove your gag so I can inspect your mouth. After that, my assistant is going to cover your head with the hood she has in her hands. If you make any sound, I will cause you a whole world of pain both right now and we get to our destination. And believe me I will do it. Do you understand?"

Paula's eyes were tear filled. She was pretty sure now that she wasn't going to be held for ransom. The stroking of her intimate parts was a big clue. She was disconcerted by the fact that the two women were going to take her somewhere. Weren't women supposed to stick together and work against female exploitation? What about feminism and all that? If she could just talk to the women and find out what was going on, maybe she could convince them to let her go. The threat of punishment, however, frightened her. Her widened, blue eyes flickered around the room, taking in the five Hispanic men, Carla and Yvonne. She was clearly outnumbered. She resolved to stay quiet. She was sure she would get the chance to bargain for her freedom later. She was, of course, wrong.

Dolefully, she nodded her head in assent to Yvonne's instructions. The tall, chestnut haired slaver, slowly undid the tape across her mouth. There was no sense inflicting unnecessary pain or upsetting the girl by harsh treatment. The removal of the tape revealed a blue rubber ball that had been jammed between her lips. It was the size of a handball. Yvonne pried it out with the help of Paula's tongue. The young girl was only too happy to have the offensive object out of her mouth.

Yvonne deftly spread the young girl's lips and examined her teeth. She was not looking to assess her age like you would do with a horse, but, rather, making sure she would not need extensive dental work nor had any obvious sores. Paula always took care of her teeth and had no sexually transmitted diseases. She had been very careful and had made both of the boys she had slept with, at different times, of course, wear condoms. The first had been her high school sweetheart. The second was a fellow journalism student at TCCC. They had been going out for about a month now and Paula had only given in to him last week.

Having satisfied herself with her examination, Yvonne signaled Carla to administer the hood. It had a built in gag and Carla started off by making sure that the thick, leather prong was seated in the girl's mouth. Paula only saw it coming at the last minute, Yvonne was still holding her head, and she opened her mouth to issue a protest. It was the usual response. Carla was able to shove the mouth filling leather past her teeth with no problem. While the girl whined and complained pitifully, Yvonne helped pull the hood over the girl's head and seat the ear plugs in her ears. The hood was of the same general design as those that had been worn by Natasha and Ilona back in Kalikastan except that they were not custom made. Burnham had twenty of the hoods sent to the Elizabeth operation from Kalikastan when he found out about them. Once the hood was buckled under Paula's chin and behind her head, Carla activated the little speakers and Paula's ability to see or hear what was going on around her was terminated.

All that was left was to unfasten her ankles from the rings in the floor, affix the ankle cuffs connected by an 18" chain to her legs, and she was ready for transport.

The same procedure was followed for the remaining four girls. It took about fifteen minutes per girl and so the work was done in a little over an hour and twenty minutes. Only the thin, blond girl gave them any trouble. She wailed and screamed when her gag was removed. She swung her body in an attempt to free herself. Yvonne had a hard time getting hold of her nipples because of her small tits. Finally, she gave up and just gave the girl a solid blow to her solar plexus. She opened her mouth easily after that as she fought for air. Carla waited until she was breathing somewhat regularly before administering the hood.

It had all gone pretty typically. Once all of the girls were hooded, Yvonne spoke to Santo about the price for Paula. Primo slice went for about $25,000. Paula was pretty near to primo, but not quite. Her thighs were a little heavy and her nose a little too thick. There was a slight scar on her right arm from a skating accident. Yvonne offered Santo $17,500. Santo responded with $24,000. They settled on $22,500.

The cash was in a safe in the truck. Due to their extended business arrangements, Yvonne and Carla had little worry that Santo's men would make off with it. The trade in female flesh was worth about 80 to 100 grand a month. That bought a lot of guacamole. No one would fuck that up.

Santo's men helped escort the bound and hooded ladies to their travel accommodations. Each of them slung one of the girls over his shoulder and brought her up the stairs to the loading dock. Yvonne took one of them herself while Carla brought back upstairs the carton of bondage materials.

When they reached the loading dock, Yvonne and Carla placed the girls in the specially made lockers inside the van. They mewed and whined while they stood around waiting to be confined. Naked and helpless, bound and blinded, their pretty breasts swayed and bounced as they shivered in fear.

The lockers for the girls were mounted on both sides of the van's interior and there was room for ten sluts. Sometimes Mary Ellen's girls made more than one stop and came back with the truck almost filled. Tonight, once Paula and her sisters in travail were safely ensconced in their tiny, sound proof lockers, five of the lockers would still be empty.

It was customary to settle up once all the girls had been loaded. Yvonne brought out six bands of hundred dollar bills from the safe in the back of the van. The bill for tonight was $104,500. Paula had been the next to highest valued of this lot. Linda Harrington, one of the girls from the car that had been kidnapped, had made top dollar at $27,000. She was a beautiful girl with full, well formed breasts and a lovely face. Her hips were slender and her thighs were well trimmed and graceful. She was primo slice indeed. The lowest was the somewhat scrawny blond, Abby Taylor. She was one of the girls from the apartment. Mary Ellen had evaluated her at $16,500, but Yvonne found an appendectomy scar that had not been shown on the photos. Santo knocked $1,000 off her price.

Yvonne handed Santo twenty-one of the banded 100's. There were fifty in each band equaling $5,000. She took five hundreds from another band and handed the rest to Santo. That was that. Their business for the night was concluded.

"Hey, Yvonne," Santo said as the women prepared to leave the loading platform and get in the passenger portion of the van. "I forgot to tell you, I got two more chicas to load in your van."

"What are you talking about, Santo," Yvonne replied.

"Two more sluts. That's what I'm talking about."

Yvonne noticed that there were seven men on the loading platform and two women. Two of the men were blocking the stairs to the van. Two of the men were between her and Carla. Two men were next to Santo and had produced from somewhere two Tasers.

"Don't fuck around, Santo," Yvonne said.

"I'm not fucking around, *chicita*," Santo replied. "You're going for a little ride."

"Bullshit, Santo," Yvonne returned. "You and what army?"

Yvonne always carried a little equalizer under her shirt behind her back. It was only a small Beretta semi-automatic, .25 caliber. It held eight rounds. But Yvonne was a deadly shot and never missed.

Carla was watching and listening with apprehension. One of the men with the Tasers was heading towards her. The other was approaching Yvonne. There was only a second to act.

Yvonne reached her right arm behind her back as she ducked to get away from the Taser. The man shot it at her but missed. Carla tried to move away too, but her man hit his mark and she collapsed to the ground, screaming and shaking like an epileptic.

It was Carla's scream that did it. Yvonne had the .25 out and ready for use, but when she heard Carla scream, she turned her head to look. One of Santo's men leapt at her just as she was turning her head back. The shot went wild and Yvonne went down. Three men were on her at once. She struggled and fought them, getting off three more ineffectual shots in the process.

"Shit!" Santo yelled. "Get the fucking gun, *stupidos!*"

One of the men had hold of Yvonne's arm and was trying to pry it loose from her hand. Another had her other arm and was twisting it behind her back. The four combatants rolled over the cement floor of the landing dock. Finally, when Yvonne managed to regain a sitting position, one of the men let fly a right jab just under her chin. Her lights went out.

Two of the men already had Carla's clothes half off. She was recovering from her shock as they pulled her blouse free of her arms revealing her plain white sports bra. One of the men had her pants and white bikini panties around her ankles. The problem was Carla's heavy work boots. One held Carla's torso down while the others, trying not to look at her blond shrouded puss, attempted to unlace her boots. Carla was not defeated yet. She grabbed the man holding her torso by his shirt and pulled him towards her, knocking her forehead against his nose. The man screamed and released her. Once freed from his grasp, Carla rose to a sitting position and cracked one and then the other of the two men at her feet with fierce chops to their necks.

Carla carried a snub-nosed .38 police special in an ankle holster on her right leg. The problem was that the men had her pants around her ankles and she couldn't get it out. If she had, the party would have been over.

One of the men had rifled through the carton containing the bondage equipment and pulled out two of the belts that Carla had applied to the five prospective slave girls. He tossed one to the men holding Yvonne, who was starting to recover from the blow to her chin. He ran over to Carla with the other one. Santo was just standing there, amazed that six of his men could not subdue two bitch dykes.

The man whose nose Carla smashed leapt at Carla and took her back down to the dirty, concrete floor. While he struggled with her, blood flowing freely all over him and the defiant blond woman, the other men wrapped the bondage belt around her waist. They got her left arm into one of the confining manacles easily. The other was a bit more of a problem. They had to hit her upper arm three times before she collapsed in pain and were able to get it in place so that it too could be confined.

Yvonne's wrists had already been confined. She was yelling and screaming as the men tried to disrobe her. One of them had gotten her pants unbuckled and the zipper down. The other had ripped open her shirt, revealing a frilly, white, lace bra and the size 34D mammaries held in by them.

The men dealing with Carla had managed to get her turned on her belly. One of the men was sitting on her back and another on her legs. The third man was removing her boots. She was screaming and yelling at the men. "You cocksuckers! Fuck you, you assholes! Fuck you! Let me go or I'll kill you, you motherfuckers!" But Carla's resistance was about over.

Yvonne, on the other hand had just begun to fight. When the man who undid her zipper tried to drag her pants down, she kneed him in the face. He recoiled and she gave him her boot, sending him sprawling. The man undoing her shirt looked up in surprise. Yvonne spun away from him and rose quickly to her feet. While not yet a black belt, Yvonne had been training in Tae Kwon Do karate. Since her arms were confined, she had only her feet with which to defend herself and her lover. She gave the man a solid blow to his head with her boot. He went down with a groan. The man who she had kicked a moment before was just getting to his feet and she gave him a toe in the middle of his forehead. The third man who was helping, or rather trying to help them subdue her, backed away.

Santo was beside himself and cursing and yelling at his men in pungent, Dominican slang. Yvonne took a good look at him, hatred in her eyes. She stepped closer to him, backing him up against the wall. He raised his hands in a gesture of self defense. Just as Yvonne started to raise her leg and give him as close to a lethal blow as she could, her pants fell down. Her leg caught in the loosened garment and she went to the floor again. The man she had not yet kicked jumped on her. One of the other men had recovered and he jumped on her too.

Santo picked up Yvonne's discarded .25 caliber Beretta. He eased back the hammer and placed it at her head.

"Cut the shit, Yvonne, or I'll blow your brains out."

CHAPTER EIGHT

Amanda Billingsgate always considered herself as a hard luck kind of girl. The most recent development in her life had, done nothing to disprove that.

Eighteen months ago she was on the brink of a breakthrough in her career. She had picked up modeling when she was sixteen and had gone through all the cattle calls and interviews only to hear each time the man or woman in charge of casting tell the photographer or the director of the video or commercial, that, "No, she's not the type we're looking for," or "I think she's a little too tall," or "I think she's a little too short."

Amanda considered herself just right thank you, and as far as being the right type, well her family had plenty of money and plenty of class. Her father was on the board of three companies and was a runner up for the right to represent Margate in the recent by-elections. It wasn't his fault that the Conservatives were taking it on the chin that year.

And so, she had finally been called back for a second look for this cosmetics campaign. The art director loved her straight, jet black hair, her little upturned nose and her saucy grin. She was the right body type for their market, he said, 5'3" tall, well developed up top and wide, curvaceous hips. Don't get me wrong, Amanda didn't have to work for a living. It was just that she wanted her own career, her own money, so she wouldn't have to hear from her father that she shouldn't stay out so late, drink so much or spend so much money. She was 18, after all! She needed her own apartment, her own car and the freedom to come and go as she pleased.

It was the night before they were supposed to do some test shooting that it happened. She had been over the house of the director, a 50ish, peevish sort of fellow, thin and definitely gay. It was a small party, just ten or so people. There had been a man there who kept staring at her. It was getting late and she wanted to be fresh for the next day's shoot and so Amanda left the party early. She had parked her car about three blocks from the director's apartment.

As she was walking, a car pulled up to her and she heard a voice call out, "Excuse me, miss, can you tell me where Lancaster Court is?"

It was dark at that part of the street and no one else was around. Amanda didn't notice those things at the time. She stopped, approached what looked to her like a Bentley, and leaned over to respond to the man's question. Too late did she notice that it was the man from the party. She was about to tell him what for when the rear driver's door opened and a man stepped out. She looked at him and the turned back to the man from the party and started to say, "What's going on here?" when he sprayed something in her face. All she remembers after that was feeling dizzy and two strong hands guiding her into the car.

That was 18 months ago. After her slave training, she was purchased by an elderly man who mostly wanted to look at her naked body and receive foot massages from her. She was with him for two weeks when he died of a heart attack during one of her foot rubs. His son was a miserable creep who treated her dismally. He beat her all the time, fucked her raw and loaned her out to his friends at parties.

The son must have gotten on someone's nerves for, after seven months as his prisoner, someone shot him on the way home one night.

There were no close relatives and so Amanda reverted back to her slave house. After a few weeks of harsh 'retraining' there, which was quite unfair since she hadn't done anything wrong, she was purchased by a wealthy, good looking young man. On the first night as his sexual servant, Amanda thanked her lucky stars. He was a great lover, had a natural grace and politeness about him and treated her like a prized possession. Amanda thought that she had made it at last. Her mistake.

About three weeks after she joined the man's household, he had a guest, a tall, broad shouldered, bearded man. He looked ferocious and her master was very deferential to him. The long and the short of it was that the man complemented her master on his taste in slave girls. The next thing she knew he had given her to him. Can you believe it?

The man was as hard as iron and everybody who talked to him was afraid of him. He brought her back to his house in the city, whipped her unmercifully and then savaged her rear. He spent three days ravaging her. He would go out, leaving her bound and gagged in some tiny, little cage, come back drunk and deliver another night of pain and unhappiness to her.

They left the city after three days. It took a long time in getting to the man's estate. Amanda had no idea how long or where they had gone. She spent the journey hogtied and gagged in the trunk of his car. It was a huge estate with ponygirls and everything. One of the other slave girls told her that his name was Axmail Grobgy and that he was this big Russian gangster. Amanda hoped that now they were at his estate, she could fade into the woodwork. But, no, he had developed a thing for her and she was assigned to him full time, 24 hours per day. Not that he didn't fuck and abuse the other slave girls too. He did that plenty. His main focus, however seemed to be on causing Amanda misery.

Finally, two months later, he got tired of her. But rather than being sent down to the general slave girl pool, one of his bodyguards took a hankering to her and she found herself for the next three months a barracks whore. Talk about cocks! She must have serviced 15 or 20 per day. And those guys liked to fuck long and hard. When they were finally done with her on one shift and placed her in her cage so she could rest, it seemed another crew got off duty and was ready to party.

A few weeks ago, she was finally set free from the barracks. She got a job in the main dining room serving meals to the staff. She had to give the occasional blow job, a daily one for the cook, and, when her duties were done for the day, more often than not, one of the staff would have her sent up to his room. It wasn't so bad. She even found a little niche on the third floor where she could hide during breaks between meals. She had made friends with a blond haired Polish girl named Gilda who spoke almost no English. Amanda showed her her secret place and the two naked young girls often spent time there just holding hands or kissing.

Two days ago, Amanda had been scurrying across the main entrance hall on her way to her little hideaway. Lunch was over and she wasn't needed for an hour. Gilda had gone up before her. Amanda just knew that today they would make love to each other. Their kissing had gotten very passionate and Amanda thought that she was falling in love with the girl.

As she tried to hurry across the marble floor on her way upstairs before anyone noticed her, who should come barging in the front door but her owner, the master of the estate, Axmail Grobgy. Amanda shivered with fright at the sight of him. She increased her pace, but just as she got her foot on the bottom step of he stairs, she heard him yell, "Hey, you! Stop!"

"Oh, he can't mean me," Amanda tried to tell herself. But an ounce of caution is better than a pound of cure and so she turned to make sure she was right. Well, of course, she was wrong.

"Come here!" the man commanded in his booming voice. Amanda hurried to obey. He looked her over as if he had never seen her before. Then he had a look of recognition. "Come with me," he ordered.

Amanda followed the man outside. There was a cart there with two black tailed ponygirls in front of it. Amanda was scared to death of the ponygirls. They were all so big and strange looking. They spent their time naked, like she did, but they had no faces! Deep down inside, Amanda was afraid that someday someone would want to make her one. It would be just her luck!

Grobgy didn't say anything to her. He just tied her hands to a ring on the back of the cart. He went into the mansion and returned about twenty minutes later with a shield gag. Amanda didn't have to wear one when she worked in the dining hall because she had to be able to relay the staff's orders or answer questions about the specials. The huge man rudely shoved the gag into her mouth and locked it behind her head. He jumped on the cart, snapped the reins and off they went.

Amanda had never been a jock in school. The furthest she had ever run was down the hall to answer the telephone. Well, if you didn't include the slave reception center where she was held after she was first brought to this strange country. The men there made the women run, run, run around the courtyard. It was awful.

The cart took off like a shot. Amanda struggled to keep up with it. Her feet were bare and it hurt to slap them down on the macadam trail. After a few minutes, gasping for breath, her lungs screaming, she realized that they we headed for the ponygirl park. She had seen them congregating there during the racing season. Then it struck her. They were going to turn her into a ponygirl!

Amanda was too out of breath to cry, but her heart sank and a great fear rose up in her belly. "Oh my god! Oh my god!" she thought. From fashion model to ponygirl in less than two years! It was bad enough that her modeling career had crashed. You can't do much modeling when you're naked all the time, and tattoos across your chest and belly were hardly a fashion statement, even if one was a way cool, roaring lion. At least they had let her keep her name. And now no one would even be able to see her face, the face that was going to launch her as a cosmetics model. It was just her luck.

When the cart finally pulled up at its destination, Amanda thought she was going to die. Her sides hurt and she didn't think she would ever be able to take a regular breath again. Her owner leapt down from the cart and came around to untie her from it. Keeping her wrist bracelets fastened together, he dragged her into a camp site.

Amanda looked up and saw a little, misshapen man and a tall, fearsome looking ponygirl. The man was sitting in a chair by the door of a long caravan. The pony was kneeling in the grass next to him. He was running his hand laconically across her head. Amanda's breath had recovered enough so that she could break out in uncontrollable tears.

Grobgy, still holding her bound wrists looked at her quizzically. "What the fuck is wrong with you?" he said.

The frightened slave girl didn't know what to say, so she just continued to cry. She hadn't been so scared since the night she found herself naked and in a cage back in London, her hands bound behind her back and a big, fat gag in her mouth.

Grobgy just stared at her perplexed. Jerzi, who had been sulking, stood when the cart driven by Grobgy arrived and stared at the girl. Lightning, awoken from a state of disassociation from reality that ponygirls are so good at, was surprised to hear English spoken. She hadn't heard that much English in months.

Amanda continued to cry. Grobgy yelled at her, "Stop crying or I'll whip you!"

The disconsolate slave girl sank to her knees. Forlornly, she begged her master, "Eeee ooooon ake e a ony url, eeee!"

"What?" Grobgy returned.

"Eeee oooon ake e a ony url, eeeeeee!" Amanda repeated desperately.

Grobgy, exasperated, reached down and undid the slave girl's gag. "Now what did you say?"

"Oh, please don't make me a ponygirl master, please! I'll do anything you want! I'll be good, I promise! Please! Please!"

Grobgy issued forth a deep, hearty laugh. "You're not going to be turned into a ponygirl," he got out despite his mirth. "You're here to take care of a ponygirl!"

The young, British, former aspiring model looked at her master with a mixture of relief and confusion. "Thank you, master!" she said. "Thank you!" And then she added, "But I don't know how to take care of a ponygirl!"

"You'll learn," Grobgy replied, "or you'll be beaten to within an inch of your life. Understand?"

A wave of fear swept through the girl. Here it was again. Just when she had gotten settled, the world turned upside down once more. Her tears started anew.

"Wait a minute, Axmailavich," Jerzi interrupted in Russian. "She can't take care of Lightning! She doesn't know anything about ponygirls! What about the slave girls from one of the teams that didn't make the tournament? One of them can take care of Lightning!"

"Well, that's just the thing, Jerzi," Grobgy answered him. "I asked all of the drivers and not one of them was willing to lend you one of their slaves. It seems your reputation in tormenting slave girls has spread far and wide."

"But you can make them," Jerzi blurted out. "Make them do it!"

"I thought of that. If I did it, no driver would want to drive for me again. No, the best I could do is get one of the other drivers to lend you a slave girl for a day or so. She'll teach this one...," he paused for a moment and lifted the slave girl's chin so that he could see her chest, "...Amanda, what to do."

"She can't learn what she needs to learn in a day. I'll bet she doesn't even speak Russian," Jerzi continued to protest. He turned to the unhappy girl. "Do you speak Russian?" he said to her in his native tongue.

Amanda just looked at him. "Huh," she said, in English, of course.

"See what I mean," Jerzi said.

"You'll take her because I said so, Jerzi!" Grobgy said angrily. "You'll take her because if you don't, I'll rip your midget head off and feed it to the pigs! Got that!"

Jerzi was taken aback by Grobgy's anger. "I, I, I'm not a midget, I'm a dwarf," he said defensively. "There's a big difference."

"I don't care if you're a cross between a donkey and a chimpanzee!" Grobgy yelled back at him. "The girl stays!"

Jerzi was cowed into silence. He was in deep shit already because of what Natasha had done. He didn't want to make it worse.

Calmer now, Grobgy said to Jerzi, "Yuri's lending you one of his girls for 24 hours. Her name is Dora. She speaks a little Russian, I'm told, and a little English so you should get along fine."

"A little Russian? A little English?" Jerzi asked. "How little?"

"I don't know," Grobgy answered, "but you'll have to make due and that's all there is to it. Now I'm going back to the mansion and get a good blow job to take my edge off. Otherwise I might murder somebody. Somebody about four feet tall. Understand?"

"Yes, Axmailavich," Jerzi answered dolefully.

Both Jerzi and Amanda watched with great apprehension Grobgy jump up on the driver's seat of the pony cart and pull away. When he was out of sight, their eyes met each other's

"She's not bad looking," Jerzi thought. "I wonder how well she fucks."

"What an ugly, little man," Amanda thought. "I can't believe I'm going to have to fuck him!"

There was one thing that had to be gotten out of the way immediately. The girl needed to be taught what disobedience would bring. "Get down on your hands and knees and put your forehead on the ground," Jerzi told the slave girl curtly.

She obeyed immediately. There were only two reasons for the little man to order her to assume this posture: to whip her or to fuck her. Amanda didn't know which one she feared most.

Jerzi went over to the caravan where he hung the whips. He selected a three foot long riding crop. He stepped back over to the girl and addressed her in heavily accented English. "My name is Jerzi. While you are assigned to me, my word is like the word of God to you. You have been assigned the duty to take care of a very valuable ponygirl. When this girl Dora comes, you will watch her very closely and do everything that she says. She'll only be here for one day, so you better learn quick. Do you understand?"

"Y,yes, master," Amanda managed to squeak out.

"I'm going to give you five strokes of this riding crop so you will know what it will be like when you fuck up, which I'm sure that you will."

"Y,yes, master," Amanda said tearfully. "The way things are going," she thought, "he'll probably whip me and then fuck me too. Why do these things happen to me?"

Amanda had a soft, full ass. It was not hard and firm like the American girls'. In her former life, although she characterized herself as a model, she didn't work out or do exercises, or anything more strenuous than carrying a shopping bag. It kept her derriere pleasantly soft and a good place to absorb blows from a riding crop.

The dwarf raised his arm and delivered a resounding stroke to Amanda's ass. She was surprised by the strength of the little man. "Ohhhhhhhh!" she called out in pain. The crop left a solid red line across her rear cheeks.

"Whack!" Another blow fell. This one hurt more than the first. "Oooooowwwwwwww!" the girl yelled. "Ooooooooo! Master!" she said.

"Shut the fuck up, slut!" Jersey told her angrily. "If you talk again out of turn, I'll give you five more!"

Amanda just hung her head and remained quiet. The third and fourth blows came in rapid succession. "Ahhhhhhhhhh!" Amanda cried out. "Ahhhhhoooouuugh!"

Jerzi put all his strength in the last one. "Whack!" The blow fell across Amanda's already red lined posterior.

"Ohhhhhhh! Ohhhhhhh! Ohhhhhhhhhhhhhh!" Amanda screamed.

The five strokes being done, Jerzi walked over to the caravan and replaced the riding crop on the hook near the door. He turned back and saw the red lined ass of the new slave girl. It was quite attractive. She was moaning and crying pitiably. Her full breasts swayed under her as she expressed her unhappiness. He didn't have anything else to do, so he decided to fuck her.

Amanda heard the cruel dwarf coming back to where she knelt. "Open your legs wider," he said roughly.

"Oh my god, he's going to fuck me!" she thought. "Just like I predicted!"

She obediently made her legs go wider and arched her back to make her hairless cleft more available. She felt the little man's hands slide over her still fiery rear and she gave a little jump from the pain. The hands continued to glide over her round hips and then over the backs of her thighs. They descended down the tender flesh and then up again.

The man's hands were rough and scratchy to Amanda's soft skin. They were small, but strong, she could tell that. The slave girl knew that no matter how distasteful the thought of it was, she needed to stop crying and make herself ready for his cock. She went to that place where slave girls go to excite themselves for their masters. She thought of all the wonderful fucks she had had before she was stolen from her life. There was Philip. He was handsome and really rich. He had done her in her parent's bedroom during a party and made her squeal with pleasure. Tom had a motorcycle. When she rode it, the vibrations of the engine made her hot. When they got to his flat, she tore his clothes off. Robert seemed a little stuck up at first, but he mouthed her for what seemed like hours. It was that wild Irish bloke, though, Sean, that really got to her. His cock was long and thick and he could go on and on and on. "Mmmmmmmm," she thought as she remembered it. Her slit began to moisten obediently. Suddenly, the coarse hands on her body were Sean's, the cock that was going to enter her was his too. She couldn't wait!

Jerzi drew the fly to his pants down and freed his manhood. It had already thickened and grown. He had fucked Natasha so many times that he almost forgot what it was like to fuck a beautiful girl. He passed his hand between her thighs and tested her slit. It had grown slick with the girl's lubrication. Her hairless labia had become engorged with blood. "She's a hot one," he thought. "Maybe Grobgy will let me keep her after the tournament," he thought, hopefully.

He placed the tip of his cock at the gates to the girl's crevasse and slowly pushed himself in. Her pussy was hot and soft. As he slid himself home, he felt her tighten herself and give his cock a gentle squeeze. "Not bad," he thought. "Not bad at all."

Amanda felt the little man's cock press at her pussy. In her mind, it was still Sean's. As it passed further inside her and pushed aside her pussy's walls, she opened her eyes. She had expected the little man to have a little dick. He didn't. It was thick, and by the way he was lowering himself to her depths, it was long. "Who would have thought," she mused. She clenched her pussy muscles to give him a little thrill and she heard him sigh appreciatively. "Maybe if he likes the way I fuck, he won't beat me as much," she thought. She decided, even though her ass still burned from her whipping, to give him a good time.

Jerzi's eyes turned to slits as the slave girl's cunt pleasured him. Her hips thrust back at his in perfect unity. When he speeded up, she speeded up too. When he slowed down, she eased her motions to match him. Her pussy kept caressing his cock, clamping down on it on every inward stroke. After a while, she gave out a low moan and her body shivered. Her cunt throbbed around his cock. She was coming.

The slave girl felt her orgasm building shortly before it hit. She was surprised how aroused the little man made her. She groaned when she came and her pussy's contractions filled her with pleasure. It was just a precursor though, she knew, to the one that she would have when the little man shot her full of his spunk.

The little man decided that he wanted to sample the new slave girl's ass. After her orgasm subsided he slid his cock from her warm environs. She gave a little moan of disappointment. He positioned it a little higher and pressed down on her rear cheeks. Easing them apart, he centered his cock on her brown star and slowly, but surely, worked his way in.

The removal of the thick manhood from her pussy made Amanda wonder what the little man was up to. When she felt his hands spreading her rear cheeks and pressing her hips downwards, she knew. Only Nigel had ever done any ass fucking with her. She thought it was naughty but it didn't really do anything for her. In her training, she had, of course, been subjected to it a hundred times it seemed. Some of the men knew how to bring her mild pleasure there, most of them couldn't have cared less. It was the same thing after she was released. The creep who owned her just shoved himself in and came, but the guy just before her current owner was really good at it, making her purr with a strange contentment. Her present owner raped her ass with a violence that astounded her. It was usually after a cruel beating, much worse than the one the little man had given her. She was anxious to see what he could do.

She was not disappointed. He entered her slow and easy, giving her time to relax her muscles. His thrusts were long and slow, dragging his cock across the entrance its full length before burying it deep inside her once more. His pace increased steadily, allowing her to follow him along. And when she heard him panting and groaning, his thrusts becoming stronger and harder, she thought she was going to lose her mind. "Ohhhhh! Ohhhhhhh! Ohhhhhh!" she called out as her pussy exploded with joy. This was a first! He had made her come by fucking her ass! Her cunt throbbed and sent delicious messages of ecstasy through her body. "Here it comes! Here it comes! Here it comes again!" she screamed in her head. Just as her pussy began another celebration, the little man groaned deeply and his cock began to shoot his hot cream into her bowels. "Ohhhhhhh! God, yes!" she screamed. "Oh, yes! Yessssssss!"

She knew that she shouldn't be speaking. He had warned her about that. She couldn't help it; it felt so good.

Two days later, she was standing in the middle of a crossroads in the ponypark at the Fall Tournament grounds bawling her eyes out. She was lost. Jerzi had sent her to pick up his dinner at the drivers' canteen. It had taken her a half hour to find it. There had been a long line of slave girls all waiting for the same thing, pushing and shoving, cutting into line. One of the masters pulled a girl aside and gave her a lashing for causing too much trouble. Amanda finally reached the window. Jerzi's meal ticket was dangling from her slave collar and the woman there took the ticket and then draped a steel food container around her neck so that she could take it back to her master. Amanda was surprised to see a woman working there who wasn't a slave girl. She was older, maybe 55 or so, and had a dress on. How nice it would be to wear clothes again, she thought as she watched her work. She was a little embarrassed to be naked in front of her. But all the other slave girls were naked too and, in the end, it really didn't matter.

The woman had to drape the dinner pot around her neck because her hands were bound behind her, like all the other slave girls. And now she couldn't ask directions because of her gag. All the slave girls were wearing them. It was as if the place had come down with some kind of epidemic that only struck pretty, naked, young women and the mouth and chin covering shield gags were their protection.

In fact, it was by a strictly enforced regulation that unaccompanied slave girls, not only in the ponypark, but anywhere inside the fairgrounds, be bound and gagged. It would be so easy for a slave girl to slip into the public camping areas and, when no one was looking, steal some clothes and try to make an escape. Within the ponypark it was a matter of standard practice to cut down on stealing and the spreading of rumors by errant slave girls. It is sad to say that some masters were not above sending their slave girls into another driver's camp to pilfer supplies and other worldly goods.

Amanda had never seen so many slave girls, never mind ponygirls, in one place at one time. There were plenty of both. The slave girls seemed to come in all sizes and flavors. Some showed the wear and tear of their bondage to cruel ponygirl drivers, others looked as clean and as fresh as Amanda did.

The place seemed to Amanda a mass of confusion. Blue, red, green, red and white, green and white, purple, almost every color and color combination you could think of came by on the head of a naked ponygirl or ponygirls hauling a cart or a carriage. It scared her when they dashed by pulling a nine pony landau. They made a rumbling sound as they ran and kicked up a lot of dust. Amanda had to dive out of their way.

It took a very capable driver to negotiate that size team at that speed along the roadway between the encampments.

Amanda knew she was going to get another beating. She had had two already today. One was for not putting Lightning's racing harness on correctly. The other was at lunch time when, like now, she had gotten lost.

"Why did I have to be going up the stairs back at the mansion just when that monster, Grobgy, was coming in?" Amanda thought to herself miserably. "It was just my luck! Here I had a decent berth for a change and, presto, it was gone! It's not fair!"

Amanda, although fair of mien, was no Rhodes Scholar. She had watched the slave girl, Dora, make the ponygirl's meal, put on and take off her various harnesses, shave her head and loins, and a few other things. But the mass of information she received befuddled her. It was too much responsibility!

There were two ameliorating aspects of her transfer to her new responsibilities, however. The first, ironically was the ponygirl herself. Amanda had followed Dora's lead with trepidation when she gave the pony a rubdown. The pony's strong, tall, broad shouldered body was laid out on a 4' high, padded board. Her hands were disconnected from the strap that led down from the back of her ponygirl collar and locked to a ring at the top of the board. This was done only after the pony's eyelets had been closed since it was a basic rule that ponygirls not be permitted to view their own hands, which, for all practical purposes, they no longer possessed.

First they did her back and the back of her thighs. Amanda watched with amazement as Dora kneaded the pony's muscles, applying liberally a relaxing salve. She told Amanda to give it a try. The young slave girl thought that the pony's body was amazing. Her thighs were incredibly strong as were her shoulders. She had never been near a female that muscular. In spite of her attraction to Gilda, who she would probably never see again, Amanda had never thought of herself as having those tendencies, although she, like all other slave girls, had been trained in Sapphic techniques, but handling the ponygirl's body made her wet.

Dora had the ponygirl flip over and they then worked on her front. Amanda saw how the other slave girl guided the ponygirl with a modicum of verbal commands. The ponygirl seemed to know what she wanted her to do by instinct.

It was the front of the ponygirl that really got her hot. She ran her hands over the steel hard front of her thighs and felt a tremor run through her. She rubbed the salve into her tight, firm belly with its tattoo of the yellow, rampant wolf. She massaged the fronts of her shoulders. All the while, the pony sighed and moaned, enjoying the attention to her body. Each expression of pleasure by the muscular creature made Amanda's pussy tingle.

When she got to the breasts, she was breathing heavily. Dora had noticed her arousal. She smiled. "Hot, eh?" she asked, in her rough, accented English.

"Oh, yeah!" Amanda replied. She massaged the large firm globes tenderly. The pony's nipples were stiffened. Her breasts seemed like two mounds of friendly, resilient sponge. No, firmer than that, like padded sponges, heavenly to manipulate.

The driver had instructed the slave girls to bring the pony to orgasm. Amanda had recoiled at the command. But now she was eager to get her lips on the twin toys and to feel the pony's hot skin on hers. She gave Dora a glance and the other slave girl grinned and gave her an encouraging nod.

The British slave girl leaned forward and captured one of the pony's nipples between her lips. Her heart began to thump in her chest as she luxuriated in the sensation of the hot button being kneaded by her tongue and lips. She was lying between the pony's outstretched legs and she could feel the heat of the pony's belly on her breasts. She shifted to the pony's other enticing mound while carefully wrapping a hand around the breast her lips abandoned, stroking and massaging it. The ponygirl gave out a moan of pleasure from behind its sealed lips. Its blue, faceless head shifted from side to side dreamily.

After sating her lust for the pony's large, round globes, Amanda began to lower her body so that she could gain access to its loins. She ran her lips over the tight belly of the pony, caressing the sides of its torso with her hands. When she found her face between the ponygirl's powerful thighs, she drank in the aroma of the pony's arousal, the sight of her gleaming divide and the smooth, clean lines of her outer labia. Guiding the lean, hard thighs further apart, Amanda brought her lips and tongue to bear on the pony's stiffened love button, sucking at it softly, gently running her tongue over it. Her hands were on the tender skin of the inside of the pony's thighs and she caressed them while her lips and tongue worked laconically on the pleasure bud. Lightning moaned and shifted her hips. Her breathing was getting heavy.

The slave girl wanted the pony's pleasure to last a long time. She lowered her lips and dragged her tongue along the cleft between her engorged love lips. Drinking in the moisture of the pony's arousal made her swoon with passion. She felt a soft hand alight on her round, rear cheeks, caress them gently and then descend between her legs from the rear. She spread her legs automatically giving the older slave girl access to her quim. When her fingers found it and began to tease her crevasse, she gave a moan of her own.

Amanda worked the pony's pussy for a long time. She licked the length of the dilated gash and thrust her stiffened tongue deep within her recesses. She sucked long and hard on her clit while teasing it with little flicks of her tongue. Surrounding the pony's love lips with her hands, she squeezed the hairless love lips together and massaged them, watching her oozing moisture spill out.

Dora's administration to Amanda's pussy was having its effect. The former aspiring model issued a long, low moan as she continued to work the pony's pussy. She was determined that they should come together. When she felt her crisis rising, she accelerated her oral efforts on the pony's quim. Lightning arched her back and raised her knees, spreading them on either side of her like wings. She was wearing her leather shield gag and Amanda could hear her low pitched groans of pleasure as they escaped it. The pony began to buck and shake. Amanda felt her cunt give her a powerful throb of pleasure. Its contractions struck her again and again.

Lightning kept moaning and shaking as if her orgasm would go on forever. Amanda kept up her assault on her sex, even as she was experiencing delirious delight of her own. The small campground resounded with the two females' groans of pleasure.

Gradually, their spasmodic motions slowed and the throbbing of their pussies receded. Amanda fell forwards, her face on the pony's belly and circled her arms around her hips. "Oh, that was great!" she said.

Dora looked around nervously. Jerzi had gone on an errand, probably to go drink with his buddies. It was only because she did not expect the dwarf back that Dora had brought the younger girl to pleasure. If he had caught her doing it, and Amanda experiencing it, they both would have been whipped severely.

Over the last two days, Amanda had taken every opportunity for physical contact between her and the ponygirl. In the morning, after her head had been shaved and her loins denuded of its daily growth, she made the pony come with her hand while watching with lascivious interest her body squirm and writhe with pleasure.

It was disconcerting for her to see the pony's pale, bald head beneath its hood. She rubbed the moisturizing lotion into it with gentle, caring hands. Dora explained very insistently how the ponygirl's face was never to be looked at or exposed to others. "Is for pony, too," she said in her broken English. "Nothing is private for ponygirl except face. It is her honor. If no one can see face, she could be anybody, any former woman. Old self is preserved, you see?"

Amanda knew exactly what the older slave girl was talking about. Perhaps, she thought, in this respect a ponygirl had it better than a slave girl who could not pretend that she was some new creature unrelated to her past life. Nothing was private for a slave girl, nothing. Was preserving some dignity worth all the other travails the ponies suffered? She doubted it. But it was something.

The second thing that assuaged the cruelties that Amanda had suffered at the hands of the cruel dwarf was his cock. She could not figure out why, but his thick manhood, so incongruous on such a diminutive figure, fascinated her. The man was a walking oxymoron! The first time she sucked it, she almost creamed. The second time she did. To feel it coursing along her paths of pleasure was electrifying. Amanda gave out great, violent moans when the little man, as she thought of him, made her come. She could not get enough of his cock.

But in all other respects, the little man was cruel and callous. On her first night in the camp on the Grobgy estate, several of his cronies dropped by, probably just to see and fuck his new slave girl. They took turns plowing her orifices. One of the men fucked her face so hard that he bruised her lips. She had to kneel bent over in the dust amidst the dancing light of the night fire while being possessed from behind like some animal. One pierced her rear passage brutally, making her squeal with pain. Another lay her on her back and fucked her with her knees bent back against her chest, his foul tongue in her mouth.

Afterwards, the little man ordered her to go clean herself up. She took some soap down to a spigot on the edge of the ponypark and rinsed and washed her abused pussy and rear. God help her though, when she returned and the little man bent her over and slipped his seemingly magical cock into her, she was overwhelmed with lust and came again and again.

He made her sit in a tiny little cage when he was off doing whatever he did. He kept a gag in her mouth almost all the time except when he was using her mouth for his pleasure or so she could eat, and, except when she had work to do, he kept her hands bound behind. She spent the seven hour drive from the Grobgy estate to the fairgrounds lodged in her little steel prison inside the caravan, hooded, bound and gagged. And it seemed that he whipped her every chance that he got.

All and all, Amanda rued the day she had not been fast enough to escape Grobgy's attention. Her life, from a general perspective, had turned to shit once again. Knowing that she had earned herself yet another whipping, the naked slave girl sat down at the side of the dirt trail, her hands helplessly bound behind her, her voice silenced by the mouth filling wad of leather, and cried.

* * * * * * * * * * * * * *

Back at the encampment, Jerzi was pacing nervously. Nothing was going as it should. The slave girl had disappeared. His food was late. Lightning was still suffering, although not as much, from her injury and a general malaise seemed to have come over the pony. It was like waiting for the next thing to go wrong.

The overnight journey to the tournament grounds had been uneventful. Lightning had been tied lying down in her pony trailer rather than made to stand for the trip. He slept while one of Grobgy's guards drove. He had to keep that pesky but delectable new slave girl all locked up lest she rattle around the trailer cleaning things like she did the two days they spent in camp.

She seemed to get along with Lightning, although she still had a lot to learn about taking care of her. He had to remind her of every little thing. When she got out the wrong harness for their practice run, he had blown his top and given her three fierce blows across her breasts with a switch to remind her to do better. At times, she seemed lost at sea. He had explained to her twice the directions to and from the canteen and still she had gotten lost again.

He had, as instructed by Grobgy, taken Lightning on a practice run around the track soon after they arrived in the encampment. The run had gone well. The doctor had made up a cushioned pad to place on Lightning's damaged foot with a hole cut out where the abrasion was to try and lessen the risk of reinjury. He was amazed at how little the pony physician knew about racing. He had to explain carefully to him why Lightning needed a pad in each shoe so that her gait would be even. Also, the first cushion he designed had to be rejected because it made the space in the boot too small for Lightning's foot. The doctor had prepared a modified version that seemed to work satisfactorily.

Of course, everyone knew about Lightning's injury and his role in it. It would not do much for his reputation and, unless he won the championship this year with her, he might go begging for a pony to drive next season. All in all, though, the workout had gone well. He had taken the pony on two leisurely laps around the track. Her gait seemed okay and when he brought her back to the encampment, her foot had seemed fine.

There had been an excited crowd in the grandstands and lining the rail. Although the first round of races would not begin until tomorrow, people came out to see their favorites take some practice laps. The ponies still wore their regular working rigs and would not be fully bedecked in their finery until the ponygirl parade which marked the opening of the tournament.

Lightning received a round of applause when she completed her first lap of the track and a stronger one when she finished her second. Jerzi made sure that the second lap was done at a brisk, if not all out pace. It wouldn't do for the other drivers to think that Lightning was vulnerable. They would go after her like sharks smelling blood, forcing her to go hard in the beginning of her races in an attempt to induce aggravation of her injury. The formal announcement, done in accordance with Racing Commission rules, was that she had suffered a small laceration of her foot and that it was not expected that the injury would have any effect on her ability to compete. Such announcements were designed to prevent gamblers with inside information taking advantage of the general betting public, a laudable but unenforceable goal.

There was something missing, though. The pony just didn't seem herself. He had treated her with velvet gloves since her injury and the slave girl, Amanda, was solicitous of her needs. Jerzi had been allowing the pony to receive regular orgasms from the slave girl, contrary to his usual practice. That would stop as of now. It was time to get tough. She would need all of her fierce determination to champion. His responsibility as her driver was to make sure that she had it.

He had been planning to have the slave girl harness the pony in her punishment rig when she got back, but he would have to do it himself now. Lightning was kneeling on the grass a small distance from his caravan. Her facial demeanor was, as always, inscrutable due to the blue hood that covered it. Nonetheless, her slumped shoulders and lack of interest in what was going on around her what was to him indicative of her malaise. When he had retrieved the leather halter, he proceeded to affix it to the pony's body, running the straps under her breasts and across her chest, over her shoulders and back again under her arms.

Lightning knew what being adorned with her punishment harness meant. A chill went through her body. She hated the whip. Her fear of it was what made her what she was today. If she had been able to draw on some inner reserve of courage, suffered the blows stoically, even unto death, she would not have taken the first step in the long journey to the beast she had become. Dreading the pain, unable to bear it, living in constant terror that it would be applied to her defenseless body yet again, had made her obsequiously follow every instruction, push herself beyond all endurance until almost everything had been taken away from her.

She had listened to the two slave girls talking the other day, conversing as if she were some beast unable to fathom the meaning of their words. Her face was her honor, the one had said. How true it was. At first, she had been distraught that she was a faceless animal for the men to use and abuse. After a while, though, she came to be glad that she could hide her inner thoughts, that her true identity was hidden beneath the soft, blue Neoprene that covered her face.

By now, it was anathema for her to consider showing her face to any of them and she cooperated fully in keeping it hidden every time her hood was removed to shave her head or clean her. Every day during racing season, her driver's slave girl would, while kneeling behind her, rub lotion over the skin of her face, massaging and caressing it. It was the only reminder that her face still existed. In a way, it was a symbol of her forlorn hope that someday she would be a person again, be able to laugh, talk, determine her own destiny. This meager hope would surface only for so long as the dehumanizing hood was free of her face. When she was readorned with the depersonalizing fabric, she would tuck that hope away as inappropriate for one who had to endure the torments of being a ponygirl.

That was what was wrong with her now. The new slave girl was soft and kind. She murmured happy pleasantries while she worked on her, calling 'pretty ponygirl" and "poor ponygirl". Unlike the scrawny slave who had put the stone in her shoe and was paying a price for her sin unknown to Lightning, this girl was kind and loving in her touch. It was too much for her to take. She needed her edge, the self-denial of her personhood, to feel at home in her role. And if she was not at home in her role, she could not compete with all the other ponygirls who were.

So, when the infernal punishment harness was strapped around her body, Lightning knew, in spite of the river of fear that flowed through her at the very thought of the whip, that she was about to receive what she deserved, what she needed. Her driver knew ponygirls well.

Jerzi used a stepstool to hoist the punishment harness up onto the gibbet-like pole set in the ground near the center of the encampment, about 20 feet away from the fire. He had to use all of his weight to pull her up so that she was standing on the tips of her booted toes. He got down and fixed her booted ankles together and to a ring in the ground so she could not dodge any of the blows. When he was done, he took the stepstool away and went and sat in his little chair, a bottle of vodka and a small glass on the table next to him.

Lightning's heart was beating hard in her chest as she stood poised to receive her punishment. She had cooperated docilely with her driver as he led her to the whipping post and affixed her to it. She fully expected her torment to begin as soon as he had tied her off and was surprised when she saw him take his seat. Her throat was dry and her stomach was rolling over. What was he waiting for? She wanted to get it over with even though she dreaded the thought of its commencement.

Jerzi sat in his chair downing shot after shot of Vodka for more than thirty minutes. It was getting dark. He interrupted his waiting game only long enough to throw a couple logs on the campfire.

The fire was blazing, casting weird shadows around the campground when Amanda finally showed up. She was led by a leash hooked onto her collar by one of the security men for the festival. He was youngish, tall and foreboding looking, with a broad back, a hard looking face and a pistol in a holster around his shoulder. Amanda looked sheep-like as she followed him.

"This one yours?" the man asked.

"She is," Jerzi answered, his frustration evident in his voice.

"I found her sitting by the side of the road, bawling her eyes out. It seems she got lost. Lucky she had the tag around her neck or I wouldn't have known where to bring her." All the slave girls had been issued tags to be attached to their collars indicating the name of the estate and the driver who they served. The campsite location was also set down. Lightning's was in area 12, camp 10. Unfortunately it was in Russian and in a position where the slave girl herself couldn't read it.

"You should be more careful," the man continued. "We've had a few slave girls go missing. I'm sure they'll turn up, but you wouldn't want your girl picked up as a runaway. You might not get her back."

"Okay, okay," Jerzi said. "Just leave her here."

"My suggestion is you have her buddy up with one of the slave girls from the camp next to you. This way she won't get lost again."

Jerzi nodded. His mind was on other things right now.

The guard released Amanda's collar from the leash. He gave her breasts a little tweak and then left.

Amanda cowered where the guard had left her. Jerzi looked at her with disdain. He noted the gleam of spilled sperm on the inside of her leg and assumed that the guard had taken the opportunity to enjoy his little slave girl before bringing her back to him. It would have served her right if a battalion of beefy security guards had fucked her as far as he was concerned.

He shot back a glassful of vodka and stood from his chair. He waved his hand, indicating that the slave girl should approach him. She moved towards him slowly, as if trying to assess whether he was going to beat her or not. When she stood in front of him, Jerzi made her bend over and then calmly took the steel food container from around her neck. He threw it across the campground. Amanda watched it clatter along the ground and the now cold food come pouring out of it. A wave of indignation arose within her. Had she gone through so much torment, fucked the guard and his two buddies, just to have the food which was the whole purpose of her trip tossed away like it was nothing? When her master turned back to her, however, all thought of protesting his callousness fled from her. His face was a mask of rage. She had never seen anyone so mad. Tears came to her eyes and her body began to shiver in fear.

"You think that this is all a game?" Jerzi shouted at her. "Do you think that this is playtime? Are you stupid or something? Do I have to whip you to the bone before you get it in your thick skull that you have an important job here?"

Amanda was cowering from the little man's onslaught. She was gagged and could not answer his questions. She also had her hands still bound behind her so that she couldn't defend herself if he decided to strike her. His hands were balled up into fists. Amanda's heart was thumping hard in her chest.

Jerzi's outburst seemed to calm him a little bit, but he was still a ball of restrained rage.

"Let me tell you how it is, fuckface," he threw out to her, his voice strained. "If I don't win the championship, I'm a dead man. Now, I don't expect you to give two shits about that, but it does affect you. If my life is on the line, then I am going to do anything necessary to get you to do the right things for me, even if I have to kill you doing it! And I mean that literally! Understand?"

Tearfully, Amanda nodded her head. Her lips were shaking. The little man was going to kill her, she just knew it! "Oh, god!" she thought. "What am I going to do?"

Jerzi continued his tirade. "As far as the ponygirl goes, I've seen you stroking and caressing her like she was your pet. Well, let me tell you, you're not fit to drink her piss! She's not a toy! She's a ponygirl! And you're fucking with her mind! Get it in your fucking head, this is not a person! She is not a human being all trussed up to look like a pony! She is a ponygirl and will never be anything else until the day that she dies! So what does that leave her, eh?"

Jerzi paused for emphasis. He saw the slave girl quaking but also the beginning of understanding in her eyes.

"This creature lives her life on a razor's edge," he told her, more quietly now, as if his rage had been vented. "If she does not succeed, there's no reason for her to exist. This pony is a champion and you're trying to take that away from her. She didn't become a champion by having someone be all lovey-dovey with her. She became a champion at the business end of a whip! If you take away her fear, she has northing left!" Jerzi's voice raised at the end as if his ire had been fueled all over again by the girl's stupidity.

"Now, I was going to give the pony a good whipping. She needs it and so do you," Jerzi said. "But I thought about it and thought of something better."

The dwarf stepped away from the girl and took a long, thin switch from a hook by the door to the caravan.

"I'm not going to whip her. You are."

Amanda's eyes lit up with shock. She was going to whip her? The distraught slave girl was horrified at the suggestion. She had been the victim of many a whipping since she had been enslaved. It had reduced her mind to servility. She had, after a long struggle, accepted her fate as a mere vehicle of pleasure. To take an active role in subduing the will of another human being, even if they called that human being a ponygirl, was anathema to her. She was a victim, not an oppressor! She wouldn't do it!

But Jerzi was not finished. "If you refuse, or if you fail to whip her with all of your might for as long as I say, you will have a very unhappy fate." he told her. His voice was low and ominous. Amanda saw from his face that he meant every word he said. She couldn't imagine what he meant by an unhappy fate. She had seen the slave girl they had buried up to her neck by the back door to the mansion the day before she was dragooned to be the little man's assistant. Would her treatment be worse than that? One of the girls said that she had been sent off to be tortured to death. Would Jerzi do that to her? His next words convinced her that he would.

"Have you ever seen anyone skinned alive? It's very painful. Do you think that I will let you continue your miserable existence if I have to die because you are a stupid fuck up!" He took a knife from his belt with his free hand and flicked its tip at the bottom of her right breast. Amanda jumped at the painful sensation. A line of blood started to trickle down it over her belly. She turned pale white.

"Do you understand?" Jerzi asked her again.

Frantic beyond rationality, Amanda nodded her head emphatically. She would do anything she had to to live.

The campfire had grown large and unruly in the mild wind that was coursing through the campsite. The shifting shadows it cast seemed like dancing demons drawn from Hades by the small man's tirade. Amanda was in a place she had never been before. Even in her life as a slave girl she had detached herself from everything that went around her. She was lost in her own little world with little thought for others. Since being assigned to care for the ponygirl, she had hardly given a thought to Gilda, the pretty Polish slave girl that she thought she was falling in love with. She realized that she was at a turning point of her life, one more dramatic and more important than being turned into a sex slave. She was passing from the role of one tormented to one of the tormentors. No longer could she pretend to herself or others that she was an innocent after this! She was going to whip the ponygirl. She knew that. She would whip her with all her might for as long as the little, devilish man said.

Jerzi made the slave girl turn around and unfastened her wrists from each other. He then removed her gag. "Come over here," he ordered her. Dolefully, Amanda obeyed. He brought her to where he had been sitting and poured out a shot of vodka into the glass he had been using. "Here," he said, "drink this."

The slave girl had not had a drop of alcohol since the night of her kidnapping. Her hand was shaking as she took the glass from him. She bent her head down and took a little sip. Jerzi reached out and, taking her wrist in his hand, tilted it back until the fiery liquid spilled into her mouth. She swallowed it in one gulp.

The alcohol burned her throat. Her mind swam with its intoxicating effect. Jerzi took the glass from her and poured another shot. He made her drink it all at once just like the first. Then he took the glass from her hand and gave her the whip.

Lightning had been following the interactions between the slave girl and her driver with more than academic interest. She had heard what her driver had said about being a ponygirl. No one had ever said those things in front of her before, at least not in English, but she knew what the cruel dwarf was saying was the truth. Without the whip, she could never be a ponygirl, never run until her heart gave out, never pull from herself what she was sure that she could not give. She shivered when she heard him say that she would be a ponygirl until the day that she died. She had thought as much. How could she ever be anything else after what she had been through anyway? Life could never return to normal for her. Her hands would always seem like strange, foreign appendages, her voice something surreal. Without someone to tell her what to do and where to go, how would she know how to live? What had been her 'real' life had been crushed out of her, and the life of a servile beast left in its place.

As to the slave girl, Lightning was glad that she would no longer be able to deny her complicity in her degradation. If Lightning had had a choice to accept what the masters deemed she should have or suffer the consequences of pain and death, so did the slave girl. She could have refused to shave her head or to apply the instruments of her dehumanization to her. She could have said no when told to administer her harness to her body, or to make her shake and groan with forced sexual pleasure. Pain and death would have followed, but that was the slave girl's choice, wasn't it, whether to die with honor, her innocence intact, or not.

Lightning quailed when she saw the slave girl advancing on her, whip in hand. Though she knew that the unreal spell the slave girl had cast on her by her kindly attentions had to be broken, she dreaded the pain and torment that she would soon feel. While under the lash, she would have betrayed anyone, done anything, agreed to any condition, in order to avoid it. Even now, she wanted to beg and plead, bargain with her oppressors, promise to be obedient and cooperative, anything that they wanted, knowing full well that even if she could it would be in vain.

As the girl raised her arm back to administer the first stroke, the ponygirl cringed. She closed her eyes within her concealing hood and braced for the blow. The lash struck across her belly, just above her tattoo. It burned like blazes and she gave out a deep, mournful moan. She opened her eyes only to take in the vision of the girl's arm coming forward once again. This time the lash was laid across her thighs. She moaned and tried to shift her bound legs, tried to sway her body to somehow mitigate the pain.

The slave girl's mind was swirling with emotion as she saw the evidence of her acts raised upon the flesh of the ponygirl. Two dark red lines had formed where the leather had torn into her skin. She paused, trying to regain her resolution to do what had to be done. The sight of the ponygirl's body squirming in her bonds, the sound of her anguished moans, made her hesitate. Then she heard the voice of her master.

"Again!" he shouted. "Harder! Whip her tits!"

His fiendish threats came back to her. She put her hand on her breast and felt the sticky residue of the teasing puncture of her skin from the little man's knife.

"Do it, cunt!" Jerzi shouted. "Do it or I'll put you up there and flay you until you are a bloody mass! Whip her again!"

Amanda reared the long, thin whip back once more and brought it forward with fierce determination. She didn't want to be whipped! It was the ponygirl or her! She would choose the ponygirl every time.

The third blow landed across Lightning's firm, rotund globes. Her body jerked stiffly straight as if she had been shot full of electricity. She shrieked into her gag. Her hands twisted behind her and she bit down on her gag with all of her might.

The slave girl didn't wait for another order to continue. The effects of the alcohol, her own terror, the force of the little man's will, all combined to make her eager to continue.

Another blow landed across Lightning's breasts, then her belly again and once more on her thighs. The ponygirl's body shifted in agonized contortions. Amanda was delirious, her body covered with sweat. Her breasts, gleaming with the light of the campfire, swayed and danced as she put her body into each blow of the whip. She struck the pony's belly one more time and the little man ordered her to stop.

"Turn her around and do her back!" he called out.

Amanda threw the whip to the ground and flew over to the ponygirl. She unfixed her ankles from the ring in the ground and spun the ponygirl until her back was presented for torment. After hooking the boots to the ring so that she could not move away from the blows, she picked up the whip again.

Jerzi had gotten up from his chair. He proffered her another shot of vodka. This time, Amanda took the glass with relish and poured the liquor down her throat. It burned, but a surge of determination, a liberating feeling of power, flowed through her. She drew back her hand and let fly, bringing the stiff whip to bear on the sobbing, piteous pony's back.

The devilish driver did not order the slave girl to stop until she had laid six more lashes across the pony's body. Her back, her rear and the back of her thighs were criss-crossed with long lines of red.

Amanda was out of breath. Her body was afire with passion and lust. A long strand of her jet black hair was plastered onto her sweaty face. Jerzi stood and grabbed the whip from her hands and threw it to the side.

"On your hands and knees!" he ordered her.

The demented slave girl dropped to the ground and assumed a subservient position. The dwarf tore off his boots and clothes. When he mounted her from behind, she could feel the heat of his small body lying against her ass, back and thighs. His cock delivered a wave of ecstasy to her. His powerful hands grabbed her hips and he began to plow her furrow with long, fierce thrusts. Amanda raised her head, opened her mouth, and roared her lust into the night.

CHAPTER NINE

Giancaro Franco did not make it a habit to be awake at the crack of dawn. More often, he was home sawing logs when the red rays of dawn peaked over the eastern seaboard of the United States. This day, however was special. A very important package, or rather a group of packages was being shipped east this morning at 6:52 a.m. from Newark International Airport, its destination, Kalikastan.

Earlier today, Mr. Franco, a made member of the Carillo crime family, had a meeting with two very distraught young women. Handling distraught people was one of Mr. Franco's talents. Big 'G', as he was known to his fellow denizens of the underworld and on numerous FBI wiretaps, was a master of the art of compromise. If you agreed to whatever he proposed, he would not blow your brains out.

The two women had been transported in the back of a large, brown van with the name "National Uniform Company" stenciled on its side. There were other guests in the back of the van, but Big G had no reason to discuss anything with them. They had nothing that he wanted beyond their physical selves, which he already had. No, the two women who sat before him, naked, bound and gagged, in the basement of a well known East Orange Italian restaurant had some very valuable information. Big G was willing to grant them one of his trademark compromises in exchange for it.

Yvonne and Carla, once their struggle with Santo's boys was over, had been stripped and stuck in the very lockers in which they had confined many an unwilling female over the last eight months. Needless to say, wearing a sound deadening hood, tied off to the wall of the van so as to be virtually immobile, confined to a space no greater than 15" deep by 28" wide for over twelve hours, was a new experience for them, as it was for the five pretty, young girls they had loaded into the van themselves earlier in the evening.

Yvonne and Carla had plenty of time to speculate on what would be their fate once they reached their destination, wherever that was. It was Yvonne's opinion that their load had been hijacked by the Hispanics and that once they got to, she assumed, the Bronx, she would be able to make a deal with them. After all, she could promise them anything since this was supposed to be their last trip anyway.

Carla had a different, more accurate idea of what was going on. While less brash and aggressive than her partner, Carla was the one who had her head screwed on right. She figured that there would be no way that Santo would jeopardize his income stream from the sale of female flesh unless he knew that it was not really at risk at all. Therefore, whoever was behind their seizure had the intention of taking over the Elizabeth, New Jersey operation. While the Dominican gangs were smart enough and tough enough to do it, it was really something just a little bit beyond their organizational abilities. They were too loosely put together with competing factions. She and Yvonne had a regular stop in one of the more desolate sections of their borough. It seemed that every other time they went there, there was someone else running the operation. In fact, very often at least part of their load consisted of the former girlfriends of the men the new operators had just displaced.

No, Carla knew that the men who were angling to horn in on the slaving operation had to have a solid organizational structure and international contacts. They had to have a reputation for stability and secrecy. They had to be men with the stick-to-itiveness to make the operation a long term thing. The only people who she could think of with all of those qualities was the Italian mob.

So when she and Yvonne were hauled out of the truck, dragged down some stairs, shoved into uncomfortable, straight backed chairs and had their hoods removed, Carla was not surprised to see a group of swarthy men chewing toothpicks and wearing gold chains around their necks.

A middle aged, slightly overweight man wearing an expensive business suit, with receding, black hair and a clean shaven face was the one who spoke to them and outlined the parameters of the deal he was willing to make.

Big G admired the naked forms of the two dykes that had been hauled into the clammy basement of the restaurant. He couldn't help but think what a waste it was for such delectable flesh to be unavailable for male enjoyment. Well, that would soon be fixed.

"Okay," Big G said to the women, "here's the deal. One of you is going to help me and my boys break into the basement of your little operation in Elizabeth. She is going to do ok. The other is going to find herself winging her way overseas in an aluminum container destined for a life of spreading her legs for anyone with the price of admission. So who's it going to be, huh?"

Carla and Yvonne exchanged glances. They were both still gagged, but their communication was non-verbal. These guys could go fuck themselves.

Neither of the women responded to Mr. Franco's proffer. He waited a few minutes and then initiated some persuasion.

The secret to interrogation was having an infallible sixth sense of who is going to crack and who is not. Big G had not gotten to where he was without a keen understanding of human nature. He looked carefully into the eyes of the two nude women. Yvonne's eyes were hostile and challenging. Carla's, while putting up a brave front, conveyed the fact that she was concerned about her future.

"Paulie, I think we need to show our guests what they have in store for them. Take the brunette here and fuck her up the ass."

One of the men, a big, strapping guy with wavy black hair and wearing an imported, hand woven 100% cashmere sweater, finely pressed slacks and shiny, pointed, black shoes, smiled.

"Sure thing, Big G," he replied. Paulie was one of Big G's underbosses. It was he who was pegged to run the slaving operation after the takeover. He had brought a few of his crew with him. He signaled for two of them to grab the tall, athletic looking brunette, Yvonne. Two men, not much smaller than Paulie, took hold of Yvonne's arms and dragged her from her chair. She had little chance for resistance since her hands were still locked into the manacles attached to the leather belt around her waist. Her ankles were hobbled by the 18" long chain that connected them.

The brunette beauty did try and put up a struggle. She twisted and turned her body in protest against her manhandling. The men draped her body over some large gunnysacks of flour. Two men held her legs still while a third held down her torso.

Yvonne was issuing a torrent of muffled expletives from her gagged mouth. Her breasts were crushed against the scratchy burlap bags. Her fine ass wiggled and twitched as she tried futilely to avoid her prospective cornholing. Paulie approached the prone, distended woman and ran his hands over her pale, white rear globes. "You've got a great ass, honey," he told her. "It's too bad you don't like cocks, because from now on you're going to get plenty."

The men holding Yvonne down laughed. Paulie had taken a bottle of olive oil from one of the shelves. He cracked its silver foil covered top open and poured a few drops into the cap. Leaning over the prostrate woman, he pushed aside her cheeks, exposing her dainty, little brown star and dribbled some into to it. He took two fingers from his right hand and, while holding the plump flesh apart with the other, insinuated them into the small, round hole. Yvonne screeched when she felt her anus invaded. She began a new round of attempted twists and turns of her torso and struggled mightily to free her legs. The men who were holding her were well experienced in subduing recalcitrant victims and they giggled and made jokes about her unhappiness at her fate.

Paulie undid his pants and dropped them around his ankles, pulling his silk boxers down at the same time. Big G laughed.

"Ya look like one of them guys in a porno movie, Paulie, with your pants around your ankles like that!"

All the other men laughed.

"I don't wanna get no olive oil on em!" Paulie explained.

"Okay! Okay!" Big G returned. "Don't be so sensitive. Just get your cock up the broad's poop shooter, willya!"

"Don't rush me," Paulie retorted, his voice a little whiney. After all, most guys didn't like to perform in front of their fellows. They might brag about how long they stayed hard, or how much some slut liked their dick, but no one liked to be put to the test.

Paulie took his somewhat average sized cock and ran it between the prone woman's rear cheeks. Yvonne moaned and struggled some more at the sensation of his meat in contact with her intimate parts. It took a little while, but Paulie finally got himself hard. His cock had picked up some of the olive oil he had spilled onto the woman's anus and was slippery and shiny. He poked its fat head at the tight orifice and began to press forward. His piece slid in easily, raising a mournful moan from the brown haired woman as the tissue surrounding her delicate, little hole cracked and tore.

Yvonne's groans and whimpers filled the small space of the basement, echoing off of the concrete walls. While Paulie began to saw his cock back and forth over Yvonne's sensitive rear ring, Big G took the opportunity to converse with Carla.

"It don't sound like she's enjoying herself," Big G told Carla. "I'm going to have Vinnie there do you. His cock, I'm told, is way bigger than Paulie's. I bet it'll hurt a lot, olive oil or no olive oil. Now one of youse is going to cooperate. It's a shame to have to go through all this for nothing. You look like a smart cookie. How's about it? Do you want to get ass fucked or do you want to make a deal?"

Carla was as close to tears as she had been in many years. Yvonne was her lover. Mary Ellen and the other girls who worked for her were her friends. On the other hand, if she didn't cooperate with the mobsters, she was cooked, that was for sure. What if Yvonne, rather than experience another violation of her body, decided to give in? What if the men figured a way to break into the subterranean slave holding area anyway? Her sacrifice would have been for nothing. She looked at Big G. Would he keep his word? She didn't know. She did know that he would keep his word about having her butt fucked and then, probably worse. If she cooperated, there was at least a chance at coming out of this. If she didn't there was none.

Meantimes, Paulie was having the time of his life. "Ohhhhh, yeah!" he moaned as his cock traveled back and forth over the squalling big woman's sensitive circle. "She's tight! Oh, yeah!" All the men watched intently as his lusts began to build. They knew that sooner or later tonight, they would have the chance to fuck one of these bitches or the other. Most of them hoped the blond haired girl held out for a least a little while, especially Vinnie. He liked them with blond hair and big tits. He kept eying Carla, much to the naked woman's dismay.

"Oh, god! Oh, god! Oh, god!" Paulie yelled out. "I'm commmmmmng! Ohhhhhhhh, yeahhhh!"

Yvonne groaned as she felt the gangster's hot spunk spill into her bowels. If she ever got free, she would cut off all their balls, that's for sure. The opportunities for Yvonne to avoid a dismal fate, though, were rapidly coming to a close.

Carla gave a whimper behind her gag. Big G asked her, "Are you going to play ball?"

Carla nodded yes frantically.

"Okay then," Big G replied; he knew it would be easy.

He looked at Paulie's men. "Have some fun boys, I'm going upstairs. He turned to Carla. "Do you like linguine?"

Carla looked back at the dapper gangster like he was out of his mind.

"Of course. Everybody likes linguine," Big G stated. "Come on upstairs, This place makes the best marinara sauce you've ever had. We'll leave the guys to their pleasures."

Dolefully, Carla, naked and bound, followed him up a set of stairs at the far end of the basement. The men had flipped Yvonne over and were in the process of unhooking her legs so that they could be spread wide. Carla looked back and saw the hatred in her lover's eyes. "But what could I do?" she thought wistfully.

Big G helped Carla mount the stairs with her confining ankle chains still on. The restaurant was empty and he had Carla sit down with him at one of the smaller tables. A somewhat subdued, older, grey haired man wearing a cook's outfit came out to the table. "Yes, Mr. Franco," he said in a heavy Italian accent. He was glancing nervously at Carla's naked, bound form.

"Let's have some linguine with marinara sauce, Giuseppe," Big G told him. "And some Chianti."

Giuseppe went to the bar and returned with a bottle of Chianti and two small wine glasses. He popped the bottle open and poured some for the unusual diners. He then retreated to the kitchen.

Big G kept up the small talk during the meal. His eyes kept returning to Carla's ample breasts which swayed and jiggled enticingly as they ate. Since Carla's hands were still bound to her waist, he fed her forkfuls of the delicious pasta and brought the wineglass to her lips so she could drink. Carla was not in the mood for much eating. She was worried about her lover being raped in the basement even as she sat here enjoying fine Italian cuisine. She was also disconcerted at her nakedness in front of the chef.

Finally, after their plates were taken away and after Carla had downed, at Big G's insistence, three glasses of wine, the man explained what was expected of her. Carla started to cry when he told her that she would be the decoy that led them into the dungeon of the uniform warehouse. But she was in over her head already, and so she reluctantly agreed.

Big G backed his chair away from the table.

"Okay, so, how's about a blow job," he asked the frightened woman.

An hour later, Carla drove the big, brown van to the entranceway to the underground facility. A camera above the door confirmed for the denizens inside who was seeking admission. Carla and Yvonne had been readorned with the clothing that had been taken from them back in Ohio. Yvonne had been given a shot and was sitting passed out and strapped into the passenger seat, something not unusual after a drive from Ohio to New Jersey. Crouched under the dashboard, holding a pistol aimed at Carla, was one of Paulie's men. The rest were in the back of the van, ready to spring out at a moment's notice.

Once inside the outer door, there was another, more formidable door to get past. Jake and his boys had blasted their way in eight months ago and had, based on their own experience, tightened up security and reinforced the door. Mary Ellen was inside the secret prison, looking at Carla and Yvonne over the closed circuit TV. Something wasn't right.

She could just sense it. There was an intercom to the outside and she called over it now to Carla.

"You're late," she said accusingly.

"Oh, y,yeah," Carla stuttered back. "We were both tired so I pulled into a rest area and caught some z's."

"What's the matter with Yvonne," Mary Ellen demanded to know.

"I don't know. She wasn't feeling well when we left Columbus. I think she might have the flu or something," Carla answered. She knew that her life depended on admission to the secure area behind the thick, steel door. If she blew it, the men were prepared to set a charge at the bottom of the door and blast their way in. It would be messy, and so they preferred the easy way. If they had to go to plan B, the instructions to the man in the front was to shoot Carla and Yvonne first.

Mary Ellen hesitated. "Why didn't you call in?" she asked.

"My phone was out of juice and I think there's something wrong with the charger," Carla replied.

It sounded good to Mary Ellen, but there was just something about the whole thing that disturbed her. Yvonne had a cell phone too, was hers out of "juice" as well? The girls were instructed to report regularly when on a mission. She had been just about ready to pull the plug on everything in case the girls had been arrested. Jake had told her that everything had been cleared with the powers that be and she shouldn't worry about police interference. But she'd heard that story before. Finally, Mary Ellen decided to let the van inside. She would grill Carla and Yvonne after it was unloaded and the new product was safely tucked away in their shipping containers awaiting export. She put her suspicions down to last minute jitters. Now that they were getting ready to close up shop, she was concerned that something would go wrong.

The tall, broad shouldered, shapely blond gave a nod to the other attractive, equally statuesque, young woman, a brunette, who was operating the door switch. All of Mary Ellen's girls were tall and well built. She wanted them to be able to stand up to the men they frequently had to deal with and so she had specially recruited tall, big boned girls like her. All of her crew was down in the basement, with the exception of Carla and Yvonne, and one other who had gone out to pick up the travel canisters that would be the new slave girls' accommodations on their trip to Kalikastan. She and the other three women would help unload the van and put the sluts in their containers. Mary Ellen wanted to get them out as soon as possible so they could get ready to split.

And there was the question of Allison. She was the thin, wan, raven haired former beauty who had been down in the dungeon serving as a nursemaid to the caged girls since long before Mary Ellen and her girls had taken over. She had belonged to the former administrators. She wore a collar around her neck which led to a pipe that ran horizontal to the ceiling the length of the dungeon. This way she could go back and forth and water, feed and clean the imprisoned girls. Due to the long time she had spent as a prisoner in the basement, she had gone way past the point where she would be considered suitable for shipment to Kalikastan. So the question remained: what to do with her?

The black haired girl also had as one of her duties to service Mary Ellen and her crew when they wanted a licking, just as she had served as a fuck puppet for the men who previously ran the slaving operation. Mary Ellen felt some sympathy for the meek, cowed girl who dutifully performed whatever service was asked of her, never saw the light of day, and never complained. If she was shipped to Kalikastan, based on what Jake had told Mary Ellen, she would probably be sent to one of the 'specialty' houses' where she would experience daily torment until she was all used up. Wasn't a simple bullet in the back of her head better than that? Probably. But Mary Ellen, although her heart was cold enough to send, by now, more than two hundred young women off to slavery in Kalikastan, was not psychopathic. She didn't enjoy killing, although she did it when she had to. Killing someone you had worked with for eight months, albeit in a master-slave relationship, was going to be hard.

Mary Ellen didn't know that her problem would soon be solved. The heavy, steel door opened up and Carla eased the van forward into the inner sanctum. As she brought the van to a stop, seven men jumped out of the rear, hitting the ground running, all armed with Tasers. Big G wanted to get all the girls alive. Mr. Burnham had plans for them.

The three, tall, buxom, broad shouldered women who were waiting to unload the van were taken by surprise. They were overwhelmed at once. Mary Ellen had been coming out of the area which held the cages. It was a half level lower than the unloading platform and had its own, heavy steel door that was kept locked at all times except when product was being moved. She had just reached the top step when she looked up and saw the men rushing towards her. There was just enough time to yell, "Oh, fuck!" and turn back towards the cage area. The prongs from a Taser struck her right in the back and she went scudding down the stairway, jerking and spasming. Two men were on her at once and it was all over.

A half hour later, Big G walked into the below ground prison. The six female captives were kneeling on the cement floor of the loading platform, their hands bound behind them and their ankles chained together. They were all nude. Yvonne had woken from her drugged sleep and Carla, once the other women were taken in hand, was dragged out of the van, stripped once more and trussed up next to her sisters. It made quite a delightful scene. Heavy, plump, breasts swayed and jiggled, bare, mostly hairless pussies begged for violation. The gang leader was not surprised to see five sets of hate filled eyes staring back at him as he inspected the line of females. Carla's eyes were subdued and ashamed. She had hoped that the man would let her off the hook for helping him, but it looked to her now that that was not in the cards.

There was one more woman to collect, the driver of the truck which held the long, round aluminum containers that would take the women to their final destination. Simone, a dark haired, black skinned, Haitian girl, drove the truck into the loading area totally oblivious of the coup that had occurred. In the flick of a lamb's tail she was kneeling down naked next to her fiends.

Big G went up to Mary Ellen. She was seething with loathing for the Italian mobster. He reached out and grabbed one of her nipples between his forefinger and thumb. She tried to recoil, but one of the other men held her in place.

"What nice tit's you have, honey. Too bad I don't have time to enjoy them. You and your girls are going on a trip, the same trip you sent so many sluts on before you. I hope you like it in Kalikastan. I'm sure I'll see you there once in a while. Mr. Burnham and I are great friends now."

Big G smiled at the big blond woman while he squeezed her nipple harshly. Mary Ellen flinched but remained silent. He would have to do a lot more than that before he got a rise out of her.

"Oh, and don't think that Jake is going to save you. He's going to be meeting an unhappy fate of his own." Big G looked up to his men. "Start loading them up, but leave this one," he said pointing to Carla, "for last."

The men began to unload the aluminum containers from the truck. Each of Mary Ellen's beautiful lesbians were given shots and installed inside. The containers were equipped with an IV drip so that the women would remain comatose on their trip and an air system that allowed fresh oxygen to be pumped in.

While the other men worked on Mary Ellen's girls, Big G went down into the lower area to check it out. All of the other cages were empty. That would soon change as soon as Paulie and his crew got to work. He saw the scraggly black haired girl who was affixed to the overhead pipe. "Who are you?" he asked her.

"A,allison," she said haltingly. She was kneeling, her arms folded behind her like she had been taught. The chain that led to her collar to the pipe on the ceiling went up behind her head. She had concluded that there was to be another change in management. First men, then women and now men again. It was all the same to her, although she preferred the women. They weren't as rough as the men and they would suck her pussy once in a while when they were bored.

"I guess you're the fuckbucket, eh?" Big G asked her.

Allison had never heard it put exactly that way before, but she guessed he was right. "Yes, Master," she answered.

"You don't look like much," Big G told her.

Again, the man was right. "No, Master," she admitted.

"Well, I think that we're going to send you on a little trip too, Allison. I don't mean to offend you, but I think that we can do a little bit better than you."

"Yes, Master," Allison replied. Her heart lit up. Did he really mean it? She had spent the better part of two years locked in this basement. She had watched hundreds of pretty, young girls shipped off. She had yearned to go with them, if only to be freed from her horrible existence. And now her wish was coming true. No matter what fate had in store for her after the trip, it had to be better than the subterranean life she had been living.

Big G unlocked Allison's steel collar from around her neck. It had worn a little groove into her skin, it had been on so long. He took her by the arm and led her up the short flight of stairs to the loading dock.

"Here, load this one too," he said. To Carla, he said, "Come with me." Carla managed to stand and shuffled her way obediently to the stairs to the cell area. She carefully worked her way down them. Big G was waiting there for her. He had Allison's collar in his hand. Before Carla could issue any protest through her gagged mouth, he had it around her neck and locked.

"I said I wasn't going to send you to Kalikastan," Big G said. "I never break a promise if I can help it. But I never said I'd let you go. We need someone to take care of the girls when they come in and to spread her legs when the boys feel the urge for a fuck so they leave the product alone. You fit the bill."

Carla moaned and her body sagged. Part of her knew that it served her right for betraying her friends. Tears flowing from her eyes, she wondered despondently how long she would be kept prisoner.

"Some day, we'll send you on, don't worry," Big G said. "But you'll have to beg us first." He laughed.

"I guess that the boys'll be plenty horny when they finish loading all that pulchritude," Big G continued. "Sos I'd get ready if I was you." Big G laughed again. Everything was turning out perfect.

A short while later, the last of the women, including the clueless sluts from Ohio, were placed in containers and taken aboard the truck where they were affixed to a temporary air pump. There was a sturdier and longer lasting pump awaiting them inside the air freight container they would all be loaded into once the truck arrived at the freight yard near the airport. Allison was the last to be loaded. Before her gas mask/gag was installed, she looked at the man working on her and said, "Thank you," tears in her eyes. The guy didn't know what she meant and put it down to being cuckoo after all that time under ground.

When the canisters were all loaded up on the truck, two of Paulie's men drove it out of the basement prison. Big G got on his cell phone and called a number in Kalikastan. The man on the other end said, "Burnham."

"This is Big G, Mr. B. Your presents are on their way." The mobster rang off of his phone and turned to go back down into the cell area. He wanted to get another blowjob from Carla before she got all sloppy.

CHAPTER TEN

When Jake awoke the morning after his pleasant luncheon with Irkut, the first morning of the tournament, his head felt as big as the whole outdoors. It was throbbing badly. "A little too much gin last night, Jake old boy," he thought as he tried to open his eyes. He felt a physical presence with him on the bed. He assumed that he had picked out one of the slave girls they had brought with them to fuck and then passed out with her still in the bed. He didn't remember a thing, which meant that he probably forgot to chain her ankle to the bed before he fell asleep. That was not a good idea in a place where a slave girl could slip away and mingle with the crowds. He was getting sloppy.

Late is better, most times, than never, and so Jake forced his eyes open. As soon as he did, he realized that he was not in Burnham's caravan. "Oh, oh," he thought. "Where the fuck am I?" The décor was nothing like the plain, white walls and ceiling of his room. He looked around and saw artsy prints on the walls, a little dresser with a vase full of fresh flowers on it and light pink walls. "Am I in a whorehouse?" Jake wondered. He didn't think that, aside from the tents that operated all day and night on the outskirts of the fairgrounds, there was any actual whorehouses at the tournament.

Jake rolled to his left to get a good look at the woman in bed with him. She was sleeping, lying on her stomach with her face away from him towards the small, curtained window. She had a long, thin back and curvaceous hips. Her hair was a light brown and ran down to the middle of her back. "I wonder if I actually fucked her or just passed out," Jake thought. He reached out and ran his hand over her soft, appealing skin. His touch made the young girl shift in her sleep. Her head moved, letting her hair fall free from her back. It was then that Jake noticed it. The girl wasn't wearing a collar. He quickly pulled back the sheet and saw that there were no bracelets on her ankles. One of her hands had slipped out from under her and he saw that there was no bracelet on it either.

"Whoa!" Jake thought. "Who is this and what am I doing here?" He laid back and tried to rethink the events of the previous day.

When he left Irkut, he had gone back to Burnham's trailer. The rich, creamy lunch he had consumed had made him sleepy. He knew that it would be a late night because of the shindig that Burnham was throwing so he thought that he better rest up.

When he got to the trailer, he saw poor Betty kneeling outside of it, her neck chained to a post. He had to look twice before he fully took in her new decoration. The little orange colored beak covered her mouth. It really did complete her appearance as a strange, bird woman. He could see the sign on her chest, "Compliments of the House" and a sheen of combined cum and saliva that had run down over her breasts and belly. She looked back at him sorrowfully, or as sorrowfully as she could given that half of her face was obscured. Jake just looked away. He knew that he was powerless to help her. Seeing what Burnham had done to her made him glad that he had promised to try and get her out.

Just outside of the van, Jake had seen four women hooded and hogtied on the grass. They wore no collars or bracelets, but had their hands and ankles tied off with rope. Remembering that, he weighed the possibility that the girl next to him was one of the four women he had seen yesterday afternoon. But no, he had seen them again later that night and the girl in bed with him was definitely not one of them.

When he had entered Burnham's large, luxurious trailer, he remembered taking stock of the three young slave girls locked into cages. Two were girls that he knew well. The third was the Malaysian girl that Burnham had insisted on bringing. He had told Jake all about his abuse of her on her arrival at the slave training center and had had a big laugh about it. Jake felt sorry for the girl. He decided that he would let her out of her cage for a little while at least.

He unlocked the cage and urged the slender, pixie like, black haired slave girl out. She exited the cage reluctantly. Jake saw the signs of Burnham's abuse all over her body. He knew that she was frightened that she was in for more of the same from him. Being confined in the cage might be humiliating and uncomfortable, to say the least, but at least while in it no one was tormenting her.

Jake led the quaking girl to his bedroom. She was gagged and had her hands confined behind her. Jake had her lay down on the bed on her belly. He loosened her wrists and brought them over her head where he connected them to a chain that led from the headboard. There was enough slack on the chain so that she could bring her hands down to chest level if she wanted to. He then unbuckled her gag and, after turning her onto her back, drew it from her mouth. She was still looking at him fearfully, but there had crept into her demeanor a certain quizzical look. Jake sensed that she was waiting for the abuse to start and was puzzled as to why he had relieved her of some of her discomforting confinements.

Not feeling it necessary to explain himself, Jake just stripped and lay down on the bed next to her. He drew her body close to his, putting his arm around her shoulder so that she was leaning into him. Within a few minutes he was asleep.

Like many men who live their lives on the edge of danger, Jake had developed a built in clock. He had allotted himself a forty-five minute nap. When he awoke, he looked at his watch and saw that he had slept for fifty minutes. "Close enough," he thought.

The Malaysian girl had fallen asleep in his arms. He looked down on her pretty face. She looked relaxed and at peace. He realized that this was probably the only peaceful moment she had had since she arrived in-country. He was sorry he had to wake her. His arm was still around her soft, smooth shoulder and he gave her a little shake with his hand. Her eyes opened slowly. They were clear and limpid. She looked at him for a moment as if she thought she was dreaming. All at once, she realized that she was not and her body tensed and her face turned into a frown. Tears came into her eyes and her lips began to tremble. She whined in fear.

Well, it was all Jake needed to see. The girl's vulnerability was like an aphrodisiac. His cock jumped to attention immediately. He did not want to frighten her though and so he took his arm from behind her head and turned onto his side. He ran his hand over her soft, black hair and her dainty face and shushed her. Her hands were joined at the level of her small, pointy breasts. Her eyes stared up at him, wide and beautiful. The irises were a deep, soft brown. Her brown skin was soft and smooth. Jake decided that he would make love to her. Not fuck her like Burnham and the guards did. Her training had been cut short and she had no yet been shown the deep sensuality she could achieve as at least partial compensation for her debasement. He would show her now.

Gently, so as not to unduly upset the girl, he pulled on the chain that locked her wrists to the headboard, slowly drawing her hands up above her head. He fixed the chain in place. Seeing her anxiety increase, he again stroked her face and her head until a modicum of calmness had returned. He smoothly slipped his leg over her hips and placed his knees on either side of them. Looking down at her with softened eyes and a smile, he stroked her hair and face some more. He saw that the girl was getting the sense that he meant her no harm. Her mouth turned into a tentative, nervous smile back at him as if she feared that there was still a chance that their encounter would lead to pain and unhappiness.

Jake knew that the girl had probably gotten over her initial shock at her fate and the fact that men would use her body for their pleasure. Most of the new slaves realized within a few days of the initiation of their training that they had best use their bodies to please their masters so as to assuage the torment and abuse they were subject to. All in all, getting fucked was usually better than getting whipped. He sensed that the Malaysian girl was no different. She knew that if she could escape their encounter without pain, she could live with all of the rest.

Seeing that he meant her no harm, the pretty, innocent looking Malaysian girl's face and body relaxed slightly. He leaned over and planted light kisses over her face and lips. His cock was hard and rested on her belly. The heat of her small body was engaging his lust. He had decided, however, that he would not seek his pleasure until she had experienced hers.

Jake slowly lowered his body so that his knees were outside of hers. He held his body up with his arms so that their flesh was gently touching. Placing his face near her thin, graceful neck, he ran his tongue and lips over it, down to her chest and up the other side. When he reached the place just under her right ear, the girl gave out a little sigh. It was his signal to move on.

Sliding his body further down, Jake let his lips drag across the dainty girl's upper chest. He saw the florid blue letters there denoting her new name, Orchid. In spite of himself, Burnham had aptly named the young woman. She was as delicate and beautiful as an orchid, and as inspiring to Jake's passion. He seized her left nipple with his lips and began a soft, gentle suckling on it while he stroked and caressed the other breast. When the nipple had grown hard and straight, he shifted his lips to the nubbin on her right breast and his hand to her left. After a few moments, the girl gave out another sigh, this one longer and deeper then the first.

It was again Jake's signal to move on. Slipping his body lower on hers, he coursed his hands over her delicate, round hips. His lips pressed against her belly. When they dragged across her lower abdomen and the fierce black mastiff tattooed there, just above her soft, hairless sex, her stomach gave a little flutter. When his lips continued their journey and alit on the small, hooded dart of flesh above her crevasse, she shifted her hips and spread her legs slightly in automatic, unconscious reaction. When he circled his arms under her lean, soft thighs and took her pleasure bud lightly between his teeth, she moaned again and her body turned soft and inviting.

Jake pleasured the dark haired girl with his mouth. He ran his tongue over her distending nether lips and lapped the growing moisture between them. He made slow, deep thrusts of his tongue within her, running it the length of her moist divide and flicking it against her stiffened clit. He could hear her hands straining at the chains that bound them as if she wished to use them to reject the pleasure that he was bringing her. But her deepening breath, her low, guttural moans and her thrusting hips told him that the effort would have been half hearted at best.

The girl received his oral attentions for a long time. Each time that he felt that she was reaching her apogee of passion, he relented his caresses and let her lusts ebb. When her breathing returned to normal, he reinitiated his attentions to her quim, restarting her writhing and moaning. Finally, as the girl's knees pressed against his shoulders and her legs trembled, he let her come. He flicked his tongue several times against the hard nubbin at her slit's apex and then, grabbing it between his lips, began to suck on it long and hard. She gave out a shout of joy as her pussy throbbed and convulsed. Her heels pressed hard against the bed and she pulled at the chain that kept her hands locked above her. Her back arched and her moans of pleasure filled the small room.

Jake let her lusts play out. When she had ceased her frantic motions beneath him, he withdrew his lips and tongue from her sweet divide. He brought himself up her body between her outstretched thighs. He seized his rock hard cock and guided it to her moist, accepting cleft. When the fat head of his manhood pushed aside the outer lips of her pussy and slipped in between them, she gave out a moan. Her eyes were alight with passion. Her lips were wet and parted. The skin over her breasts was flushed and her passion induced perspiration made her small, firm, pointed breasts glisten. The girl's nipples were as hard as darts. As Jake let his piece sink deeply within her cunt, he lowered his chest so that her breasts pushed against him. Placing his hands on either side of her head, he lowered his face until his lips met hers. When he begged entrance to her mouth with his tongue, her lips parted and welcomed him.

The two lovers, and it would not have been wrong to call them lovers for this brief moment in time, were trance like in the enjoyment of each other's flesh. Jake's mind was suffused with pleasure as his cock slid gently along the soft, tight walls of her sex. Her hips gyrated as he slowly sawed his prick against her bud of pleasure. Her ankles wrapped around first the back of his shins, caressing his flesh, seeking his heat. As their lovemaking became more intense and their bodies began to rock hard against each other, they slid up to the backs of his thighs and pressed against them, encouraging him to a deeper and deeper penetration of her womb. The girl came first. The lovers' lips were still joined and Jake felt the vibrations of her excited moans in his mouth. Her pussy contracted hard against his cock and his forces were unleashed. The couple groaned and struggled to draw as much pleasure as they could from their encounter. Jake felt each jerk and spurt of his cock deep inside his brain. When the eruptions of his stiffened and enraptured rod finally slowed, Jake gave out a great groan and let his body sink into the soft, hot flesh beneath him.

The master and the slave girl lay intertwined for a long time. Jake's cock was still within her and he could feel the delayed echoes of her orgasm as her pussy shuddered. Their chests heaved. Jake laid his head next to the girl's and sighed.

As Jake lay there, his mind returned to his gnawing dilemma. How was he ever going to leave all this behind? He was sorry for the girl's fate, but he had not enslaved her. He had brought her more pleasure than she had probably experienced in all the short time that she had been a slave and more than she probably would for a long time. The freedom to use her body as he wished was intoxicating. The knowledge that he could have his choice of any number of beautiful, pleasing women to attend his needs any time, day or night, filled him with lust. It a few days it would be all over, for him at least. He would miss it.

Jake drew his body off of the girl. He loosened her hands from the chain that had bound them over her head. "I have to go," he told her softly. She smiled, a grateful, sad smile. She placed her hands on the sides of his head and kissed him.

When she withdrew, her eyes were glistening. "Thank you, Master," she said in a light, accented voice. Jake kissed her back.

She waited patiently on the bed as he dressed. He took her hand and guided her up from the bed and into the hallway outside his bedroom. Her cage was there, empty and waiting for her. "I'm sorry," Jake said, his own eyes tearing as he contemplated the girl's dismal future. She nodded dolefully in response.

He took her gag and gently placed it between her lips. She accepted it without struggle. He turned her body and locked her wrists back together behind her. When he was done, he pushed gently on her shoulders until she was level with the entry to her small, steel confinement and she crawled inside. He closed the door after her and locked it. She turned within her tiny prison and looked up at him. A tear had escaped her right eye. Jake watched it as it descended her cheek, leaving a small trail behind it.

It was later in the afternoon than Jake had planned on and he was anxious that he had missed the beginning of Czarina's match. He hurried across the restricted campground, passed through the security gate and hustled towards the field where the contest of ponygirl strength was to be held.

When he arrived, he saw that a large crowd had gathered but that the meet had not yet begun. A loudspeaker was announcing, in Russian, the names of the contestants. His Russian was improving and he heard and deciphered the names Gargantua, Juno and Thumbelina, an obviously ironic appellation. Czarina's name was next to last. There were eight contestants in all.

Grandstands were lined up along the long sides of the two 100 yard dirt tracks that constituted the field of battle. At the far end of each, there was a circular turn around. The mammoth ponies were to drag their sleds along the tracks to the end, circle about and return. Although they were competing in pairs, they would not go directly head to head. It was a timed contest. He could sense, though, that being pared with a proficient competitor would be beneficial for each pony's time.

Jake looked through he grandstands for Irving. He had come down with some of the security guards. Jake had tried to talk him out of it given his feelings about Czarina, but he had been adamant that he wanted to witness everything, in his words, "the poor girl" was made to suffer. Jake had seen some of the pony's workouts and her reactions to being used and he doubted the "poor girl" was the proper term to use. He had, in deference to Irving's sensibilities, not made use of the pony, yet, but he had been sorely tempted. It looked like it would be an exciting ride.

Irving was sitting near the top of one of the bleachers near the finish line. The bleachers were all slightly turned so that the onlookers would have a good view all the way down the track and back. Irving's seat was ideal and Jake assumed that he had gotten there early so he could insure he had a good view.

He bought two pints of ale from a vendor and climbed the stands to where Irving sat. The technician/scientist gave him a glum look when he saw him approaching. Irving blamed all the pony's troubles on him, Jake knew that, but he struggled to keep up at least a polite relationship with him. Making his apologies to the other fans sitting in the row, Jake carefully worked his way down to Irving, trying not to spill his beverages. He was only partially successful.

When he reached the slight, nerdy looking man, he proffered one of the ales to him. Irving, at first, looked upon it with disdain and then, glumly accepted it. It was warm in the late afternoon sun and the cool drink was refreshing.

The first heat was just about to start. The first loads would be at 250 pounds. The regulations for the contest required a driver to sit on the bricks and he was permitted the use of a whip. To equalize the loads of the ponies, the drivers had all been weighed and compensating weight had been added or subtracted from the loads so that the weight each pony hauled would be exactly the same.

The pennants of the estates which had enlisted contestants fluttered in the strong breeze. Jake saw Burnham's black mastiff amidst them and he thought that the billionaire would be appalled to see it there. Two of the large ponies were lining up to do their first runs. There was a large tote board on which their times would be posted. In each round, the ponies with the two worst times would be eliminated.

When there were just two left, the last two would go head to head.

The two house sized ponies took their places at the start line. One, named Collette, was wearing a deep purple hood and the other, named Thumper, a red one. Their breasts were large and bulbous and their thighs thick as Ionian columns. The tattoos on their vast, hard bellies, a fierce bear for the red hooded pony and a coiled snake for the purple one, were stretched out. Thick, leather harnesses covered their torsos with straps then ran underneath them alongside their love lips and squeezed the fat, bulging flesh of their pudenda together. You could not call them fat, overall. They were big, yes, but their bodies were mostly muscle. They were less like sumo wrestlers and more like guards or tackles on an American professional football team.

The riders tugged the ponies' reins and the ponies set themselves. A gun sounded and they were off. The pony in red, the taller and more muscular of the two, took an early lead. Collette, the purple one struggled to keep up. Jake could see the straining muscles of the large animals and wondered what it would be like to roll in the sheets with either of them. You would have to be careful that they didn't crush you.

All and all, though, it was a remarkable display of determination and strength. The drivers snapped their whips at the ponies' backs and the sled glided along the dirt tracks. The crowd cheered them on although there was an undercurrent of jeers and catcalls.

The ponies reached the end of the 100 yard track, circled and started back. Thumper still had the lead, but not by much. It was clear that the early rounds would go to the lighter, faster ponies while the later ones would tend to favor the stronger, larger ones. The contest was designed so that a merely muscle-bound pony would have a hard time succeeding. It would be eliminated in the early rounds. The fast ones would make the early cuts, but would be left behind by the stronger ones as the match went on. The winning pony would have the optimum balance of strength and speed.

By the time the two sweating, grunting ponies neared the finish line, Collette had caught up. Their heavy boots dug deeply into the dirt track. The closer they got to the finish line, the louder the crowd grew. The ponies were now neck and neck. The excited spectators leapt to their feet. With a mighty lunge and with its boots churning the track, the purple hooded pony pulled ahead in the last ten yards and won the heat by almost a full length. The crowd gave a great roar and there was appreciative applause all around.

The chests of the ponies were heaving from their exertion. They pulled their sleds to the side and, after being unhitched, were led off. While two more ponies, a green and white hooded and a yellow and blue hooded one, Gargantua and Athena, were hitched up, the first two ponies' times were mounted on the tote board next to their names. The new contestants were lined up, there was a pistol shot and they were off.

Czarina's heat was the last. The green and white hooded pony was in the lead followed by the purple one. An orange and blue hooded pony, named Bison, was last. The red pony was next to last. Clearly the results of this heat were crucial to those two contestants. Jake could see Irkut rubbing Czarina's legs and uttering encouraging words to her. Her driver, Andreyev, dressed in a silken jockey's outfit colored black and gold, matching Czarina's racing hood, sat on the sled and was flicking his whip nervously at nothing. Czarina's opponent was the pony called Thumbelina, who wore a three colored hood, green, yellow and red. She was very big up top with large, fluffy breasts. Her hips were narrow but her thighs looked very strong. She stood a few inches higher than Czarina who looked like a cruiser next to a battleship. Jake hoped for the pony's sake that her lesser stature would translate to a greater speed.

Irving fidgeted next to Jake. He had religiously watched Czarina's practices from his room in the mansion with a pair of binoculars, wanting to stay from her sight. It was his theory that seeing him would only add to her misery of having been dehumanized. Over the last few days, Irkut had concentrated on working on the pony's turns, trying to develop a neat, tight circle. Hopefully, Jake thought, it would pay off today.

The gun sounded and the ponies leapt forwards. Thumbelina, being stronger, had the advantage for the first thirty yards. By the time they had reached the 100 yard mark, Czarina was a half length ahead. She came out of the turn well, increasing the distance between her and her competitor. Thumbelina made up some ground as the ponies accelerated up to speed again, but Czarina soon was on a quicker pace once more. You could have turned off your sets right there since, once she reached the mid mark, Czarina was a full length ahead of the other pony. It seemed like she could have pulled away even more, but Andreyev, having a feel for her time based on the big digital clock over the finish line, kept her in check. When she crossed the finish line, she had the third best time overall. Her competitor, Thumbelina, unfortunately was out of the race, finishing ahead of the orange and blue pony, but behind the purple.

In the second round, Czarina was matched against the fourth place finisher, Juno, a midsized, blond tailed pony. She finished just behind her, two seconds off. The first and second place ponies won their matches easily against the fifth and sixth ranked ones. However the slower pace of their opponents told since their times slipped. It was enough to put the second pony into third place. Czarina was fourth.

Being fourth meant that she would probably lose her heat to the front runner. But being matched against a faster pony meant that her time would probably be better. She finished about half a length behind the purple pony, Collette, but moved up a notch in her time placement, qualifying her for the semi-finals.

Jake ordered two more dark, bitter ales from a vendor. He was excited for Czarina, and Irkut, who had so much pride in her. Even Irving was getting into the spirit of the thing calling out "Go, Czarina! Go!" as she neared the finish line. It was the first time that Jake had heard him use her pony name.

In the semifinal round, Czarina was paired against the purple pony again. The weight that they drew was increased to 350 ponds now, increasing by 50 pounds in each round. Jake had the sense that the cumulative effect of pulling the weight was taking a toll on the other pony. She had a dark black tail and Jake swore he could see it drooping. Her shoulders seemed a little slumped and it had taken her longer to recover from her last match. She was still breathing rather heavily. She was the smallest of the remaining contestants and, at this stage, strength was having a greater part in the heats.

When the gun sounded, the crowd gave a sympathetic moan as Czarina seemed to slip. Collette pulled ahead quickly. Andreyev was shouting and cracking his whip at Czarina's back. Although she had made up most of the ground by the turn, the smaller pony was more practiced at this stage and increased her lead when they entered the straightaway once again. But Czarina wasn't finished. Her chest heaving, her big breasts swaying and jumping, she plowed forwards. The straps of her harness dug deeply into her skin. The crowd was on their feet as they neared the finish line. The purple pony seemed to be lagging as her strength wore out. In the last thirty yards, Czarina pulled ahead and won the heat decisively.

In the next heat, the green and white pony, Gargantua, was defeated by Athena, the yellow and blue. It was all set for the final match and the gold medal round. There was a twenty minute interval for the two finalists to rest and catch their breath. This match would not be decided by which pony had run last. From a distance, Jake could see Irkut's excitement. He was rubbing Czarina's naked thighs and caressing her thick labia. Andreyev gave her a little to drink from a narrow snooted jug. Athena had had the better time of the two ponies in the last heat. She was slightly bigger then Czarina. Her driver was a lanky lad, similar to Andreyev. Her trainer, too, was busy attending to her.

There was a thick air of tension in the crowd when the two large ponies ambled up to the starting line. Czarina, the former Maureen Donaldson, stood tall, her left leg poised behind her and her right forward. Athena, equally fearsome in her aspect, stood next to her in a similar pose. The drivers looked at each other anxiously. Irving was tapping his feet. Jake felt a lump rise in his throat. The starter called, "On your mark! Ready!" and the pistol went off.

Athena and Czarina plunged onto the track. As they passed the bleachers on which Jake and Irving sat, Irving could see the strain of hauling a 400 pound load on Czarina's chest and shoulders. The racers pulled their loads slowly but surely down the track. At this weight, 100 yards might as well have been 100 miles. The thighs of both ponies were tight and their boots dug deeply onto the track as they leaned forwards trying to gain an advantage against each other. Their ponytails, Czarina's a dark brown, Athena's a dirty blond, swung back and forth, recording their efforts.

Athena led by a ¼ length at the turn. It was here that Czarina's training paid off. When they emerged from the turn, the lead had changed hands and Czarina was in front. It was now a pure test of strength and heart. Andreyev and the other driver were whipping their charges unmercifully. The crowd was cheering for their favorites. There was no official betting permitted on the exhibition events such as this one, but many a side bet had been made.

Jake felt tense and on edge as he watched the two large ponies make their way to the finish line. Their progress was slow. The track had been churned up by the prior heats although the passage of the sleds did much to tamp the earth back down. Athena was slowly regaining the lead. The ponies' groans could be heard over the yelling of the packed grandstand. At the twenty yard pole, they were neck and neck. Suddenly, the yellow and blue hooded pony screamed through her bit. She collapsed on her right knee. She had apparently torn something from the strain of hauling the 400 pound weight along the track. Czarina coasted to victory.

There was still a bit of drama left, however. If Athena did not finish, she would be disqualified and the silver medal would go to the green and white hooded pony, Gargantua, who had the third best time in the last heat. The other pony, Collette, would move up to third. Athena's driver was not permitted to leave his perch, but he yelled and screamed at the pony, whipping her frantically. The pony writhed in the dirt for a long minute and then struggled to her knees. The crowd had turned silent as they watched the heroic effort. Athena was able to climb to her feet, screeching loudly as she put her weight on her damaged left leg. She paused and then staggered forward, pulling the straps that led back to her load tight. Using only her right leg, bringing her damaged left one up after she had moved her sled a few feet, she was able to inch her way to the finish line. The rule was that the sled had to pass all the way over the line to be a complete race.

Once the pony started in motion again, the crowd erupted into a cheer. The yelling and applause became louder and louder as she approached her goal. Finally, against all odds, first her head, then her shoulders and then her hips crossed it. She had about four more feet to go. She paused and took a deep breath, making her large, round breasts jut out. Her body was besmeared with the dirt of the track which had stuck to her sweat laden skin. She pulled at the sled once, twice, three times. The race official stood by the finish line, watching to see when and if the end of the sled passed it. It looked like Athena was out of gas. The crowd hushed. And then the pony gave one last yank of her reins, digging her right foot deep into the ground. The sled shifted forward. The official, holding a stick in one hand to measure whether the finish line had crossed and a flag in the other placed the stick at the end of the cart. The sled came to a halt. He peered down and looked for what seemed to be a very long time. Then, dramatically, he stood and waved the checkered flag over his head. She had done it! Athena, injured and defeated, had won the silver.

The fans were jubilant, slapping each other on the back and cheering. Someone slammed into Jake and he spilled the rest of his ale over the people standing one level down from him. They turned and laughed, too excited to care.

Beneath all the excitement for the heroic efforts of the yellow and blue hooded pony, Jake was ecstatic at Czarina's victory. It was a shame that it came at the expense of the other pony, but a victory was a victory. She had endured and that's what counted.

Jake and Irving hurried down the bleachers to join Irkut and Andreyev in the winner's circle. The crowd had surrounded Czarina and her driver and it was with great effort that they fought their way through. Czarina was on her knees, huffing and puffing, her body gleaming with the sweat of her effort. Her harness had worn deep, red grooves into her flesh. Her breasts shook with the effort of her breathing. Andreyev had leapt form his perch and was hugging first the other driver, then Irkut and then the exhausted body of the huge, victorious pony girl. Poor Athena was on the ground moaning. Her trainer, after receiving congratulations from the crowd, hurried to her side. Someone handed him a hypodermic and he shot it into her knee. After a few moments, the pony seemed to relax, her pain assuaged. A way was made through the crowd for a sled drawn by two strong, brown tailed work ponies. Athena's driver and trainer, after releasing her from her traces, rolled the big pony onto the sled. A signal was given and she was hauled off to her camp.

Meanwhile the event officials had come down to the winner's circle. Andreyev stood before Czarina and clapped his hands twice in front of her. The big pony rose from her knees with a grace quite anomalous with her size. She stood proudly as a great, floral wreath was placed around her neck. One of the officials held up a large, gold medal up to the crowd to another round of cheers. He then turned to the pony and affixed it to her collar. Jake thought he saw the pony's knees sag as she received her honor. She had no other way of showing her emotions of the moment. Irkut was handed a enormous, silver cup commensurate with the enormity of Czarina's victory and her size. Irkut and Andreyev stood on Czarina's sled and held the trophy high.

The crowd took a long while to dissipate. Some workers removed the bricks from Czarina's sled. When they were done, Andreyev stepped onto the sled, gave Czarina's reins a snap and the victorious pony began her trek back to her camp. Someone had handed Andreyev the banner of the Burnham estate and as Czarina hauled him away, he joyfully waved it in the air.

Now Jake remembered where he had begun his serious drinking. He and Irving accompanied the delighted Irkut back to his encampment. The celebration had already started. Bottles of vodka had been opened and were being passed freely around. Czarina was on her knees, freed from her harness and giving the blissed out Andreyev an energetic blow job. Jake tried to imagine what the ponygirl was thinking. A few short months ago, she had been the former pig-whore, a large, embarrassing presence on the Burnham estate. Now, through her own efforts and Irkut's expert training, she was a champion, a true Czarina.

The party went on until darkness started to close in on the encampment. Jake took his turn at the pony's mouth. A blowjob from a champion ponygirl was considered a lucky thing and he was going to need all the luck he could get. As the pony drew her lips and tongue along his cock in seeming joy, Jake knew that she would never leave Kalikastan. Where could she go that she would be celebrated like this? Who would ever value her as much as her trainer, Irkut? She had finally won self respect. No way would she ever give it up.

Irving had stayed a little while, hanging back from the celebration. He gave Jake a dirty look when he got his blowjob. "Fuck him!" Jake thought as his cock jerked and spasmed in the pony's mouth.

Someone tilted the ponygirl over and began to ride her pussy from the rear. The revelers paused when they heard the pony start to moan and groan in pleasure. "Czarina! Czarina! Czarina!" they called as her lusts mounted. When her body began to shake and quake with her orgasm, the group of hardened ponygirl trainers and drivers cheered.

Jake was half in the bag when he left the encampment. The party was still going full blast. He had other business tonight. As he walked through the ponypark on his way back to the restricted camping area, he noted all the fires glowing in the campsites, slave girls attending to ponies, drivers and trainers sitting around the fire calmly awaiting tomorrow's dawn. When he left the ponypark, he could see what looked like two hundred campfires burning in the public camping area. Lights had been turned on in the fairgrounds, and at several tents slave girls were dancing for the enjoyment of the crowds or were performing unusual acts of passion on each other for their amazement.

When Jake reached the Burnham encampment, the fete was already underway. Three large sides of beef were roasting over huge open fires. A vast caldron of chili cooked on another. There was American style corn on the cob, baked beans, a wide variety of vegetables and salads. People were happily stuffing the food down their faces. Jake got in line and had some succulent slices of steak placed on his plate by a white uniformed chef and helped himself to the other fixings. There were three half kegs of dark, rich, American ales out. Jake helped himself to a stein full of one. Long picnic tables had been set up. He found an empty spot and began to consume his meal. Slave girls ran around the place delivering seconds, refills on beer, and anything else the diners required. Here and there, one or two were bent over getting part of their daily quota of dick. Burnham had issued his well known tokens and brought down a trailer full of his household slaves, so they knew the drill. They would have to turn in a certain number by the end of the party or take a whipping. Several punishment stakes had been hammered into the ground and a couple of the girls had apparently run a foul of one master or another since they were bound to them, hands joined together above them, awaiting a whip.

Jake finished his repast and tossed down two or three flagons of ale, he couldn't remember specifically, and wandered over to where the show was to commence. He passed by the large dessert table which was overflowing with rich temptation and waved away two slave girls who offered themselves to him, seeking tokens, no doubt.

Seven rows of comfortable chairs had been set up, about 25 seats across. Burnham was in the middle of the front row holding court. Betty was on her knees in front of him facing the stage. He had her on a leash and the refined looking men and women around him were marveling at her decorations. One woman was raising and lowering her bright orange beak and laughing.

A number of notables were present. Jake recognized the president of the Commission and one or two other Commission members. He had met them at a banquet thrown by Burnham some months ago. Jake took a seat in the third row so as to remain relatively inconspicuous.

The stage in front of the chairs was about seven feet high and thirty feet away from the front row, so there were no bad seats. A large, heavy, red curtain covered the thirty yard long stage. It was an immense construction, suitable for a more permanent installation. Who knows, maybe it was, Jake thought. Burnham rarely did things half-assed and it would be just like him to build a permanent outdoor stage so that his largess could be appreciated by everyone. Everyone that mattered, that is, since only the upper crust of Kalikastani society was invited.

Jake recognized a few of the people who were starting to assemble for the show. There were a few estate owners he had met on his travels, some drivers and trainers he knew. Occupying a front row seat next to Burnham was the tall, broad shouldered man he recognized as Axmail Grobgy. At his shoulder, hovering like a good security minion, was Anton Drabik.

Jake felt his heart go cold. He believed, although he had no proof, that Drabik was behind the kidnapping of his slave, Klara, several months ago. He had sworn to kill the bastard if he could before he left Kalikastan. Even if he was not guilty, Jake doubted that the world would miss him much.   They had met at Grobgy's big celebration at the end of the Spring Tournament. Grobgy's teams had won the overall championship for the season. Jake had pegged Drabik as a stone cold killer at the time and he knew that Drabik had done the same for him. If anyone was going to smoke out the plans involving Maddy, it would be Drabik. Jake only hoped that Klara had not known enough to be helpful to him. But his boys sometimes had loose lips and so you never knew. Nothing had happened so far to make him believe that Drabik was on to them.

The eyes of the two hard men met. Jake saw that Drabik recognized him too. A sly, killer smile crossed his face. Someone passed between them and when they were gone, Drabik was too. It was just as well. Jake didn't want to have to stare at the man all night.

Lights flickered and the chairs started to fill up. Jake's seat was on the aisle, giving him a good view of the stage and an easy retreat should he decide he had enough of Burnham's show.

A fanfare announced the beginning of the program and the lights surrounding the stage went down. The curtain opened. In the middle of the stage stood two pyramids of young women accoutered with slave regalia, but dressed in what could only be described as cheerleading uniforms. Their tops were gold and had necklines that descended under their ample, naked breasts. They were wearing short, little pleated, black and gold skirts. These were Burnham's racing colors. On their feet were pink sneakers and they had pink bows in their hair. The pyramids consisted of three pretty girls on the bottom, two on their shoulders and one on top. Three more girls were kneeling on the floor in front of them holding large pom-poms. There was a round of polite, appreciative applause from the audience.

After a moment, the music commenced. It was the Beach Boys singing California Girls: "Oh, East Coast girls are hip, you know, I really dig the styles they wear...." The music was a signal for the girls to break formation. The topmost girls jumped forwards and after making flips, landed in the arms of the girls who were standing at the bottom. The second row flipped and landed square on the floor. What one couldn't help noticing when the girls turned over in the air was that they wore no panties. A merry cheer arose from the spectators.

The girls may have been dressed like some pornographer's fantasy, but they were otherwise well practiced in their craft. They ran around the stage doing flips and cartwheels and assembling themselves in a number of athletic and artistic combinations. The music continued as a medley of American surfer music from the Beach Boys and Jan and Dean to the Ventures and the Safari's. The girls timed their flips and leaps to the music, their breasts swaying and jumping, their pretty little bottoms flashing each time. The act went on for about twenty energetic minutes. When they were done, the young women bowed and all ran off of the stage. The audience, mostly unfamiliar with the phenomena of American cheerleaders, had reacted, at first, coolly to the girls' performance, but by the end they were won over by their lewd acrobatics and gave them enthusiastic applause.

The next routine was a series of vaudeville gags based on the old nurse and doctor shtick. The nurse was put through a variety of ribald and lascivious situations and poses. Then the female patient came in and she was soon stripped and performing various sexual tasks as therapy for her ailments. A second and a third came on stage and they joined her. By the time the act was done, all of the actors were involved in a large daisy chain, fucking, sucking and humping each other. The audience was rolling in the aisles with laughter. They say that humor doesn't translate, but you couldn't tell by this performance.

When the vaudevillians left the stage, the next group of beauteous, young women performed a series of traditional, hot, vaudeville strip routines including a bubble dance, a fan dance and a very good imitation of Gypsy Rose Lee. For an audience used to seeing their slave girls naked all the time, it was especially prurient to see the lovely, well proportioned young women stripping off their clothing in time to the music. When they were all naked as the day they were born, they folded themselves into several erotic tableaus. After all three had exhibited what looked like mind blowing orgasms, they ran off the stage.

The next was a comic juggler. He had a number of assistants on the stage with him, pretty young things with large, round breasts. He came out dressed in a classic clown outfit. He bowed and started to juggle plates. As he did, he gestured for one of the young ladies lady to approach him. Tossing the plates aside to be caught by someone off stage, he reached out to her with both hands and pulled her breasts right off of her chest. The breasts went flying up in the air and the girl went screaming off of the stage. Of course, they were not really her breasts, but well designed aerodynamic simulacrums.

Each girl in turn was beckoned to contribute her mammaries to the flying bosoms. By the time he was done, he had five sets of boobs flying all over the stage. He flipped them between his legs, over his shoulders and around his torso. He had them going in a large, high loop and then flying up in alternate curves above him. After about ten minutes, one of the young ladies, seemingly wearing nothing but a slave collar and bracelets, came back on stage holding a big, green dildo. She mimicked asking him for her breasts back and offered the dildo in exchange. Jake figure that she was wearing some kind of Velcro garment over her chest and that her real breasts had been bound tightly, because, since she was naked, there was no question that she was a girl.

The juggler shrugged his shoulders and took the dildo from the slave girl and tossed it into the air. She spread her arms out from her body and he tossed two of the breasts at her. They landed directly on her chest and stuck there. The girl turned to the audience with a large, grin and a gesture of happiness and ran off the stage. One by one, all the girls returned and received their breasts back, exchanging them for a different colored dildo. When all the dildos were flying in the air and all the breasts had been restored, the clown tossed the dildos into the crowd one by one, bowed and left the stage.

There was thunderous applause. Jake found himself laughing and enjoying the show. It was just the type of show that the audience would appreciate.

For the next act, the lights were brought way down low and a single spotlight was shown on the stage. The music was slow and languorous. A plinth came up in the middle of the stage. In the middle was a naked slave girl, tall and slinky. Well that girl tied herself up into knots, as the song goes, that sailors never knew. There were oohs and ahhs and generous applause when she twisted herself into particularly impossible looking poses. Near the end of her performance, her hairless pussy presented to the crowd, she reached her hand around her contorted frame somehow and began to stroke herself to lust. The crowd hushed, fascinated by her delivery of pleasure to herself and cheered when she brought her self off.

The next two acts were just as good. There was a magic act in which, among other things, the magician made several large objects disappear up his assistant's snatch, and a knife thrower who cut some rather diaphanous clothes off of several slave girls while they were spinning around a wheel.

The cheerleaders came out again, this time to the tune of Buddy Holly, La Bamba and some other oldie tunes. Their performance was as original, athletic and obscene as their first.

The came the showstopper. The stage closed and then opened again. In the middle of the stage was a man dressed in full cowboy regalia replete with a broad brimmed 10 gallon Stetson, chaps, a leather vest and a lariat. A Gene Audrey tune played in the background. He did some tricks with the rope with which the audience quickly got bored. Suddenly, a naked young girl ran across the stage. Jake recognized her at once as one of the hogtied women outside of Burnham's trailer earlier in the day. She was running as if she was on fire. The cowboy looked at her casually and then jerked his lariat towards her. It caught her in mid-stride, falling around her thighs and then tightening suddenly. The cowboy dragged her to the middle of the stage. The girl was kicking and screaming. Jake realized at once why they needed girls fresh to the country who had not yet been given any slave training. No slave girl could have duplicated her unhappiness and panic.

Once the cowboy had her in the middle of the stage, he deftly removed the lariat from around her legs. Before she could get up and run again, he pulled a five foot or so long strand of rope from inside his cowboy vest and, in a trice, had the slave girl's wrists and ankles tied together. The audience applauded his dexterity with the rope. Then, the curtain that hung over the top of the stage was withdrawn. It revealed a wide circle of steel piping. The cowboy produced two much longer ropes that were tossed to him from off stage. He bound one end of them both about the girl's trussed ankles and wrists. He then tossed one of the ropes up over the overhead pipe. When he pulled on it, the anxious, screaming girl was hauled up into the air, about twenty feet. There was a hook on the ring and the cowboy jerked the rope that he was using to lift the girl up until her bound ankles and wrists were captured by the hook. He then gave the other rope a yank and both ropes fell to the ground. At this, the circle of steel began to whirl around. As it sped up, the centrifugal force made the girl's body fly out from the pole.

The audience clapped furiously and cheered at the cowboy's skills. But that was not all. Someone off stage tossed him a long, thin bull whip. The girl was traveling clockwise, ass first. The cowboy raised he bullwhip and, as she came around towards the audience, he snapped the bull whip into the air catching the girl right on one of her pale, white, rear globes. The girl screamed in pain.

At this, the audience went wild. It was indeed a deft display of the man's skill with a whip. He caught her three more times coming around. She screamed and cried each time as the whip struck her. Her vulva was exposed between her raised legs and one of the blows caught her spot on, producing an anguished scream of pain.

Just then, another girl ran across the stage. While the other girl had blond hair tied off behind her head, this one was a brunette. Her hair was long, down to her waist and flew behind her as she ran. Without missing a beat, the cowboy had her captured by his lariat. When she was dragged to the center of the stage, he tied her off like the first girl. The revolving ring stopped and he hoisted the brunette up on the opposite side from where the blond girl dangled.

The ring started to whirl again and the man picked up his bull whip. He struck the brunette first. She screamed in pain, as would be expected. By the time the blonde had come around, he had brought the whip down and snapped it off again, catching her as well. The girls flew around the ring, receiving each time a painful kiss of the whip on their rears, their sexes or on the backs of their thighs.

A third girl came out, a lovely, big breasted girl with a long, black ponytail. The cowboy spun around and roped and hooked her up above as well. He then repeated his demonstration of skill by striking all three girls in rapid succession.

Once they had gone around three or four times, a fourth girl ran out. She had fiery red hair and alabaster skin. She ran out on the stage like she was being chased by King Kong. But instead of running across the stage, she stopped about halfway across. She looked up and saw the other three girls flying through the air, moaning and groaning their pain, especially the blond girl who had been struck at least twelve times by now. Then she looked at the rope in the cowboy's hands. She frowned and began to cry. When the cowboy flinched the rope at her she jumped back. He did it twice more and, having seen her prospective fate, she frantically dashed back to where she started. The cowboy looked at the audience and shrugged his shoulders. There was a round of laughter.

Suddenly, the girl came running out again, screaming. There was a deep red welt on her ass. She tried to make it to the other side of the stage, but at the last minute, the lariat encircled her. She soon joined her mates up in the air. As the circle spun, the cowboy flicked his long whip up in the air four times, catching each girl in turn.

It was a remarkable display of skill. After they went around a fourth time, the cheerleaders came running out in front of the stage carrying four large nets. Three of the girls held their net up over their heads. The cowboy looked down at them. He moved to the side of the stage where there was some kind of switch box. As the whipped young women came spinning around, the cowboy turned a switch. The blond girl came flying off of the steel circle and was flung off of the stage. Screaming with fear, she landed, all trussed up in a ball, right into the net. The cheerleaders gathered her up and ran back behind the stage. Three more cheerleaders caught the second screaming girl, et cetera. A resounding applause met each capture of a flying girl. When the fourth girl landed in her net, the audience stood and cheered.

Jake did too. He wouldn't have wanted to be at the business end of the man's whip, especially in the blond girl's position, but skill was skill and this guy had it. The cowboy bowed several times and then all the performers came out onto the stage. The cheerleaders hopped and tumbled, the clowns chased the women around the stage, the magician and his assistant bowed. The whipped young girls were rolled out on trundles, bent over, their legs splayed wide and their heads raised. They were wearing ring gags. The Beach Boys came over the loudspeakers once again singing their trademark song about what they wished all girls could be and then, to the audiences' intense appreciation, the Beetles came on singing, "Back in the USSR".

It had been a grand performance. Burnham had outdone himself. Jake had to hand it to him.

A few moments after the curtain closed, lights went up on a stage on the other side of the field and a five man rock band began to play. Jake thought he recognized the song as something he had heard on the radio back home, but for the life of him, he could not recall the band's name. It was then that things got really exciting. The cheerleaders and all the other slave girls from the performance came running out and started to drag men and women out into the field to dance with them. The flying burrito sisters were rolled out and made available for anyone who wanted a taste of them at either end. Their bottoms were all marked up and Jake didn't want to add to their miseries, although that didn't seem to faze some of the people. What he did want, as did a hundred other men and women, was a shot at a cheerleader.

It was at this point that Jake remembered starting to drink gin. He should have known better. Gin was almost always his downfall. But the excitement of the night, the wonderful, starry night sky, the enticing, beautiful young girls prancing and dancing around in their short, black pantyless skirts, brought out the party animal in him. In the back of his mind, of course, was the fact that he would soon be leaving Kalikastan behind. This time in a few days, either he would have fled it forever or he would be buried somewhere out on the steppes. Eat, drink and be merry for tomorrow we may die, he thought. After three glasses of gin, he was finally able to corral one of the cheerleaders. She had shoulder length strawberry blond hair and a cute little nose. She danced with him lasciviously, rubbing her butt up against his crotch, flipping up her tiny skirt, or holding and massaging her delicious bare breasts.

After three songs, Jake hauled her off the dance area and out of the lights. He found a place behind one of the trailers and took her in his arms. He kissed her and she kissed him back passionately. Jake didn't care if her passion was feigned or not, the product of intense, coercive training or not, the girl was hot and her wriggling, hot tongue set him on fire.

He pulled her down on the grass and tore off his clothes. He knew that someone might come by, but he didn't care. The girl leaned back, smiling, her legs spread, her tiny skirt flipped up, waiting for him to mount her. Well, he didn't need an engraved invitation. He slid himself between her knees and targeted his stiffened rod at her fleshy gate. She was wet with arousal and he slid right in.

What followed was ten minutes of torrential humping. The gin, the beer, the vodka, all seemed to combine to ignite his passion. The girl held him tight and brought her heels up the small of his back. She rocked her hips back at him furiously. Her mouth inhaled his tongue and she sucked and played with it lustfully. When he finally came, he groaned so loud that he was sure someone would hear. He couldn't stop himself, however and he kept moaning and groaning as his cock pumped out a river of his spume. She was coming too and she screamed her delight into the night.

Afterwards, he lay in the girl's arms panting for breath. His heart was pounding wildly. He could feel hers too, and when she caught her breath, she sighed, "Oooooooo, Master! That was wonderful!"

Jake felt the same way. Between breaths, still entwined in her arms and legs, his cock softening, but still lodged in her steamy twat, he asked her, "What's your name?" It was too dark to read it on her chest, and, with his head lagging over her shoulder, he couldn't see her chest anyway.

"Darla, Master," she replied.

"Will you be here tomorrow night?" he asked hopefully.

"Yes, Master. Tomorrow we perform in the public campgrounds. Our tent is on the western end. I'll be there all day taking guests, but if you talk with my master, you can have me all night after the show."

"I'll give it some thought," Jake said. By her accent, he placed her from somewhere in the American Midwest. He wondered if she was one of the girls brought over by the Elizabeth operation since they took it over eight months ago.

"I have to entertain some more guests, Master. May I get up?" she said pleadingly.

"Oh," Jake answered. "Of course."

He rose to his knees and the cheerleading slave girl squiggled out from underneath him.

"Please come see me tomorrow, Master," she asked sweetly.

"I'll try," Jake answered.

He watched her run away back to the dancing crowd as he searched for his pants. He heard the sound of soft, clapping hands and he turned around. It was a slender, young woman wearing a long, green and yellow sheath dress. She was sitting on a log not more than ten feet away from where Jake and the slave girl had been fucking. She had a pleasant, impish, round face and a shapely figure. Her straw colored hair was cut into a mop around her head and descended to just below her ears. Her breasts were loose and unhampered under her dress and Jake watched as they shifted slightly while she clapped her hands.

"Very good!" the girl announced. "I'd give that a ten out of ten."

"Why, thank you," Jake answered while fishing around in the dark for his pants.

"They're over here where you threw them," the girl said, a hint of mirth in her voice.

"Do you mind?" Jake asked. He was trying not to get embarrassed at his wet cock dangling between his thighs.

"Not at all," the girl replied. She threw Jake's pants and jumbled up undershorts to him along with his shirt and shoes. Jake hurriedly started to put them on.

While he was dressing, the girl continued the conversation. "You're the American, Jake Barnes, no?"

"I'm the American, Jake Barnes, yes," Jake replied.

"It's my pleasure, my name is Tanya."

"Tanya is a pretty name," Jake said while he was pulling his trousers up.

"Do you dance with regular girls or just slave girls?" she asked.

"It depends on the girl," Jake answered. He had finally managed to get his shirt on and was working on his boots.

"Well, take me for instance. Suppose I asked you to dance with me?"

Jake looked up. He hadn't had a come on from a female who wasn't wearing a slave collar in a long time. He wondered what it would be like to fuck a woman who could say no. But then again, every girl is somebody's daughter and although from the girl's voice and what he could see of her, she looked sufficiently over 18, you never knew who her father was and whether, in this trigger-happy land, he might take umbrage.

He looked at the girl again. She was very pretty and well formed and she seemed pleasant enough. Maybe she would and maybe she wouldn't. Maybe he would or maybe he wouldn't. But it wouldn't hurt to just dance, would it?

"Okay," Jake answered.

His boots back on his feet, his cock tucked away in its cave, Jake stood. He held his hand out to the young woman and she took it. Her hand was warm and firm.

"Come on," he said.

Jake remembered dancing with the girl for a long time. They took several breaks during which he remembered laughing with her and downing several iced glasses of gin. She was drinking vodka, of course. At some point in the night, his memory faded. He did remember her warm body, her pleasant breasts and coming inside her with a delirious groan.

But how he got to where he was and how long they had fucked, he didn't recall.

But it was nice to remember her name. Tanya. Jake looked at his watch. It was a little after 7 a.m. The ponygirl parade was at 8. If he just snuck out, maybe no one would see him, father, brother or, for all he knew, husband. He was just about to crawl out of the bed and retrieve his clothes when the girl moaned and turned over. Her breasts swayed as she turned. Her nipples were short and fat and were surrounded by dark rings of silky smooth skin. Her belly was tight. Her new posture revealed the front of her long thighs and the inviting, trimmed divide between them. He was about to jump out of the bed when the girl's eyes popped open and gave him a good looking over.

"Do you always fuck and run, Mr. Barnes?" she said teasingly.

End of Book 9